Emerald Knight

By

J.M. Sampson

8 7 of **100**

To D.R. Gorull

I hope you enjoy the story.

J.M. Sampson

Pittsburgh, PA

ISBN 1-56315-225-8

Paperback Fiction
© Copyright 2001 J.M. Sampson
All Rights Reserved
First Printing — 2001
Library of Congress #00-106122

Request for information should be addressed to:

SterlingHouse Publisher Inc.
The Sterling Building
440 Friday Road
Pittsburgh, PA 15209
www.sterlinghousepublisher.com

Cover Design: Jeffrey S. Butler — SterlingHouse Publisher, Inc.
Book Design: Kathleen M. Gall

Printed in the United States of America

Sincere thanks to those who made this book possible:

Karen Sampson
Shirley Keen
Ruthann Conway

**A special thanks of gratitude
to those who encouraged my efforts:**

Todd, for his recommendation that I put my story on paper.

Joseph III, who is responsible for old Iron Hide.

Josey Marie, for her editing help.

Terri, my wife, for her patience and understanding.

Michelle, for proof reading, and editing.

Frances Humphreys, high school history teacher.
Please forgive my liberties with a few of the events of English history.
You had a positive influence on me, and all of your students.
You are the example of what a teacher should be.

Marilyn Centner, college English teacher.
Thank you for encouraging me to write.
It has been many years since I had the privilege of being your
student, but your interest in a young man's
literary efforts has not been forgotten.

**In every respect, the Emerald Knight is composed
from a little of each one of you.
Thank you.
I hope you enjoy the book.**

EMERALD
Time Line

Year	Event
650	King Arthur
580	Seven kingdoms, one king
485	Emerald Knight
470	Scot Hold destroyed
445	Rome leaves Briton
440	Last high king before Germaine
43	Claudius of Rome invades

A.D.

B.C.

Year	Event
34	Emerald Sword forged
37	Titan's Blade to Volstad
54	Julius Caesar, second invasion
55	Julius Caesar, first invasion
57	Mallock Scott born

The trees towering above the waiting combatants intensified the darkness of the predawn hour. Germaine stretched his senses to the fullest in an effort to detect the enemy's approach. He could see the nearest of his fellow defenders, but the rest remained hidden by the darkness and fog. The early morning mist formed droplets of water on his skull helm and weapons. *Will my ears and eyes prevail over these elements? Too much thought. I must trust in my instincts.* Germaine shifted his weight slightly. The knight found the long hours of standing in the forest to be but a minor inconvenience. *It could be worse. I could be wearing full battle armor.*

A slight hint of sound in the fog-shrouded darkness caught his attention. His right hand moved to the haft of the sword, Lightning. The sword rested in its belted sheath on his left hip. On his right hip hung the short sword, Stinger. Germaine left his other weapons and heavy armor in the keeping of his page, in the safety of Fenn Castle. Small glints of emerald light danced upon his chain mail with a power of their own. Germaine knew the light was born by the special metal from a meteorite of which his armor and weapons were made.

"This cursed fog. Will it prove to be a sword to aid our foe?" the First Prince of Fenn Hold swore in a whispered tone to Germaine. When no reply came, he looked at the man dressed in emerald mail.

Germaine raised his left hand in a motion to silence the man. The prince did not say another word but turned his gaze intently toward the fog-shrouded glade that lay unseen beyond the trees.

"Swords at ready!" Germaine spoke calmly, his voice curt. "The enemy comes." Germaine's insides felt cold as ice as he slid Lightning from its sheath. The knight, Germaine of Scot Hold, narrowed his eyes to slits as he drew Stinger with his left hand. In the early morning hour he wore not the cumbersome armor used for cavalry warfare or joust, but the lighter mail and skull helm that were ideal for close in battle. The skull helm did not give protection to his face, as did the heavier battle helm with its visor and emerald plume. This helm covered from a point just above Germaine's eyes and swept up and over his skull to a point where it flared out away from his neck. Germaine knew the Romans, one-time occupiers of Briton to the south, were the ones responsible for the design.

As Germaine tensed his six-foot frame in readiness for action, he recalled the words of the old code. Nay, more than words, the code defined his way of life. *For might on the side of right, truth, fidelity, and allegiance to Jehovah God, do I expend all my strength and, if necessary, my life.* As these thoughts flew to his heart, Germaine saw a movement in the mist.

"ATTACK!"

The Emerald Knight surged into the advancing enemy, his blade biting into flesh and sinew. Germaine's mind rose above feeling or sane thought as his honed reflexes carried him through the fray. His lithe body moved in a warrior's rhythm as he parried an enemy's battle-axe with Lightning. His forward momentum carried him close in for a simultaneous thrust of Stinger to pierce the axe wielder's throat. Even as he pulled Stinger free of the slumping foe, Germaine sent Lightning slicing through another attacking warrior's chest. As Germaine swung the blades forged from a meteor, an emerald haze of light seemed to shimmer in their paths. The metal could slice though armor like a knife through cheese. Past experiences told Germaine that the unearthly emerald light radiating from the swords had a demoralizing effect on the enemy. The thrust of one enemy sword marked his left forearm, but he noticed it not as he continued his advance, decapitating the one who had wounded him.

Germaine looked upon his work as a science and had his abilities honed to perfection. As the Emerald Knight wielded his swords, time held no meaning for him. For Germaine, time no longer mattered.

As Germaine pressed the attack, a dark warrior with black wings adorning the sides of his helm swung a wicked mace at the knight's head. An upward parry with Stinger deflected the weapon as Germaine cut deep with a sweeping arc of Lightning. Blood burst forth as the body was nearly severed at the waist by Germaine's sword. The mace had struck a glancing blow to Germaine's helm as it was deflected.

"Germaine!" A voice invaded his world. "Germaine, it is won, the day is won!". The knight recognized Jahil's voice as he pulled Stinger free from its last bite.

The fog had thinned. Once again Germaine descended from his aloof, mental set of battle to the painful realization of the death around him. He clearly saw the devastation left by the battle. Bodies and pieces of flesh stained the ground red with blood. Germaine saw enemy and ally alike held in the indifferent grip of death. A few moans reached Germaine's ears as testimony that some were unfortunate enough to still live, though grievously wounded. Once again the Emerald Knight felt remorse for such great loss of life. *Perhaps men will learn to live together in peace one day. It is sad that it takes violence to stop violence. Sad, but a fact*. He could not allow his disgust for wanton death affect his resolve. To do so would mean his own death. Germaine sighed with relief that the rebellion had been crushed. He knew his task of defending Fenn Hold to be finished.

"You've been wounded, man!" The prince spoke, wiping his blood-spattered face and reaching for the knight's shoulder. "By the planets, I have never seen anything like the way you waded through the enemy! You must have slain twenty warriors."

Germaine reached out his sword and wiped it across a dark pant leg of his dead foe, freeing it of blood. After placing Lightning in its sheath, he repeated the process with Stinger. "Your enemy is defeated. Are you satisfied that my oath is successfully completed?" Germaine asked tersely. He removed his skull helm, noticing, as he did so, the new dent in it.

"Well, yes," the prince almost stuttered, "but it's not necessary for you to terminate your service now. The men respect your leadership, and I—"

"No!" Germaine said, cutting off the prince. "I must go. I make it a rule never to overstay my oath. Thank you for the offer, but I must decline." Germaine felt a twinge of sadness. He had grown to regard the prince much like a younger brother. Germaine had found forming attachments to be a dangerous habit to get into. Other than his wife and children, Germaine only allowed Mikial, his young page, into his life. *It is hard enough for me to look upon the bodies of fallen allies without having to see a close friend laying in the carnage.*

"It will be as you wish, Sir Knight," the prince spoke sadly. "Will you consent to stay until we celebrate our victory? It will mean only a few days delay while I make preparations."

Germaine looked at the prince, and his narrow mouth curled into a smile at Jahil's facial expression. Jahil, usually quite jocular, now displayed a manner that Germaine recognized as quite serious. "Let us clean the filth of battle from ourselves so that we may prepare for your celebration."

The prince laughed in relief. "You will not regret the delay. This celebration cannot demonstrate my thanks fully enough. Sir Germaine, if ever you need my aid, you have only to ask. It is true that you were hired to help rid my Hold of these invaders, but you far exceeded the terms of your oath. Now, let us get your wound tended, and then we will have a small celebration of our own!"

Germaine said earnestly, "There is one favor I would ask." Germaine could see his wife's image in his mind. He had not allowed himself to dwell on their long separation caused by his present oath term.

"Just name the favor. It will be done." Jahil answered with a broad smile.

"Would it be possible for a military escort to be sent for my wife and children? The escort would provide safe passage should they encounter some stragglers of your former enemy roaming the country side. We have not had the opportunity to spend much time together, and this would be a good holiday for them." Germaine ended with a smile as he thought about his family.

"It will be done, Sir Knight. I will dispatch an escort immediately. How long is the journey to your family?"

"My wife is staying at her sister's lodge, a day's ride to the west of Fenn Hold." Germaine raised his arm, indicating the direction. "I will give directions to the escort before they depart. I have not slept in the past twenty-four hours, or I would go."

"It is best that you rest and allow your wound to heal. Do not worry about your family. They will be delivered safely."

As they approached Fenn Castle, the Emerald Knight felt the fatigue and pain that had accumulated over the last few months. His body and mind protested every step, reminding him of the need for rest. He would gladly enjoy the hospitality of Prince Jahil's hold.

Germaine spied a familiar figure, his page, Mikial racing across the castle's drawbridge as they neared it.

"Sir Germaine, how did the battle go?" Germaine would not yet allow Mikial to go into battle. Germaine still saw him to be more a boy than man. Though common for a lad of thirteen years to serve as page for a knight, Germaine did not want to chance the boy's death. He had found him in a village leveled by war. There was no way to know who had attacked the village. In those days, Germaine knew, one could rely on the fact that attack is not a possibility, but a probability. The enemy had been gone from the village for more than a day when Germaine arrived. Germaine found the boy, a lone survivor of the raid. In an act of compassion, the knight reached out his hand to Mikial. As he remembers the scene, Germaine again feels the sobbing boy's tears against his cheek as when he comforted him on that now distant day. Germaine could feel the boy's excitement at being part of the knight's daily routines. Mikial had often talked about being a knight himself one day.

"The battle went well! God has given us a great victory this day! Now, we will rest and enjoy a celebration of our victory. How is Silver Cloud?" Germaine asked about his great, white stallion. The knight knew that Mikial loved to be in charge of the horse. The boy proved to be the only person other than Germaine whom the horse would allow on his back. Germaine had not ridden Silver Cloud in this day's conflict due to the forest terrain and poor visibility. With experience, the knight knew a man on foot in a thick stand of trees could use a lance to great effect against riders.

"He is well, Sir Knight! He has a full belly and is quite content."

Germaine, Jahil, and Mikial made their way across the moat bridge. The men walked wearily with the weight of the past days of conflict burdening their shoulders as they passed through the castle gate to a much needed rest.

A few days before the battle, far to the north of Fenn Hold, Lady Estella Merelda is in a discussion with her chief advisor, Bildad Genoha.

"Estella, you are not listening to me," whined Bildad Genoha. "Your life may be in great danger!"

Estella looked calmly at Bildad's aged face and thought about how much she had grown to depend upon his guidance. She recognized that he had been the advisor to her family for many years, long before her own birth. She had always looked upon him as a member of the family. Before the death of her parents, she did not think of him as a hired advisor. That he had actually been in their employ, and not a family member, became painfully clear with the sudden death of her parents.

Her dark brown eyes twinkled as she smiled charmingly and said, "Oh, Bildad, I still think you are overreacting. The death of my parents was an accident. You are the only member of this hold that suspects foul play." Speaking of the accident caused her sadness to rise nearer to the surface. Estella's smile turned to a frown as she fought to hold back the tears that began to rise from her heart.

She watched as Bildad screwed up his face in a scowl, "Estella, as the new ruler of Lyon Hold, you owe it to your people to protect yourself. I know your parents have been in death's keep for two months now, but you have to consider Lyon Hold and its welfare."

Estella walked gracefully to the window overlooking the great, east meadow. She could see the activity of the peasants and freemen in the village. *Bildad is right. These people are now my responsibility*. Had only her parents produced a son to inherit leadership of the hold. She knew it not to be an unusual event for a woman to rule a hold. In fact, quite the opposite was true. The truth of the matter was Estella never considered the possibility. Her parents had been healthy and appeared to have many years ahead of them. She never aspired to be the ruler. She wanted to find the right man to wed, and one day he or their offspring would rule. Estella's smile returned as she considered her rapid approach to the old maid age of twenty-three without a serious prospect. With this thought, she turned back to Bildad and said, "we still have the men-at-arms here to protect me. Do you not believe them to be sufficient?"

Bildad's face twisted in a frown. "Estella, the men-at-arms are not combat hardened. We have enjoyed peace for many years, and I fear we would be remiss to expect them to be capable of protecting you."

Estella thought about the men who were counted as the common soldiers known as men-at-arms. Several looked to be quite old, and the rest seemed to be younger than herself. "All right, Bildad, what do you suggest?" *May as well humor the old worrier*, thought Estella. *Even though I believe him wrong about the death of my parents, I will keep an open mind. Should not a good ruler have the patience to listen?*

Bildad pivoted and pointed to the south, as if to emphasize his words. "I have heard of a valiant knight to the south who swears liege oaths to those on the side of right, who need protection. His current oath is nearly ended, and he could be here within a fortnight."

"What kind of man is this knight? I do not want some cutthroat on my doorstep."

"My Lady," he answered, "by all accounts, the Emerald Knight is a man of the old code. He has never lost in combat or joust. He is a man known to be of great honor and would never violate his oath to protect his liege."

Bildad paused. Estella felt he considered another point. "I am told he belongs to a religious sect that seems to be harmless, though its basis came to this land by way of the Romanos. Even though the influence of Rome has all but disappeared from our land, their religion still influences some, especially in kingdoms to the far south. The members of this sect call themselves Christians."

Estella watched Bildad's craggy face as he spoke. She could feel his great respect for this knight.

"And my Lady," Bildad continued, "he would train our men-at-arms so they would be better defenders of this hold and its lady. Your father and I had been lulled into a false security with the many years of peace that have fallen behind us. We have been taking peace for granted."

"You have convinced me, Bildad. Send for this Emerald Knight at once."

She turned and, once again, stared out the window, deep in thought. *I have loved this meadow and my memories that have lived in it for all these years. How many times did my dear mother and father play with me among the wild flowers? My innocence is gone, but my memories will be cherished as long as I have breath.* The death of her parents brought her the greatest sorrow she had ever known. A tear fell from her cheek as she remembered how her father was always trying to spark her interest in finding a husband. Just the day before his death, he had walked with Estella through her meadow. "Stella, you need to settle on a husband, not because I want you to, but you need someone to share your life. You are in your mid-twenties, and I fear you will grow to be an old maid, bereft of love and companionship. You know that your mother and I will not live forever, and we would like some grandchildren to spoil." With this memory, Estella's tears flowed freely. She did not hear Bildad as he left the chamber.

Estella thought for a few moments about the knight. *What kind of person will he prove to be? I hope that Bildad is correct in his assessment of this knight. We will see.*

Five days after Estella sent Bildad on his journey, Germaine waited impatiently at Fenn Hold for the arrival of his family.

Germaine's family arrived just before noon of the day of the victory celebration. Germaine helped his wife as she dismounted. Even with their years of marriage, Germaine felt the quiver of emotions tug at his heart. He marveled within that she was as beautiful as the last time he saw her. *When was that last meeting? Three months? No, it seems more like an eternity. Our separations are growing too long.*

Daren, Germaine's son, was already at his father's side. The knight watched his daughter, Durelle, as she easily dismounted from the horse she had ridden.

"Ana, I find you more beautiful with each meeting between us." Germaine removed her riding bonnet and ran his fingers through her golden hair as he gently pulled Adriana to him, embracing her with a kiss. Releasing Adriana, Germaine turned to his daughter and son and encompassed the two in a great hug. "How much you have grown since I last held you. Durelle, you are near to a full-grown woman, and beautiful as your mother. Daren, you are no longer a boy, but a man. It will not be long before you will not wish to be hugged by your father."

Adriana placed her hand on Germaine's shoulder. "We have missed you, Scotty. The days are much longer, and the nights have greater cold and darkness without your presence in our lodge." Germaine smiled at her nickname for him. When he had first brought her to his castle those many years ago, she loved the sound of his surname, Scot. He remembered how she corrupted the name into Scotty, her personal view of his identity.

Germaine turned to Adriana and gently placed a hand on each of Adriana's arms as he looked deep into her blue eyes. "You do not know how much pain I feel at times because of our long separations. This last Oath of service has been much longer than any before it. Even the previous terms I have served have been longer than usual. It seems as if the world is turning upside down in conflict. I hope to spend some time with you and the children now that my service to Fenn Hold is completed." *It is a strange irony in life that for my family to live I must protect others. While I serve as liege, I must depend on family and friends to see to their protection.*

Adriana smiled. "Perhaps it will be so, my knight, but should those plans fail, you know that I understand your code. I would never try to separate you from doing those deeds that help others. It is true that you earn a living for us with your service, but we both know helping others has been your greatest passion since the loss of Scot Hold."

Germaine held his wife close once more as he spoke softly. "You know me as well as I know myself, yet you are wrong about the source of my greatest passion. You are that source. Every thing I do, every breath I take, is for you. Make no mistake of my motives in serving liege oaths. I want to return us to the life we had at Scot Hold. My fear is that I should awake one day to find that your love for me no longer lives in your heart."

Adriana kissed Germaine and whispered, "My love for you will last until my final breath is drawn in this life. Do not fear losing my heart. It will always be yours. If we succeed in rebuilding our castle, it will bring joy to me because I know it will fully restore your life. If it should befall that we do not recover what was lost, I will still be happy as long as I have you."

The knight took Adriana's hand in his. "Come, I will show you our quarters. Jahil insisted on his finest rooms. I fear the young prince is trying to spoil us. There is time enough for us to freshen ourselves for tonight's celebration." Germaine beckoned to two servants who waited nearby. "Bring these bags, please."

"Daren, how was your birthday? Was my gift to your liking?" Germaine asked. He had happened upon a finely crafted chess set made of whale bone while traveling through a coastal town. He purchased the set and left it with Adriana on his last visit, to be secreted until Daren's birthday.

"It is as much fun to look at as it is to play. I have beaten Durelle many times."

"I have beaten him as well, father," Durelle flared.

Germaine laughed and said, "I will be happy if you confine your conflicts to the movements of chessmen on a board." Germaine held Adriana's hand as they made their way through the castle courtyard to a high, arched portal. The knight knew the opening in the gray colored stone wall gave access to the lower level with two stairways, one going upward and the other going downward to the cellars below. The entry hall to the ground level rooms lay between these two stairs. Germaine, who led the group up the stairs, spoke, calling Adriana by her nickname. "Ana, how is your sister's health?" Her sister had been ill when Germaine last visited his family.

"I fear her end is near. She has waged a valiant battle, but the illness has beaten her down." A tear formed in the corner of one green eye as she spoke. Germaine thought about how beautiful Ana was, even in sadness. He found her green eyes and blonde hair the right balance to her lightly tanned face.

The knight turned his thoughts once more to his dream. He hoped that one day he would have the resources to rebuild Scot Hold. He wanted Ana to have all that had been wrenched away from them by the barbarian Picts. Not for the first time, Germaine wondered if the horde could have been turned back if he had been present during the attack those many years ago. *No, my brave captain and his men-at-arms defended the castle to the last man. Who could have done more than those loyal servants who gave their lives defending Scot Castle?*

Germaine and his family, followed by the two servants, entered the room in the upper level. As they talked, Germaine's thoughts returned to the present. In just a few short hours, they would be celebrating the victory over the dark invaders. *Yes*, Germaine thought, *I am going to take some time for my family. We have been apart for too much time in the last few years. My dream can stand a little delay.*

10

The afternoon hurried in its passage to evening and found Germaine reclining comfortably on cushions with a long, low table before him. On the table were vast quantities of beef, pork, vegetables, and fruits of many sorts. To Germaine's left was Prince Jahil of Fenn Hold. On Germaine's right was seated Adriana, wearing a beautiful, green gown with white frilly trim on the neckline and hem. Germaine noticed she sat upright upon the cushions while she dined, her golden hair pulled into a bun. The knight could never understand how she remained as beautiful now as she did when they first met. Around her neck she wore a dainty, silver chain with a crucifix suspended from it.

Germaine looked at the children, Durelle seated to Adriana's right, and next to her sat Daren. He saw the two youngsters were obviously excited about the festivities.

A wide-eyed Mikial was seated to Jahil's left. The dancing troupes before them were very skilled and colorfully dressed. Germaine noticed that Mikial was especially interested in a blonde, blue-eyed girl who performed with the dancers and looked to be about his age. Germaine was amused with the youngster's expression. He realized the boy approached the age where girls were less of an annoyance and more of an attraction.

Mikial turned to Germaine. "I believe I could dance like that, Sir Germaine."

With a smile Germaine looked at the boy and said, "Why not give it a try, Mikial? I believe Prince Jahil will not object."

Jahil grinned at the youngster. "By all means, let us see if you have a future in entertainment."

Germaine was astonished at how quickly the boy jumped up and joined the dancers on the floor. *No shy wallflower this lad*! Germaine saw that Mikial spent a few minutes in adjusting his steps, then the boy fit right in with the others. The knight had found Mikial to be very open when dealing with his page duties, but away from them he was usually very reserved.

The evening was very entertaining and relaxing for the knight. A troupe of jugglers who performed without error, tossing knives and swords into the air and from one performer to another, interested the knight. Germaine leaned toward Jahil and said, "I am well familiar with my swords, but I would not try to throw them about like that. I wonder how many jugglers lose hands trying to learn this skill?"

Jahil pointed to one of the troupe. "That fellow has many scars on his arms. He must have been a slow learner." Germaine joined the prince in a good laugh. The knight felt a lightness of spirit that he had not experienced in many months.

A magician followed the jugglers, and Germaine found himself unable to detect the fellow's sleight of hand. The man made many objects disappear, among which was a full size sword that vanished in a hand cloth. *This fellow is very good at his art. It is a pity I cannot pull Scot Castle out of a cloth, making it whole as it was of old.*

As much as Mikial had enjoyed the dancing, Germaine noticed that the boy liked the magic tricks even more. The magician came to where the boy was seated and appeared to pull a dove from Mikial's ear. The knight smiled, seeing the lad taking advantage of this brief respite in life to be a carefree youngster. Too much of the boy's childhood had been torn away.

Germaine noticed Durelle and Daren were as awed over the magician's tricks as Mikial. Germaine was happy that he had sent for his family and hoped they would always remember this time together.

Much of the evening Germaine watched Adriana, noticing how the juggling acts and dancing enthralled her. The knight smiled as his lady laughed melodi-ously at the antics of a juggling jester. Costumes worn by the dancers seemed to light her eyes with wonder. Germaine was amused by her rapt expression as she watched the jugglers.

Germaine's favorite part of the evening was having his wife's hand in his as he relaxed in the company of his family and friends. *Yes,* Germaine thought, *it is a good evening!*

As Germaine watched the magician, he saw a messenger approach the prince and say something in his ear. When the messenger left, Jahil turned to the knight. "It seems you have a visitor who wishes to do business with you. He will await you in the foyer."

Germaine raised his brow at that revelation. He had intended to go to his home and spend time with his family before looking for another term of service. *I will speak with this visitor after the celebration ends, but it would have to be something of dire consequence to cause a change in my plans.*

The evening flew past with the speed of an eagle. Just as all things good or bad must end, good things seem to end more quickly. With a twinge of regret that their evening together in celebration was ended, Germaine rose from his cushions to take his leave of the prince.

"God be with you, Sir Knight," said the prince, "remember my hold is always at your service!"

Germaine bowed. "My thanks and eternal gratitude to you, sir!" The knight held Adriana's hand as the children followed them to the foyer.

When Germaine had entered the outer foyer, he was greeted by an older, graying man, who was slightly stooped due to the weight of his years. Germaine noticed he had a hint of mirth about his eyes. He could see the light of a great mind in the old man's clear, blue eyes, eyes that seemed younger than the wrinkled brow above them.

"Sir Knight, I greet you on behalf of the Lady Estella Merelda, mistress of Lyon Hold." The old man bowed. "I am her servant, Bildad Genoha."

"Greetings to you, Bildad, and to your mistress. How may I be of service?" Germaine smiled as he returned the man's formal greeting.

"Sir Knight," Bildad appeared nervous to Germaine, "we at Lyon Hold have need of a warrior such as you. It is possible that Lady Merelda's life may be in grave danger!"

Germaine turned to Adriana. "Would you allow me a time to talk with this man whilst you and the children return to our chambers?" The knight felt conflicts rise within his chest. *Perhaps Bildad is overstating the danger. If he is not, I will weigh the need for my intervention with great care.*

Adriana nodded. "I will see you later, my knight."

As Adriana and the children left, Germaine noticed that Bildad's hands were shaking slightly. He looked to be quite nervous. Germaine decided a change of scenery might put him at ease. "You look as if you've had a difficult journey, Bildad. Let us go to the pub and finish our discussion over some ale."

Germaine and Bildad made their way across the castle drawbridge, walking to the village that was nestled in the shadow of Fenn Castle.

Meanwhile, as Germaine and Bildad walked to the inn, a sorcerer sat in deep thought within a cave nestled in the mountains far to the west of Fenn Hold.

III

Camron sat alone in the darkness of the cave. He heard not a sound nor did he see any movement in the chamber hewn from a mountain's rocky heart. He sat shrouded in the dim light that cast a twilight pall over everything. The old man sat at a table in the middle of the room. The object of his attention, a gemstone faintly glowing with red light, sat at the center of the table. On occasion the stone would flash, illuminating the room in a red wash before subsiding to a faint glow.

Time had no meaning for Camron. Only the pulses of bright, red light meant anything of importance. "The power of evil has increased its influence over the stone. See how bright it has become in the last two days." The old man spoke to himself, a habit born of being alone.

Again the stone pulsed. A ruffling of pinions caught Camron's attention, causing him to remove his gaze from the stone. In the momentary glow, the gray figure seated at the table widened his brown eyes that peered from beneath bushy, gray eyebrows. Camron threw back the hood of his gray cloak, revealing his long gray hair. Beneath his beaked nose grew a gray beard and bristling mustache. His eyes seemed to burn with the light reflecting from the stone's pulses. The lines on his face hinted at great wisdom. Camron looked to his left where stood a huge tree branch that had been placed there as a roost for a great owl. "Well, old Gryph, what do you think about this annoying light?" The owl sat watching the stone, in much the same manner as Camron had been doing. "If you could learn to speak, I would not have to talk to myself like a man struck by lunacy." Camron returned his attention to observation of the stone. He stared intently, not moving a muscle.

When the dark walls of the room were illuminated by the recurring flashes of red light, Camron could see the shelves and workbenches that lay beyond the table. The shelves were haphazardly laden with piles of books and manuscripts.

On the workbenches were various sizes and shapes of equipment. Camron used the equipment in the art of sorcery. Shifting his attention to the twists of metal tubing and cube-shaped devices, Camron spoke again. "What good is this equipment and all these books? What knowledge can I glean to dim the light of this power stone?" The man again turned his attention to the owl. "The red light of the gemstone is pulsing more frequently, Gryph."

Camron saw that the owl returned his look with an owlishly wise stare. "Do not look at me that way, Gryph. You know perfectly well that I cannot do anything about the evil that is being wrought by Craitor. The man is mad with his hunger for power. Here I sit, a sorcerer with almost no power at his command." He paused to look, once again, at the stone's ominous pulse. "It's been twenty years since I had an ally that was worthy of the power. Twenty years since the death of the last king selected by the power sword, Titan's Blade. Without such an ally, my powers are weak. It is a cruel fate that the powers controlling the world have tied my sorcery to that sword. Perhaps there will never be another that can fuel my talent." Camron frowned. "This has been the longest span without a choice by the sword. Can it be that the world no longer has room in it for a sorcerer and a mystical sword of power?"

The old man slowly pushed himself up and out of the chair. "If you suddenly decide to speak, Gryph, do not answer my last question. I fear the answer would prove that the world is also void of room for a leader of virtue and honor, the kind of man the sword would choose. The hour is late, and my bed awaits me. I am sure, old Gryph, that you are ready to strike out on your nightly hunt."

As Camron walked toward the chamber door, a blinding white light flashed, causing the entire chamber to disappear in its brilliant burst. A momentarily blinded Gryph was startled into a fluttering flight from his perch and almost collided with the old man before landing on the floor. As the light ebbed, Camron turned quickly and looked at the stone. He saw the light coming from the second gemstone that had been sitting anonymously next to the red one. The white stone had been unobtrusive for twenty years, residing near its red twin without showing any glimmer of light within its crystalline shell.

"By the heavens!" The old man was almost dancing. "Gryph, the power stone has awakened!" Gryph blinked his eyes and fluttered back to his roost.

The owl turned its head toward the opening that led out of the cavern chamber. "Ah. So you are no longer interested in the power stones, my wise old friend. Do not let the white light frighten you. It is of good, not evil. Let us find out who it is that has stirred the slumber of the stone. Perhaps I, Camron, am back in the realm of sorcery."

Camron rushed to one of the workbenches and picked up a small cauldron. The surface of the object was covered with runes and mystic symbols. As he carried the cauldron to the table, Camron spoke. "Califern, I need your mystic visions to answer my questions." The cauldron, Califern, contained oily liquid. He gently set it on the table, carefully placing it between the stones. "Now, Califern, show me the one who has awakened the white crystal."

As he released his hold on the bowl, ripples began to travel across the surface of the liquid. Reaching into a fold in his robe, Camron brought out a small vial from which he removed a stopper. After placing a little of the contents from the vial into the liquid, he watched intently as images began to appear. On the surface of the liquid appeared a knight dressed in brilliant green armor.

"I see you, Sir Germaine. Perhaps you will be privileged to see me soon as well." Camron walked over to a bookshelf. Pressing the secret latch in it caused a portion of the wall to open, revealing a small room. On a pedestal within the room lay a sword that was glowing with its own light.

"Titan's Blade is showing its long-hidden power, too! It seems that I must prepare for a journey." With that, Camron placed the sword in its scabbard and bound it in cloth for concealment. He would not chance to carry the sword openly, for someone might try to touch it. He knew the sword brought death to those who touched it without being chosen.

Camron then began to gather up various pieces of equipment from his lab, placing them in a heap to be loaded on his horse-drawn cart. The old man talked to himself as he labored. "I will not need all of my alchemy equipment. For this journey, I travel with the necessities." He picked up a bulky object from the pile where he had just laid it. "I will not need to transmute metal. Back on the shelf you go. If I need to make gold, I will expend some power on a minor spell to do so. Even now, I feel my power growing with the awakening of the white stone."

As Camron prepared for the journey, back at Fenn Hold Germaine prepared to question Bildad about the mission that had brought him.

IV

Germaine allowed Bildad to settle into a seat with ale in hand before he spoke. "This is much better." He noticed the old man did not seem as nervous as he had been at the castle. "What manner of danger is your mistress in, Bildad?"

"Sir Knight, until two months past, Lyon Hold had a kind and generous lord. He and his lady were well liked by all his subjects and associates. A tragedy struck one evening. Their bodies were found in a narrow pass, crushed by great stones from an avalanche. Two bodyguards were also killed so that none lived who witnessed the event. It has been called an accident, but this I do not believe."

Germaine looked sharply at the old man. "How is it that you have come to this conclusion?" *The old man may be thinking with his heart and not his head. I will listen, and perhaps I may find only an overactive imagination, vapor instead of substance.*

Bildad slowly withdrew a pouch from his tunic. "This is how." He opened the pouch and let something fall to the table.

Germaine reached over and picked up the object, turning it slowly between his fingers. His eyes narrowed as he recognized what he held in his hand. "A link of metal from chain mail armor. It could be from a knight or man-at-arms. Where did this come from?"

Bildad said, "I have been a long time servant of Lyon's rulers. After the bodies were found, I went to the site to satisfy my grieving heart. I was accompanied by a young officer, Byrone. It was his sharp eyes that found it, sir, at the top of the pass where the avalanche began. We also saw one footprint in evidence."

Germaine looked at Bildad. "So you returned to Lyon Hold and made this evidence known to others?"

Bildad grimaced. He replied, "Yes, Sir Knight, but others do not believe what is before their eyes. Our hold has been at peace for many years. I am afraid Lady Merelda is not overly concerned."

Germaine shifted in his seat. In these days of fragmented kingdoms and power seekers, this small bit of evidence was cause for Germaine to suspect foul play. "But did she not send for me?" *If the lady of the hold does not seek my aid, then this man is wasting my time. I cannot force a person to seek help.*

The knight recognized a pensive look on Bildad's face. "She did, but she did so only to humor an old man. That is all right with me, as long as it serves the purpose of getting her the needed protection."

Germaine sighed, hoping that he could still find reason enough to refuse swearing a new oath. "Do you not have a standing military unit that can handle this problem?"

"As I stated, we have been at peace a long time. We have a small garrison, but they are woefully under-trained and inexperienced. They could be an adequate guard, with your training." Bildad smiled slightly. "I can see that you are not eager to leap into another term of service. Once the men-at-arms are trained, we can reevaluate the danger. It is possible that the term would be quite a short one."

Germaine had one more question, though he already knew the answer. "You spoke of the former lord and lady being well liked by their subjects. Surely they had hearts that stood on the side of right and virtue. What kind of ruler is Lady Merelda? Is she of a like mind and manner?" Germaine would not serve a liege that did not conform to his code.

Bildad smiled. "Sir Knight, she is the reflection of her parents. She is a reluctant ruler, but she is worthy of your code."

"You spoke of term length. Make no mistake. I serve until the liege is satisfied of completion." Germaine paused as he took another quaff of ale. "Your lady has asked for my aid, and she will have it, sir. I ride tomorrow for Lyon Hold." Germaine rose from his seat. "I must prepare for the journey. Good night, sir." Germaine reached out to clasp the old man's hand in friendship.

Bildad stood up. "Sir Knight, may I impose to travel with you?"

"I will travel at a brisk pace. Do you believe you can keep up with me?" Germaine was eyeing the old man closely, ready to weigh his words and manner.

Bildad laughed. "I am not as frail as you seem to think. I will maintain your pace."

"Your company is welcome, sir." Germaine gave a curt nod as he took his leave. As he walked to his quarters, his thoughts were on his family. *How can I tell Ana about this new oath? It seems that I can never turn my back on those in need, and yet, I sacrifice the company of my family. Once I regain Scot Hold, I will then be able to turn my attentions to my family.*

When Germaine once again faced Adriana, he asked her to sit with him as the children settled down in the chamber adjoining theirs.

"I have been asked to serve another oath term. I believe it to be of great importance in life or death of the liege I would serve." Germaine felt a pang of guilt. *Why must I feel concern for the problems of others? Am I ever going to have the strength to say, 'Your need is great, but I will wait until another needs my help?' No. I would not be living by the knight's code of honor.* Germaine saw that Adriana had a slight twist of a smile on her lips. He knew she was trying not to appear disappointed.

"When will you leave, Sir Knight?"

"I must leave in the morning. I regret the shortness of our time together. Perhaps this oath term will not last long."

Adriana allowed a full smile to light her face. "Do not fret. I know your code well. We will await your return. Just be sure that you do return to us, Scotty. My great fear is that an enemy sword will take you away from us."

Germaine felt guilty as he thought about the fear Adriana must hold for him because of his dangerous occupation. "I will do my best to return to you, my love. I will also pledge to you that I will not accept another oath term until we have spent at least a year together."

Adriana continued to smile as she pulled Germaine close to her breast. "We must not worry about the days we do not yet hold. This day, right now, this moment, is in our grasp. Let us make the most of it." Adriana reached out and extinguished the oil lamp as she lay back and pulled Germaine to her.

The night passed too quickly. The dawn found Germaine departing from his family, once again.

Germaine maintained a calm, unconcerned manner on the first day of the journey as he rode Silver Cloud. Behind Silver Cloud, a mottled gray horse carried Bildad. Bringing up the rear were two packhorses for the knight's equipment. Mikial rode upon the back of the first pack horse.

Germaine led them along a narrow track through a dense, black forest. *At times it seems as if the trees are great sentinels, reaching out to grab at us as we violate their domain with our presence.* Germaine thought about the tales he had heard about fairies and elves living among the trees in the Black Forest. He had never placed much value in such tales. Even so, these trees were of great girth and very old. *Perhaps such beings could live here*, Germaine thought.

Bildad interrupted Germaine's thoughts as the travelers made their way beneath the leafy canopy that filtered the sunlight. "I have traveled this trail many times and still find myself disquieted by the gloom."

Germaine heard Bildad, but his attention was focused elsewhere. The knight had detected others in the forest. *There it is again. A brief glimmer of reflected light. The fools do not realize that the occasional rays of sunlight in the gloom of this forest lights them like a beacon for my eyes. There are at least three men shadowing us. Could they be robbers, looking for an opening to waylay us, or*—Germaine turned in the saddle at looked at Bildad. The old man was obviously unaware of their company. *Or do they have a more singular purpose?*

About an hour before dark, Germaine called a halt as they entered a small clearing.

"We will make camp for the night here," Germaine said softly. "There is forage for the horses, and we can safely make a fire." He turned to Mikial and said, "Search up some fire wood, but don't go more than fifty feet from this clearing."

As they dismounted, Germaine narrowed his eyes as he strained to pierce the surrounding forest. He tested the air with flared nostrils, and his ears were pricked for any sound. *I hear birds to the west of the clearing, but none to the east. The watchers are still abreast of us in that direction.* The knight turned quickly, strode to the second pack horse, and began untying thongs from one of the bundles. As the knight unwrapped the bundle, he knew Bildad approached and must have noticed that he had removed a bow and quiver of arrows from the pack.

"Ah, do you intend to hunt game?" Bildad asked.

Germaine turned from the pack horse and walked toward the old man.

Germaine saw Bildad squint as a ray of the evening sun found a momentary gap in the leaves to strike the polished emerald knob of Lightning, where it hung in the scabbard at Germaine's side. The knight always kept the sword at his side, even when he had been enjoying the celebration at Jahil's castle.

Germaine pulled the green cloth hunter's cap from his head and dusted his britches with a couple of quick swipes. He wanted to give the hidden watchers normal-appearing camp activities that would keep them from becoming suspicious. "Not so, Bildad, at least not four-legged game. We have had company for several hours. Do not look about! Act as if we are simply setting up camp."

Bildad looked puzzled for a moment, then said, "As you say, Sir Knight."

Germaine made a slight motion with his free hand to silence Bildad from further speech. "We have company, and I am going to greet them. I will leave the clearing as if to hunt. As I reach the trees, you call out, 'Good hunting, sir!' This will serve to allow our listeners to think we are unaware of their presence."

Mikial came trudging into the clearing with a great armload of wood. "Clear a place over there." Germaine pointed. "Build your campfire. Use but a third of the wood you carry, and do not leave the clearing again until I return."

"Yes, sir, it will be done!"

Germaine turned and walked into the woods. Bildad called in a loud voice, "Good hunting!"

Germaine waved, but did not answer. When into the woods a good fifty yards, he began circling the camp in a wide arc, making his way back toward the south. His eyes were constantly darting, looking for signs of his quarry. The knight's efforts were dedicated to moving silently. Movement in a tree thirty feet away brought Germaine to a halt. He stood as if frozen in mid-step. His spine prickled as he realized how close he came to being discovered.

Germaine saw the watcher about two thirds of the way up a tree. The man had not yet seen Germaine because he was still in the act of settling into his precarious roost. Smoothly, Germaine slid behind a tree. Peering around the trunk, he spied two men. He could see they were in a small clearing, with three horses standing near them. At times, they looked up into the tree, as if for a signal from the watcher above. Germaine watched as they nervously swung their attention to staring around at the encircling trees. Germaine knew they were concerned about the whereabouts of the hunter that had slipped into the forest.

Germaine studied the men. Their clothes were similar to those of men-at-arms. The knight noticed they wore light mail armor that reached to the thigh, the type he himself favored as opposed to the heavier, knee length type worn by many. Over the mail, they wore black over-tunics that were adorned with a hold insignia over the left breast of each. Germaine could see well enough from his vantage point to recognize the shield and crest emblems that distinguished each hold insignia. Germaine noted the watcher in the tree had left his weapons hanging on the pommel of his saddle.

Germaine inched closer to better hear the words they were quietly speaking. As he painstakingly maneuvered his way, Germaine kept glancing up at the watcher, waiting until he swung his head away before moving again.

Finally, he could hear their words. "I say, kill them at first dark. There's no need to wait longer. Our lord will be satisfied when they disappear without a trace."

"Quiet, fool!" The second man said. "Lord Prince told us to wait for the others. They will be here at first light. Together we will catch our quarry in a crossfire."

Germaine had heard enough. These were not thieves or innocents, but assassins. Drawing two arrows from his quiver, he loosed his first shot and had the second arrow away even as the first slammed home. The speaker fell forward with an arrow through his throat. The second man lost his throat and voice in the next moment. They dropped without a sound.

Germaine looked up. The watcher was still unaware of the fate of his fellows. He wanted to take this man alive to get more information about the plot. As Germaine moved closer to the tree, he saw the watcher look down toward his comrades. The knight watched as the man lost his balance when startled by the scene below.

Germaine yelled, "Hold on, man! I will spare your life."

As he got the words out, the man did grab a small limb. He still held the broken branch when he hit the ground. Germaine hurried to him, but his neck was obviously broken.

Germaine strode to the two men by the horses and quickly searched their bodies. The insignia on their tunics displayed a shield with a black falcon holding a curved sword. The field behind the falcon was blood red and the crest on the shield was the shape of a skull. *I have never seen an insignia such as this. What hold could it represent?* Continuing the search for clues, Germaine found a little money and jewelry, but nothing to solve the mystery. The body of the watcher yielded little else. Germaine sighed as he looked through the men's belongings that were strapped to the horses. *Just the usual kit carried by warriors. They were traveling light. Not many provisions. Perhaps they were planning to use our food.* Germaine pulled a belt knife from the waist of one of his victims and used it to cut away one of the insignia. He folded it and placed it within his tunic's inner pouch. Germaine had a feeling that this would not be the last time he would see the black falcon insignia.

Germaine made his way to the clearing and summoned Bildad and Mikial.

"We have some work to do before dark." Germaine told them about the three men as they made their way to where the bodies lay.

Germaine saw Bildad look aghast upon the scene. "Who . . . Why were they following us?" The knight knew that, even with the suspicion Bildad had presented earlier, the old man was not prepared to face the reality of his fears.

Germaine said, "I heard some of their conversation. It seems we were to die early in the morning. These three were expecting reinforcements to arrive before sunup. I believe that they are part of some plot to prevent us from reaching Lyon Hold. We must conceal these bodies and move ourselves away from the beaten path before dawn."

Germaine dragged the bodies behind two trees that edged the small clearing. He lay them side by side and directed Bildad and Mikial to cover them with branches and leaves. As they covered the bodies, Germaine spoke to Mikial. "We will take their horses and weapons with us. If we were to free them, the enemy may come across one and become suspicious too quickly. It will be to our benefit for the comrades of these slain to ride, not knowing exactly where their prey may have camped. Secure the weapons to one of their horses." Germaine could not kill the horses. They were fine animals, and they did not share the fault of those who had ridden them.

After returning to camp, their labors completed, they ate a light meal. The knight would not allow himself or his companions any sleep before they broke camp. Germaine removed all signs from the clearing and brushed over their spoor with a leafy branch. They stayed upon the beaten path, maintaining a fast pace, until two hours after midnight.

Germaine reined Silver Cloud to halt and motioned to the trees as he turned to face his companions. "We leave the trail here." Germaine hid their tracks where they had left the trail. With luck, the riders would range far beyond the point where the spies had been slain before discovering their mistake. The knight led them through the trees about a half mile to the west of the traveled path. The underbrush did not hinder them, because the heavy canopy above allowed little sunlight to nurture the stunted growth. Their progress was much slower now that Germaine had to concentrate on keeping his bearings with few reference points. He knew the slower pace would allow the horses to recover some vitality.

Just before dawn, they heard the muffled pounding of many hooves as riders hurried toward the south. Fifteen minutes after the riders had passed, Germaine led his companions back to the trail. He knew they would make better time than they would if they tried to continue moving among the trees. Germaine hoped it would be time that their pursuers would not be able to make up with their hard-ridden mounts.

Bildad pushed his horse alongside Silver Cloud and asked, "Sir Germaine, last evening, how did you know we were being spied upon by those assassins?"

Germaine glanced at Bildad and then away. "It is an instinct that comes with many years of conflict. Is that not why you have hired me?" *Can it be a sign that I have been doing this work for too long, when I can almost smell the enemy? Feel his presence without having to see him?*

"Yes, Sir Knight. It would appear you are well worth your price."

Germaine and his companions kept sharp vigilance as they rode. The knight motioned them into the trees, again, just before noon. "A rider comes this way. He is traveling in the direction from which we fled." Germaine had his group well out of sight when the lone horseman passed.

"We will move farther from the trail and grant ourselves and the horses a short rest." Germaine wanted to keep his horses fresh. "If that rider belongs to the ones looking for us, his presence on the trail will be our boon. If he reports not seeing us on the path, perhaps their leader will think we have not yet entered the forest." About a mile from the path, they came to a stream.

Germaine signaled a halt. After dismounting, Germaine strung a rope between two trees that edged the stream. He secured the horses' reins to the rope, insuring that they could reach the water to drink.

Germaine spoke to Mikial. "You and Bildad sleep, whilst I keep watch." Germaine sat with his back to a tree, listening for intruders. He allowed his companions two hours sleep, then roused them to ride again.

The knight led them back to the trail, and they rode until late in the night on that second day. Germaine finally allowed a longer rest at about midnight, leaving the trail for a safer camp a short distance away from the path they had been traveling. They did not make a fire. Instead, they ate dried jerky from Germaine's pack. They washed down this meager meal with a little wine from Bildad's flagon.

As they sat in the darkness eating their meal, Bildad asked, "Sir Germaine, I am a man of much experience in the things that make up our world. However, something has been tickling my curiosity. If I may be so bold as to ask, where did you come by the green metal of which your sword is made?"

"It is a story much older than most of remembered history. My ancestor, the founder of Scot Hold and the first of the Emerald Knights, Sir Mallock Scot, is the one responsible for the green blades. The tale has been passed down to each generation to keep its knowledge alive."

Germaine paused for another sip of wine, "Early in the evening of a clear spring night, generations ago, Mallock and a group of his warriors were settling into a new camp near a marsh land. As they sat around the fires that night, a fiery omen flashed across the sky and crashed into the marsh with the sound of thunder. Mallock and two of his warriors were the only ones who dared to approach the site where the glowing ball had crashed into the ground. The object was on the edge of the marsh and half-buried in mud and water. It was so hot that vapors arose from it, and the water hissed with its heat. Mallock set a guard around the object until it cooled enough to be approached. For two days, the heat was so intense that they could not come within fifty feet of it without singeing their hair. After four days they could get close enough to strike it with hand-held stones. The heat was just bearable at such proximity. When they struck the object, it did not sound like stone, but like something with which they were not familiar. Using heavier stone to hammer on the object caused several large pieces to separate from it. Fine metal was not widely available in those years, but Mallock recognized that the object was composed of quality metal. Lifting the shards with their crude iron swords and pikes, they placed the pieces on a nearby outcrop of granite. They pounded the shards into rough billets by striking them with heavy stones. Mallock found an armorer who shaped the green metal into swords. They were crude in appearance when compared to those of the Romans, but they were strong enough to slice through Roman iron. The Romans were making their first incursion into Briton and were equipped with fine metal swords. Most of the people in Briton and the kingdoms to the north, including Valeria, were using cruder iron to forge their weapons. Do not misunderstand me. There were many in Briton who wielded swords as fine as those of the Romans. There were several master armorers who had been trained in the art from their fathers, and their fathers before them. However, their production was limited. As time passed, Mallock had the swords reworked and honed to greater sharpness."

"The source of the green metal still lies hidden on Scot Hold land. Through the years, metalwork has improved enough to produce these swords that I carry, yet even these are very old, having been reworked over the years." *More than weapons, these two are old friends.* Germaine rested his hands on the hafts of the swords as he thought about the years he had wielded them.

Bildad broke into the knight's thoughts. "I have heard of mystic swords of power. Are these swords mystical? Is there magic in the green metal from the heavens?"

Germaine laughed. "Other than the emerald light that shines from within the metal, its only outstanding property is great strength and sharpness. It will slice through armor as easily as a knife cuts lard."

"That is an amazing story," Bildad stood up and stretched as he spoke. "Thank you for being kind enough to share it with me. Now I must rest my weary bones."

"We will all sleep until first light." Germaine spoke as he settled down on his blanket.

"Should we set someone to watch?" Mikial asked.

"No, we all need rest badly. Do not worry for I am a light sleeper, besides Silver Cloud will rouse us should someone approach our camp. He is a light sleeper as well."

Germaine and his fellows did not experience any more skirmishes on the journey, and Lyon Hold came into view on the third day. Germaine surveyed the lay of the land, with an eye toward possible need for defense. A small castle surrounded by a water-filled moat sat nestled in the Black Forest. A village crowded about the area adjoining the apron of the castle drawbridge. As Germaine examined the scene, he noticed the buildings of the village were unremarkable and occupied a narrow stretch of land in front of the castle. He nodded in appreciation of the layout as he looked across the wide, defensive grassy area that lay between the village and the forest that bordered the hold to the north, south, and west. Germaine could see a great meadow to the east of Lyon Hold Castle. He relinquished the lead to Bildad, as he led Germaine and Mikial in their passage over the drawbridge which spanned the moat. Two men-at-arms guarded the gate to Germaine's new liege.

Bildad spoke to Germaine when they had reached the courtyard of the castle. "You will be shown to your quarters first, to bathe and change from your traveling clothes before you meet Lady Merelda." As Bildad dismounted, he beckoned to a young man wearing stable livery, "This lad will see to the horses."

V

It was nearly two hours before Germaine and Mikial were escorted to the evening meal. Germaine wore his emerald green tunic and pants. Mikial wore a simple, blue tunic and pants, with a black sash around his waist. Upon the left breast of their tunics was the Scot Hold insignia. The shield was of a silver background with emerald green sword and lightning bolt crossed. The crest above the shield was an emerald green, battle helm resplendent with a plume of the same color. They met Bildad outside the dining chamber. He announced them to the assemblage as they stepped into the room. "My Lady Merelda, I present Sir Germaine, of Scot Hold, and his page, Mikial."

Both guests bowed at the waist and moved to the seats indicated by Bildad. Germaine noticed the appetizing fare that lay upon the table. He looked at his new liege with a critical eye. She wore a scarlet gown with white, lacy frills on the sleeves and hem line. Around her dainty neck rested a string of pearls. She was about a foot shorter in stature than Germaine and her hair of fine texture and dark brown, almost black. She wore it in a kind of bun held in place by a comb set with pearls to match her necklace. Her nose, though small, fit the proportion of her face. Germaine's gaze rested upon her eyes. He felt them to be an asset to her appearance. Her large, dark brown eyes gave a wide-eyed look of innocence to her face. *She is not unattractive, nor is she of great beauty. The lady looks to be a person who bears the weight of leadership with dignity.* Germaine had served other female lieges and had found most to be sensible. A few had been quite the opposite. Germaine felt a knot in his stomach when he thought about the lady who had almost gotten him killed with her 'good' intentions. Of course, there had been some lords who had caused him problems as well. He saw a smile stir on Lady Merelda's delicate, painted lips.

"Sir Knight, I hope I have passed your inspection," she said, laughing musically.

"Pardon my manners, Lady Merelda. It is my habit to analyze my liege each time I take a new oath. I meant you no disrespect." Germaine felt a twinge of embarrassment. *I am getting careless, to allow someone to read me so easily.*

"I do not take offense, Sir Germaine. Tell me of your journey to Lyon Hold while we dine."

Germaine began recounting the events, noting that Merelda raised her eyebrows when he reached the point about killing the spies. When he had concluded the tale, she began questioning him.

"Sir Germaine, is it not against the old code to kill without warning?" She had an intense, serious look on her face as she spoke.

"No, my Lady, not when on the field of battle or anywhere lives are at stake. These men had stated their intention to kill us, and they were well armed. Their actions placed them on a battlefield, and I was their foe." Germaine felt impressed with the young woman's question. Germaine knew the knight's code did not contain a great volume of rules, but he knew it as a way of life that few outsiders could understand. The basis of the code was simple. Common sense on the side of what is right. *This young lady has taken time to acquaint herself with at least some of the code. She demonstrates herself to be of potential leader quality.*

Lady Merelda's smile returned. "I am curious. Why do you wear emerald colored clothing and carry weapons of the same hue?"

"I wear emerald because of my ancestor, Sir Mallock Scot. He was the leader of a band of men that fought a desperate war against invaders from across the Sea of Storms. Mallock and his men wore green clothing to help conceal them in the forest. When the conflict was finally ended, Sir Mallock chose to use emerald as the color of his family crest. The weapons also played a part in the color selection, as the metal they are made of is emerald in color, but that is another story."

Estella Merelda had a rapt look on her face. "What an interesting history. We may talk about it again, Sir Knight. I notice you wear a red emblem on your left shoulder. What does it represent?"

Germaine reached over and tapped the emblem with his right hand. "This, my Lady, is a cruciform emblem, a reminder of the cross upon which the Son of God was crucified."

"Oh, yes, your religious belief. Someday you must tell me about this deity that was killed by mere mortals."

Germaine smiled broadly. "It would be my pleasure."

"May I ask why you hire yourself out in Liege Oath?"

Germaine said soberly, "I was once lord of a hold much like this one. While my family and I were attending a festival at a distant hold, Scot Hold was destroyed by Picts, barbarians from the north. My family was left with only the skill I possess. I have earned a living for my wife of sixteen years and our two children by swearing Liege Oath to those who need protection or those who desire training in knighthood." Germaine again felt the twinge of guilt that stabbed at his memory. In his mind he could see his men dying without their leader's aid.

He paused and then asked, "What of the insignia that I described with the black falcon and the sword? Has its like been seen in these lands before?"

The lady slowly shook her head no, then raised her hands in a helpless gesture. "Do you believe these men were part of some larger plot, one that may have included the death of my parents?"

Germaine carefully weighed his words. "It has been my experience, my Lady, that one must always expect the worst and hope for the best. While expecting the worst, keep your sword at ready, and be resolved to use it." The knight did not wish to alarm the lady with his opinions concerning the assassins. He would await further proof before stirring hot embers into open flame.

"You will be my sword, Sir Germaine." Estella said. "My advisor will work out the details of your contract. I trust that you enjoyed your meal, even though we had so much to discuss." With this, she stood up. The rest of the party stood, as was proper respect. "I will look forward to seeing you tomorrow."

Germaine watched her glide through the door as she made her exit. Bildad guided Germaine into the library where he and Germaine agreed upon the letter of their contract. After agreeing to terms, Bildad and Germaine drank a flagon of wine. Germaine allowed Mikial his measure, as page.

That night, as Germaine lay upon his pallet listening to Mikial's snoring, he reviewed his appraisal of Estella Merelda. Though she was short in physical stature, she seemed to exude a strength that could carry her through difficult times in her role as mistress of Lyon Hold. She did not seem to be overbearing, so his term of Liege Oath shouldn't be too difficult. Germaine soon drifted into a much-needed sleep.

Germaine arose an hour before daybreak and stirred Mikial from his sleep. After an early breakfast, the knight set Mikial to work cleaning the weapons and armor. The boy would have everything at a high polish before the noon hour.

Bildad arrived a half hour after daybreak to escort Germaine on a tour of the castle and its defenses. Accompanying Bildad was a man-at-arms wearing a captain's badge of rank on the breast of his chain mail corselet. "This is Crom Vilad, captain of the soldiers of Lyon Hold."

Crom was a giant of a man. Though Germaine gauged him to be about an inch shorter in stature than himself, he carried at least fifty pounds more weight than Germaine, and it wasn't fat. Red hair streamed from under his silver helm, and a red beard all but concealed his mouth. The knight observed that the green eyes of the captain peered out of a craggy face that showed the lines of middle-age.

"May your sword be strong and true against your enemies." Germaine said, greeting the captain with the warrior's code.

"And victory to you, Sir Knight," returned Crom, swinging his right fist up to thump his chest in salute.

Germaine pointed to the ramparts above them. "Let us begin there."

Crom turned to a nearby ramp-way and led the way as Germaine and Bildad followed.

Germaine was impressed with the preparations that had been made for defending the castle from the ramparts. He saw strategically placed vats of oil with firewood stacked nearby. Stored in armory niches along the wall, he saw crossbows with bolts. Long bows with arrows had been placed in other niches, as well. Along the walls at regular intervals hung repelling poles to be used to push away the ladders of would-be invaders. Around the entire inner perimeter of the rampart ran a wide walkway, four feet below the highest edge of the rampart wall. The knight estimated the walls formed a rough rectangle of about two hundred fifty by two hundred feet. The east and west walls were the longest. Germaine noticed a spacious terrace located at the midpoint of each of the four walls of the rampart. The terraces were widened sections of the walkway, and provided a place for a catapult mount. Each mount could be swung on a pivot to provide a wide range of a barrage on any attackers below.

Germaine walked to one of the catapults and remarked, "This is much smaller than a siege machine." Piles of round projectiles lay near each of the four catapults, ready for use. "The projectiles are not large, but their effect would help hold attackers at a distance." Germaine stepped over heavy ropes that were connected to iron rings set in the rampart wall. He noted that the ropes encircled the catapult base. "These ropes keep the catapult from throwing itself backward, into the courtyard or the roofs of inner rooms. Is it difficult to swivel the mount with these ropes binding it?"

Crom answered. "No, Sir Knight. Two men push against the extended launch beam before pulling it back for another volley. The movement is slow, but the mount maintains its set when launching."

The knight walked over to the rampart wall and peered out over the meadow to the east. Looking down at the moat, he gauged the distance to the ground at about twenty-five feet.

"Well, Bildad, I am impressed with the weaponry you have in place for resisting a frontal assault. How efficient are the men who will use this equipment?"

Bildad frowned and said, "Sir Knight, this is our weak link. Our men-at-arms lack training."

Germaine allowed a half-smile to twist his lips. Training warriors paid well, but Germaine never looked forward to the task. "Then it looks as if I must begin to earn my keep."

Turning to Crom, Germaine said, "Assemble your officers on this eastern rampart in fifteen minutes."

"It will be done!" Crom answered, with another chest thumping salute. He then turned and hurried down the nearest ramp.

When the officers had gathered, Germaine put them at ease. There were ten men, including the captain, and they ranged in age from about twenty years to Crom, who appeared to be the oldest. The knight looked out over the meadow to the distant hill on the horizon.

Drawing his sword, Lightning, he gestured with its point to the distant hill. "What you see around you, the village, this castle, that meadow, may have to be defended with your lives. Is there a man here who does not wish to chance losing his life in battle for the defense of these things?" Germaine looked intently upon the face of each man as he spoke, evaluating the character of men he would have to fight beside. He did not detect a lack of resolve.

"Have any of you ever been in battle?" Crom stepped forward, as did two others. "Good. We have a core to build upon. Over the next days, I will show you techniques in using long bow, sword, catapult, and spear. It will be your job to teach your subordinates the techniques you will learn. I believe that time may be shorter than we wish, so we will act as quickly as possible. Muster is sunup tomorrow."

Germaine knew how difficult the two weeks of training would be for the officers, but he knew that it would be physically and mentally draining for himself as well. Germaine used the rest of the day to familiarize himself with the area surrounding the castle. He spent some time within the village, evaluating what would need to be done to prepare the people for a possible attack. At the end of the day, Germaine and Mikial ate with the soldiers who were assigned quarters within the castle. Most members of the garrison, Germaine knew, were residents of the village, entering the castle only during their official duty time. Germaine turned in for a well-earned rest, knowing the days ahead would be hectic.

When Germaine rose before sunrise, he was ready to meet the day and the challenge ahead. After the men had their quick breakfast, Germaine led them outside the castle to a more open area.

"The swords you now hold are made of wood. Treat them as if they were sharp iron." Germaine paused. "Notice you have not been given shields. There is a reason for this. In man-to-man combat with broad swords, a shield is excellent for parrying. However, in a battle with many men involved, reflexes and your sword will prove to be your best protection. A shield can actually hinder you. Suppose you are fighting with a man in front and to your right, a man to your left may thrust past your shield while your own sword is obstructed by the shield you thought would protect you. Do not think I am condemning the use of a shield. In the days to come, we will learn how to use the shield for defense, and on offense as a means of throwing your opponent off balance. I am saying that if you learn to parry with your sword, even whilst you are using it offensively, you will make better use of a shield. I prefer to use two swords, one for defense when the other is on offense."

Germaine pointed to a young officer with the tip of his wooden sword. "Step forward, Jarod. Stand as if you are preparing to duel with me."

The officer did as Germaine directed. Germaine lowered his sword and said. "Move your feet further apart, with your left foot a little in front. Bend your knees, and be prepared to spring in any direction. Remember. Your offensive thrust, or sweep of the sword, may have to become defensive in an instant." Germaine nodded as the man adjusted his stance. "All of you practice this stance. From it, you can thrust, like this." Germaine demonstrated as he took a half step with his right foot and thrust his sword forward. "Now, Jarod, I want you to attack me with a thrust motion."

Jarod stepped quickly and thrust at the knight's midsection. Before contact could be made, Germaine parried the thrust and had his sword point at the officer's chest. "As you have seen, anyone can make a thrust. The difference is the ability to parry and turn the enemy's attack to your advantage. Separate yourselves into pairs and practice thrust and parry."

Germaine walked among them and gave pointers and advice. After twenty minutes, he showed another strategy and combined it with the first. It was a building process, and Germaine was setting one stone at a time. By the end of the first day, the knight had the men performing all the moves in a kind of dance. Germaine sensed a rhythm in battle, and this was the best way he could teach what he felt.

The days passed with Germaine teaching the men a new weapon daily, and spending part of each day reinforcing their use of the weapons already learned. Germaine found the officers to be quick studies, and the drills went smoothly. One of the men did send an errant arrow on a path that came near to striking a villager, to Germaine's chagrin. When Germaine had succeeded in teaching the use of the weapons they had, he spent the balance of the two weeks in honing their skills with mock combat and drills. All of the training was conducted in a section of the defensive perimeter outside of the castle walls.

During these two weeks the knight saw no one other than the officers and Mikial, though he did on occasion see Lady Estella watching from a tower in the castle.

The month following the training of the officers was not as hectic for

Germaine, because he now served more as an observer while his officers trained their men. Germaine set the pace a little slower for the men, thus allowing the officers to achieve some respite from their own grueling two weeks of training.

In the third week of training, Bildad came to visit Germaine early one morning. "How goes it with the training, Sir Knight?" he asked.

Germaine smiled and said, "You have good men in your service, Bildad. They learn quickly. If our foe allows us another week of preparation, we will be capable of making a proper defense of this hold." *I hope we have that week. I want to send out squads of mounted men to patrol the surrounding area. They are not yet ready.*

"This is excellent news, which brings me to the reason for my visit. The Lady Estella requests that you join her for dinner. Be prepared to give her your evaluation of the progress that our men have made."

Germaine smiled and said. "A diversion from the soldier's mess is a welcomed occasion. Convey my acceptance to Lady Estella." Germaine felt relief with the training nearing its end. He wanted to do some investigation on his own concerning the insignia he recovered in the forest. Training the men had been his priority. As the day drew to a close, Germaine prepared to attend the dinner.

⇝ VI ⇜

When Germaine arrived at the dining chamber, he was wearing an emerald chain mail vest, breeches and tunic. High-top, black boots and a black sash about his waist accented the emerald colors. Upon the left breast of his tunic was the Scot insignia, with its emerald green, battle helm crest resting atop the shield with its crossed lightning bolt and sword. Germaine's sword belt was partly concealed by the sash and held his sword, Lightning, nestled in its sheath.

"Welcome, Sir Germaine," Estella said. "Is it necessary to dine with a sword at your side? Surely you do not expect the beef to be that tough." She smiled at the jest.

"No, my Lady," returned Germaine. "I would not so anger the cook. However, as I once explained to you, one must keep his sword ready. It is my experience that a jackal will not attack when and where he is expected. Perhaps this sword will ensure that I will be allowed to complete my meal."

"Germaine, your humor is refreshing. Please be seated." Estella indicated the chair to her right. Bildad was seated to her left. Unlike his previous dinner, Germaine discovered that on this night they would be the only ones eating at the great table.

"Tell me, Germaine. Are the men doing as well as they appeared during my observations?"

Germaine began, "Lady Estella—"

"Please," she interrupted, "just call me Estella. Leave the *lady* part for the benefit of other listeners. Tonight the three of us are simply comrades."

Feeling uncomfortable, Germaine began again. "As you wish, Estella. You have a good eye for the progress that has been made by your men. They will be capable defenders for Lyon Hold." *This group of warriors reminds me of my old hold force. They will not quit when the going is difficult.*

Bildad said, "Estella, you will never regret having hired this knight on behalf of your Hold." The old man paused for a sip of wine. "He has been most thorough in training the men."

Germaine smiled sheepishly. He really did not feel at ease with praise. He was merely doing the job for which he was being paid. Germaine's fear was that, in all of his preparation of the men, he might overlook something of importance to the saving of a single life.

Germaine bowed his head and silently asked a blessing on the meal.

Estella spoke. "I remember you bowing your head and making some pronouncement over the food on the first occasion we dined together. I must confess that my curiosity was roused. May I ask the meaning of this ritual?"

Germaine noticed her right eyebrow lifted in a high arch and a slight parting of her lips in genuine curiosity. "It is because my Savior demonstrated the blessing of food before He would eat. My mother was taught about such things by a Roman monk many years ago, and she taught them to me." Germaine could see his mother, holding him upon her lap and retelling the stories she had been told.

As they dined, Germaine and Estella continued the light banter with an occasional comment from Bildad. The knight found the evening the most enjoyable since the night he last spent with his family.

As they finished eating, Estella asked, "Do you know how to play Fox and Hounds, Germaine?"

"Why, yes, I do. I've been told that I'm quite skilled at it." Germaine had almost stuttered as he began. The question had been abrupt and caught him off guard as he was about to ask leave of himself for the evening.

With a motion to a servant, Estella stood up and beckoned to Germaine. "Come to the library with me, and we shall see how skilled you are."

Germaine could not remember, afterwards, how many games they played that evening. What he did remember was how much he enjoyed the time in Estella's company. She spoke knowledgeably upon many subjects, among them was that of hunting.

"My father expected a son, and had to settle for a daughter. I am afraid that he taught me a lot of unladylike activities. He taught me how to hunt when I was old enough to ride. I remember killing my first hare. I was so happy at first, but then I felt sadness when I looked at those eyes that seemed to be staring at me. I would go on to make many more kills during the many hunts with my father. I never truly enjoyed the killing of animals, but it was necessary to eat. My mother did not always approve of Daddy treating me like a son. She did her best to make a lady out of me, but without much success. My mother introduced me to several eligible princes. Unfortunately, I would end up defeating them at arm wrestling or steeple chasing."

Germaine laughed as he imagined the scene. "Were you hoping to find a worthy suitor by finding the man who could defeat you?"

"No." A shadow of sadness passed across Estella's face. "Competing was the thing I knew how to do best. I had learned my father's lessons well. I fear that most of my suitors found me to be an adversary, rather than a potential helpmate." Estella's face brightened. "However, as of late I have been more successful at remembering my mother's attempts at teaching me the finer points of being a lady. I have not frightened away too many suitors recently."

He was fascinated at the number of subjects she could converse about. It seemed that she was not afraid to ask questions. Germaine detected a genuine curiosity about his religion.

Estella smiled as she removed one of Germaine's game pieces from the board. "This religion of yours is fascinating, tell me how men overcame the god you call Christ."

Germaine paused as he remembered his mother's words. "Men did not overcome Him. He was sent to mankind by God for the purpose of dying on the cross. His death served as a sacrifice to cleanse the dark blot of sin from men who believe in Him." The knight moved a game piece. "My mother found it to be quite interesting that the instrument of Christ's death, Rome, was also God's method for spreading the news of Christ through the world. Rome invaded Briton in the year forty-three and brought more than their roads and fortifications. Christian monks were among them, with Rome's blessing."

"And you," Estella paused, a game piece held above the board as she spoke, "do you find it difficult to follow the teachings that your mother gave you? It seems that so many years would weaken your belief."

Germaine continued to smile as another of his game pieces was removed. "It is difficult at times to abide by teachings from so long ago. However, I have happened upon Christian monks, and enclaves of Christians over the years. My knowledge has expanded because of those I have met. I also keep the code of knightly valor, which includes duty to God." Germaine sadly remembered one of the enclaves he used to frequent. They had been destroyed by raiders. Germaine, once again, felt sadness over the price of peace.

Estella's curiosity was refreshing. What was more, he found himself glancing at her face often. True, he had earlier appraised her as no great beauty, but she had a beauty about her that flowed from within.

Once, during a move of game pieces, their fingertips touched for an instant. Germaine felt as if that touch surged through his arm right to his heart, causing it to leap in his chest. He felt like a giddy, young boy. He was both elated and concerned about these feelings toward Estella, because of his religious beliefs and the sanctity of his marriage vows. The knight could not remember ever having to question his feelings in the years he had been married. During some of those years, he had served oaths to attractive women. Never had he developed an attraction toward any of them. He knew he would have to examine these feelings at length.

"Germaine, I am about to defeat you again! You have not won a single game."

Germaine could see the competitive fires burning in her eyes. He could not, however, see any evidence on her face that she had felt any of the things that he had experienced during the evening. For some reason, this made Germaine a little sad. "Estella, I have enjoyed being trounced by you, but now I must go. Allow me to retire for the evening."

"Of course, Germaine. Be careful of the shadows, and keep your sword ready," she laughed as he walked out.

Deep in thought, he barely acknowledged the two guards that bracketed Estella's doorway as he left. He walked slowly to his quarters. By the time he gained the entrance to his sleeping chamber, he believed that he had the problem solved. It had been quite a while since he had spent any time in the company of a female. In his service to Fenn Hold, he had rarely spent any time away from soldiers. He had enjoyed two brief visits with his wife, Adriana. Considering that his service to Fenn Hold was for a full year, time spent with his family was rare. No wonder he felt some happiness while in Estella's company. His feelings were not those of lust for physical favor. As he thought about the time spent in her company, he could not recall anything outstanding about her that would cause a sexual attraction. In fact, other than her face, and demeanor, she was somewhat average in appearance. With these thoughts, Germaine decided that his enjoyment of Estella's company did not conflict with his beliefs.

Thinking of his wife made him long to see her again. Perhaps this crisis at Lyon Hold would prove not to be serious, allowing him to visit her soon.

Germaine remembered the day he first met the woman he would marry. He had been riding through a forest, hunting for game. Hearing shouts nearby and the clanging of swords, he rode to investigate. He found a small coach being defended from robbers by two men on horseback. They were bravely fighting against six attackers. As Germaine drew Lightning and charged into the fray, he noticed the driver of the coach was already dead. Germaine's charge turned the battle, as he slew two of the attackers. Two survivors of that raid fled for their lives. As Germaine rode near the coach to check on the condition of the valiant defenders, a blow to his head knocked him unconscious. When he came to, a beautiful woman was dabbing at his brow with a damp cloth.

"Please, forgive me. I thought you were one of our attackers." She was beautiful. Germaine discovered that his heart had been smitten, as well as his head, by that timely blow.

Germaine, feeling much better with these revelations and memories, fell into a peaceful sleep.

On that same evening, many miles away, a gray hooded figure continued his journey to meet the Emerald Knight.

Camron sat unmoving, save for the jostling caused by the rough trail. The old man, wearing his gray hooded cloak, was perched upon the small wooden shelf that passed for a seat at the front of the two-wheeled cart. Camron's gaze was directed above the old, swaybacked horse that pulled its burden with a steady beat of its hooves. The cart's load was heaped high above the low sides. A heavy, waterproof cloth stretched across the cart to protect the contents from the weather and to hold everything in place.

He traveled along a trail through hill country where there were few trees growing in the rocky soil. In the distance, Camron could see the tall trees of the Black Forest.

His gaze was not fixed on the forest, but what he saw between himself and that distant forest held his attention. At the edge of the forest was an encampment. It had all the trappings of a military camp. Camron knew he would have to pass through it to reach the forest. *I cannot turn aside. Delay is out of the question. Perhaps these men will allow me to pass without incident.* Camron moved his hand to the inner fold in his robe. Feeling the power stone and his wand, the old man nodded his head slightly.

As he neared the camp, he counted ten men, all heavily armed. As Camron's little cart approached the camp, the men moved to block its path.

"Old man, halt your cart. We may have need for your belongings." The big warrior who spoke this command laughed ominously. Camron noted that the warriors were clad in black, with bird wings mounted on each side of their helms.

Camron spoke in a friendly tone. "Please, do not detain me. I have a long trip ahead of me, and I do not wish to harm you." The old sorcerer frowned as the men ignored him and began to pull his belongings from the cart. They paid little attention to him as he sighed and lowered himself from his perch to the ground.

Camron did not speak as he walked twenty feet away from the cart.

Suddenly, one of the warriors noticed that the old, gray figure was standing with his arms held straight up, above his head. In Camron's right hand was a slender metal rod and in his left was a glowing crystal.

The warrior in charge yelled. "Get the old man! Kill him quickly!"

The order came too late. A bright white light arced through the air between the rod and crystal. At that instant, a blinding flash of light erupted from the center-point of the arc, forcing screams of agony from the warriors as they died.

As the light ebbed, the sorcerer placed the crystal and rod in a fold within his robe. Camron walked to his cart, stepping over smoldering clothing that now held ashes instead of men.

"Delays, delays! Now I must reload the contents of my cart. Are there not people with manners in this land?" Camron picked up his scattered equipment and secured it for the journey.

Again, a gray hooded figure sat stone still on the front of the little cart as the swaybacked horse pulled its burden into the forest. *I have seen the clothing and insignia these men wore. These men belong to Craitor. Does he know of my presence, or was this a happening of chance?* The old man continued in thought, as he drew closer to Lyon Hold, and the Emerald Knight.

The next few days were uneventful for the knight. He spent his time checking guard duty rosters and directing men in the repair and upkeep of their weapons. Crom proved to be a very able captain, and Germaine left him to the execution of the day-to-day operations of the military.

Crom followed the defensive plan that Germaine had formulated. The knight had posted guards on four-hour watches at each of the four turrets that formed the four corners of the upper parapet. Two more guards walked a continuous route on the walkway of the parapet. On the lower level, Germaine set two guards to stand watch at the drawbridge gatehouse, while the captain of the guard remained in a booth at the center of the castle courtyard. The knight had assigned a sentry detail of two guards outside of Estella's chamber door when he first arrived at Lyon Hold.

Germaine felt that they were well prepared for unwelcome guests. Just the same, he conducted inspections at different hours during the night.

On this night, as Germaine walked up the ramp-way to the parapet, he was looking carefully around him for anything that might indicate trouble. The knight's eyes were narrowed as he came to a sudden stop near the top of the ramp-way. His blood became icy at the sight of a puddle of water near the outer wall, and the wet footprints that led to the ramp before they faded out of sight. Turning quickly, he raced toward the stairway that led to Estella's chamber, bellowing, "To arms," at the top of his lungs.

Lightning was already in his right hand as he came into view of the chamber door. He was just in time to see one of the guards at Estella's door go down, mortally wounded.

Germaine saw a stranger in black garb standing with a small sword in his hand, watching the guard fall dead to the floor. It was not the stranger's sword that had struck the death blow. It was the second of the two guards who had committed the evil deed. Germaine realized the treachery had caught the loyal guard by surprise. The poor fellow did not have the chance to draw his sword.

The knight whirled into action. Lightning appeared to leave a continuous green haze in its swinging arcs. "By the planets, surrender or die!" Germaine was wielding the emerald sword with unbridled fury as he struck without mercy. His anger was fueled into a frenzy by the murderous action of the traitor.

Striking swords with both the man in black and the traitor, Germaine pulled Stinger from its sheath and, in almost the same motion, cut the man in black about midway of his right rib cage. The wound was not serious and served to spur the stranger to a more fervent, desperate attack. Germaine parried the stranger's thrust with a swish of Stinger, at the same time deflecting a blow from the traitorous guard. Germaine's forceful counterblow caused the traitor to stagger back two steps. Germaine seized the opportunity to bring both swords to bear against the stranger. Although the stranger deflected Lightning away, there was nothing he could do about Stinger. It burst through his heart. The stranger's dead body struck the floor, and Germaine pivoted just as the traitor's sword grazed his calf. The traitor did not have time to relish his wounding of Germaine. Lightning struck at the same instant, removing the traitor's head.

As sane reality regained its hold on the knight, he heard a woman crying. Looking away from his fallen foes, Germaine saw the sobbing chambermaid of Lady Estella standing in the now-open doorway. Germaine saw that she stared horrified at the guard's head lying at her feet. At her side stood Estella. The knight noticed the lady had a rare frown on her brow as she viewed the carnage, but he could see no sign of tears on her face. Her shoulders were trembling, and her face was ashen. Germaine felt she was struggling to maintain a strong facade.

"Well done, Sir Germaine, well done!" Bildad's voice broke the silence. Germaine saw the old man hurrying toward him from his opened chamber door. "You have served the hold well this day."

Holding up his left hand to stop Bildad from saying more, he turned his attention to the two women. He said harshly, "Ladies, do not ever open that door unless you recognize either my voice, Bildad's, or Crom's on the other side. Is that understood?" Germaine did not want Estella to needlessly expose herself to danger. Even if the attacker should be losing the fight, Germaine knew the lady could place herself within reach of a dying man's weapons.

The sobbing chambermaid nodded her head. As Germaine turned his gaze upon Estella, he noticed for the first time that she held a short sword in her right hand. He also saw a glint of fire in her eyes.

"Has the world been struck by lunacy?" Estella turned her gaze from the fallen men to Germaine. "What purpose would someone have for harming me? Are the days of living in peace to be replaced by the sword?"

Bildad moved to Estella and put his arms around her shoulder much as a father would do to comfort a child. Germaine stepped forward and herded the three into Estella's chambers.

"Do not touch the bodies yet," he called over his shoulder to the men who had arrived soon after the fight was over.

Once inside with the door closed behind them, Bildad tried to comfort the chambermaid by offering her a glass of wine. "I know this is a difficult time, but you must settle yourself. I know you do not wish to further upset your lady." The old man's words seemed to help, or perhaps it was the wine.

"Estella, do you know how to use that?" Germaine pointed to the sword in her grasp.

Estella nodded, "As I told you earlier, my father taught me things that are usually reserved for a son to know. He showed me how to defend myself. I fear that I never took the training seriously enough and did not see a need for such skill."

Germaine raised the corner of his mouth in a half-smile. "It seems that I have neglected one of my students. At three this afternoon we will conduct your first lesson in the art of sportsmanship. We will complete the training your father began." Germaine studied Estella's face to see if she would reject his order. What he saw there was a small smile as she nodded her agreement. Germaine marveled at the strength the young woman had shown. She had never seen such as had transpired this night, but she stood firm.

"Sir Knight, it is as you command. Now I must ask you and Bildad to take leave of my chambers so that I may dress."

Germaine gave a start as he realized that he stood in the presence of two women in their nightgowns. He blushed, as he bowed, and left the room.

The moment was not to be lost on Estella as she laughed at his discomfort. "Do not worry, Sir Knight. We shall not speak of this impropriety."

As he closed the door, Germaine was glad to hear her laugh. He knew she had been stretching her will in an effort to maintain the appearance of being the strong ruler of Lyon Hold.

Now to see what the dead could tell the living, the knight thought as he approached the bodies. He walked over to the fallen guard. Crom was standing by the body. Germaine got his first good look at the face frozen in death and recognized it as that of Jarod, the young officer he had singled out in sword training. *Did I fail to teach him everything that was necessary?* Germaine turned to Crom. "This man will be given a hero's burial. I will speak to Estella about assistance for his wife."

Germaine walked over to the man in black and rolled the lifeless body of the stranger over. Under the black cloak, the man wore a black tunic and breeches, the tunic bare where the hold insignia should have been. In fact, Germaine could tell where stitching had been pulled out where an emblem had once been. "I believe that this tunic once held a shield with the crest of a skull upon it. Unfortunately, believing is not proof." *I can visualize the black falcon holding a curved sword.*

"We've seen clothes such as those before." Bildad had walked out of the door of the chamber after Germaine and was peering intently over the knight's shoulder as he searched the body.

Germaine did not look up at Bildad's intrusion but continued his search for clues. Two thin ropes were coiled up and hanging on the stranger's belt. In a pocket of the breeches was a rolled-up strip of cloth. The only weapon on the body was the small sword with which the stranger had unsuccessfully tried to defend himself. Germaine looked up from the bodies and found Crom standing before him. Finished with his search, Germaine stood up.

"Crom, I want this man's body placed on public display today. Secure the body to a plank, and prop it against the wall of a building in the village common area. Have every person in Lyon Hold view this corpse. If anyone has informa-tion concerning the stranger, bring them here."

Crom thumped his chest in salute and motioned four soldiers forward to remove the body. As the soldiers carried their burden away, Germaine pointed to the traitor's body. "What of this trash? How long has he been a man-at-arms for Lyon Hold?"

Crom walked calmly to where the head lay upon the floor. Stooping over he grabbed the grisly object, lifting it by its hair.

Crom looked at the face and said. "This is Dirk Arnot. He was received into service about four months ago."

Germaine frowned and asked. "How long would he have been in your service when the lord and lady were killed?"

Crom looked away from Germaine and then back. "About three weeks, Sir Knight." Crom had a look on his face that Germaine could well understand. The captain felt blame, himself, for hiring the spy, much as Germaine had blamed himself many times for the death of Scot Hold.

"Do not place the guilt on yourself, Crom. You could not have recognized this viper for what he was. Remember, no one considered the possibility of attack upon the rulers of this hold at the time of his enlistment. Even after the death of your lord and lady no one, save Bildad, thought the deaths to be anything other than an accident."

It was clear to Germaine, as he weighed the evidence before him, that this spy had infiltrated the military of the hold for the purpose of removing the ruling family. His efforts were first directed against the elder Mereldas in the form of the passing of information. Information that allowed a deadly ambush to be set. Tonight was a different story. He would have to speak to Bildad about the evidence he had discovered tonight. Perhaps the old man could shed new light on the motive of the unknown adversary.

Germaine stepped away from the knot of men who were still standing by the bodies and motioned for Crom to join him. When they were out of earshot, Germaine said. "Crom, after you have posted a new guard at Estella's door, check your roster for any men enlisted in the past six months. Do so quietly without arousing suspicion in the ranks." Germaine kept his voice low to prevent anyone from overhearing. "Perhaps this man was not the only spy set in place." Germaine felt anger twist within his gut like a knife thrust. A spy sent into a field of battle, or in a time of war, he could understand. The knight found the death of innocent people in a time of peace, by a spy, to be intolerable.

As Crom saluted and took his leave, Germaine turned to Bildad. "We must discuss this evidence."

Bildad said, "Let us go into the library, Sir Knight."

After they had settled in the library, Germaine said, "This stranger was not here to kill Estella."

Bildad raised his eyebrows.

"The stranger carried bindings for her legs and arms and a gag for her mouth. He would have carried her away in the night, if events had not gone in our favor." Germaine glanced toward the window and discovered the sun was up. The knight had lost track of the time.

"To what end, Sir Knight? Ransom?"

Germaine shrugged his shoulders. "The motive behind the actions of these men is not yet clear, Bildad." Germaine stood and walked to the window. "Is there anything of unusual value within this hold that would so attract someone's attention?" He remembered the tale of a kingdom rumored to own a great diamond, set in a tiara. Raiders attacked and destroyed the kingdom in search of the diamond. The raiders could not find that which did not exist.

Bildad shook his head. "There is nothing of value. Our treasury is no greater than many other holds. Most of our transactions are by barter."

Germaine continued to look out the window as Bildad spoke. The late fall air carried with it the promise of winter. Soon, the first snows would be upon them. *The identity of our adversary is still a mystery. Raiders in search of booty would not be so indirect. They would attack openly if they suspected anything worth the effort.*

"If our unknown enemy does not show his hand shortly, perhaps the snows of winter will give us a respite from this intrigue." Germaine knew that the very nature of the hold's surroundings would create a more difficult environment for any force attempting to attack in the winter season. The castle's storerooms would be well stocked for the winter, while an attacking force would find forage and shelter a problem. A siege force would face great difficulty in maintaining supply lines through the forest. Shaking himself from that thought, he came back to the subject at hand.

"When you originally told me the story of the deaths of the lord and lady, I felt there may have been an inside man to pass along, in advance, the activities of the lord. How else would it be possible for a trap to be set up without knowing that the lord's party would be traveling through that narrow ravine at that particular time? The traitor came into service here in plenty of time to perform that act of villainy. Our own experience, with the men who stalked us on our way here from Fenn Hold, indicated prior knowledge that you had come to me for aid. Perhaps there are others hiding in our ranks. We must remain alert for any activity by a soldier that is suspicious. It is difficult, at best, to draw a viper from its lair."

As Germaine again slipped into thought, he considered the possibility of moving Estella to another hold, perhaps Fenn Hold, for her safety. *No. It appears that someone is trying to remove her from this hold. Moving her would possibly aid the unknown adversary. Besides that, I do not believe Estella would consent to such a move.* Germaine was shaken from his thoughts by a loud knock at the library door.

"Sir Germaine, it is I, Crom."

"Make entry, captain." The knight strode toward the door. He noticed a man was accompanying Crom.

"Sir, we have one from the village who says he has information about the dead man." Crom said this in what Germaine recognized as an excited tone of voice for his usually staid personality.

As Germaine surveyed the newcomer who stood beside Crom, he felt as though he was looking at a gray shadow. The man was wearing a full-length cloak with a hood that covered his head. His face was mostly concealed by the hood. The color of the man's garb was gray, and what Germaine could see of his face also appeared to be gray.

"What is your name, sir?" Germaine felt a strange uneasiness pass across him like a cloud. *There is something about this man that seems familiar. Perhaps we have met before.*

"My name, Sir Knight, is Camron. I am at your service."

As he heard this name, Germaine gave a start. "Camron … Surely you are not *the* Camron. I mean the sorcerer, Camron!"

"One and the same." Camron gave a slight bow of his head with this acknowledgment.

"Forgive my manners, Camron, it is just that it is widely believed that you died at the time of the passing of the last, great High King of Valeria, twenty years ago," said Germaine. The knight remembered how the great, northern kingdom had fragmented into the many independent holds that now existed.

The gray figure chuckled. "Alas, as you can see, I am still walking upon the earth. What do you wish to know of Lord Craitor?" Camron threw back his hood. Thus uncovered, Camron appeared to be nothing more than an old, white-haired man.

"Craitor! I've heard of him but have never had the pleasure of meeting him.

What has he to do with this filthy work?" Germaine was trying to remember what he had heard about Lord Craitor. He could vaguely recall a conversation with another knight some years back. The Craitor of that long ago exchange was a knight of great strength.

"He is lord of a hold, and he calls himself, Falchion Raptor. He considers himself to be a knight but shuns the term in preference to *falchion*, an ancient term used by some cultures to identify a special warrior."

Germaine repeated the name, "Raptor. That is a bird of prey, such as a falcon." Reaching into a pocket of his tunic, he pulled out the insignia that was cut from the would-be ambusher.

Camron eyed the emblem. "Sir Germaine, the insignia you have in your hand, the black falcon holding a curved sword, is his emblem." Camron paused. "The crest represents his hold, Skull Fortress. It is well that you have not met him! He is evil and does not live by the old code as you do."

"How do you know about me, sir," Germaine asked? *Perhaps my feeling of having met this man has some substance.*

"I make it my business to know the affairs of many men. Besides, the exploits of the Emerald Knight are well known by many in the realm." Camron again paused.

Germaine felt uneasy as the old man seemed to be staring into his soul through the windows of his eyes.

During the old man's pause in his tale, Germaine noticed that Estella had entered the room, and now listened as the old man continued his story.

Camron said, "The Falchion Raptor has never lost in a joust or true combat. Unlike you, however, he makes up his own rules as he battles opponents. If you should ever face him in combat, remember to expect ungallant tricks on his part. He has slain many of his foes with a device in his sleeve that shoots small, deadly arrows. He has beaten many men who were far better warriors than himself."

"I shall remember your words, Camron, but what is his motive in this plot?"

"The Raptor wants to be High King of all Valeria. You already commented that a raptor is a bird of prey. Another meaning for the word is one who seizes. Several holds have already fallen to his subterfuge. He used poison to kill the crops of Glenn Hold. After staging riots, Craitor had the lord killed by his henchmen. Craitor then showed up as a benefactor to the starving people. They are now loyal followers of Lord Craitor, Falchion Raptor. He used various tactics on other holds. This hold is the next in line. Your actions here, and at other holds, have undoubtedly delayed him."

Camron again paused as Estella said, haltingly, "The evidence shows this evil Lord to be the probable murderer of my parents." The old sorcerer saw the tear that traced her cheek. "Realizing that someone intentionally took their lives ... it is difficult to bear the pain of knowing ..." Estella's voice trailed off before finishing.

Germaine asked, "Why have you stood by and allowed these other holds to fall before coming forward? Why have you made yourself known now?"

As Germaine asked this question, Camron was struggling with how much he should reveal to the knight. "I came to you because I have a personal interest in stopping this evil. My reasons for not appearing sooner are my own business for the moment." *I must wait until the right time to tell my full purpose to Germaine. I will not yet reveal that my powers are tied to a sword and a power stone.*

Germaine narrowed his eyes. Camron could tell that the knight did not care for the vague answer he had offered. "If you will not tell us the reason for your delay, perhaps you can tell us of your 'personal' interest?"

Camron's eyes became glassy, as if he were in a trance. "I served the last high king for twenty-five years. It was early in his reign that the Romans removed their last legion from the land. The Romans had left the northern kingdom intact during their occupation. The high king did not carry war to the Romans, and he provided a service by keeping the Picts, and other wild tribes of the far north, at bay. The high king paid a small tax to the Romans, and allowed a garrison to be stationed within his kingdom. The king was wise, and a worthy ruler. Valeria experienced an era of peace during his reign. Even the wild tribes that were usually troublesome seemed to respect his rule. When years had taken their toll, and the specter of his death approached, I swore to the high king that I would not stand by and watch his kingdom be destroyed by an unworthy leader. So far, there has not been a man worthy of being high king. I have waited these many years for such a man to come forward." Camron could not yet reveal his entire reason for coming to Lyon Hold. For now he would let them believe that preventing the unworthy Craitor from gaining control was his motive.

Germaine asked Camron. "Why not use your powers of sorcery to dispatch this evil knight?"

"Unfortunately, it does not work that way. My powers are available to use in helping a man of valor and honor, but, for me, I can only use them for self-defense. I believe you may be worthy of my assistance. If not my sorcery, perhaps my counsel, alone, will be of benefit." Camron knew there was a lot he had left unsaid, but that was the way it would have to be. *Germaine will have to be willing to accept what I will offer to him. Though he is worthy, he will still have to prove himself further.*

Germaine asked, "Would you agree to stay here in Lyon Hold so that you may provide us with the wisdom of your counsel? That is, if Lady Estella will permit you shelter?" The sorcerer watched as the knight looked to Estella and received her approval by way of a nod in agreement.

"If it is your wish, Emerald Knight, I will stay." *Just as I had hoped*, thought Camron.

Germaine asked Bildad, "Do you have appropriate quarters available for our new ally?"

"Yes, Sir Knight! We have a large room that was once a dungeon. I presume the, er, sorcerer must have alchemy equipment and such for which he would need room." Camron wryly noted that Bildad did not sound too eager to have this new guest under the roof of Lyon Castle.

"You are quite right, kind sir. I do have equipment. The gear is in my wagon that sits in the courtyard just inside the front gate." Looking at Germaine, Camron's eyes twinkled. "Do not be puzzled by the fact I conveniently brought my luggage with me, Sir Knight. After all, I did foresee that you would ask me to stay." With that the old wizard went out with several men to direct the moving of his equipment.

So began the sorcerer's stay at Lyon Hold. Within days, Germaine would watch as winter brought an early snowfall.

VII

With the first snows, Germaine's hopes were realized, as no further attempts were made on Lyon Hold. As part of his job, Germaine was personal bodyguard to Estella and spent many long hours in her company. During these hours, which were long in time but, seemingly, short in length to Germaine, he became a confidant to the lady. He found that he enjoyed the role.

Shortly after the first snow, Germaine was completing Estella's training in self-defense with the sword. He noticed she now wore the weapon at all times, even with her elegant dining gowns. "Always be prepared," she had laughingly asserted to Germaine on that first occasion she had worn the sword.

"Today we will see if your training will serve you in battle." Germaine smiled as he looked at the diminutive swordswoman before him. *I will have to be careful not to hurt her,* he thought as he prepared for their mock combat. "Remember, the swords are made of wood, so do not be afraid of injury."

"It is you who should fear my blade, Sir Knight." Estella spoke in a stern tone.

I must not be too tough on her. I would not wish to shake her confidence. As he thought this, Germaine noticed that Estella looked confident. "Now take your stance and prepare for my attack."

As Germaine took his position, Estella leaped forward without waiting for the command to begin. Germaine swiftly parried her jab and could have struck a grievous blow, but he hesitated. He thought the lady had lost her balance from his blow against her sword. From appearing to fall one instant, to whirling about and thrusting upward the next, Estella managed to force her wooden sword into Germaine's now unguarded left armhole of his chain mail. "Yeow!" The knight dropped his own wooden sword and swung his right hand to his bruised chest.

"Oh, I did not mean to hurt you. I am afraid that I became a little over zealous. Here, let me tend to your wound."

Before Germaine could answer, Estella had dropped her sword and was helping him remove the tunic and mail. She gently touched the bruise as Germaine looked down at her upturned face. As he looked at her dark eyes, she looked up, and his eyes caught hers. She hesitated a moment and removed her hand as she blushed.

"I do not believe there is anything broken. Will you forgive me for striking you so hard?" She turned her eyes away from him as she spoke.

"Forgive you? I am proud of my pupil. You have learned your lessons and taught me one as well." Germaine laughed as he pulled his under-tunic on and gingerly donned his chain mail. He tossed his over-tunic across his shoulder instead of pulling it over the mail. "I hope you deport yourself as well in the event of actual need." Germaine hoped that she would never have to resort to swordplay.

Germaine saw Camron on those occasions when Estella invited them to dine together, and at other times he would go to the dungeon to question the old sorcerer. Camron proved to be reclusive, but he allowed Mikial to spend much time with him in the dungeon.

On several occasions, the old man told Germaine that he had been farseeing but had not turned up any new information. Crom's earlier report concerning his scrutiny of the men indicated that there were probably no other spies. This was also the opinion of Camron. The old sorcerer told Germaine that he would be able to detect any of Scul's men who might enter the castle. From time to time, Crom would report to Germaine that the sorcerer had instructed that individuals should be turned away from the castle. Germaine did not know if the sorcerer was correct in his appraisals of suspicious persons, but, for now, he would allow the sorcerer's judgments to stand.

The knight also found that Camron had a curious aversion to being called a wizard. He had referred to the sorcerer as a wizard on several occasions until one day the old man retorted. "I am a sorcerer, a man of unknown sciences, not a carnival magician!" Camron had said with upraised eyebrows.

Germaine could not see the difference between a sorcerer and a wizard. The knight would sometimes resort to calling Camron a wizard, just to see his reaction.

Germaine continued spending time in Estella's close company during her waking hours. He knew that there was little danger of a military action during the winter, but he could not rule out another daring attempt to remove Estella.

He found himself on frequent, long walks with his liege within the halls and courtyard of the castle. During these occasions, they would have interesting conversations that made the hours hurry by quickly.

During one of these walks, Germaine was answering Estella's questions about knights. "Not many lords aspire to knighthood, at least not as many as in times past." Germaine paused as he remembered how his father taught him the elements of being a knight. "My father was a knight, and I asked him to teach me. He started me from the bottom, shoveling the manure of his charger. I became his page and worked hard enough to earn my knight training. My father said only men who were willing to work for knighthood could obtain it."

"What of your mother? Did she want you to become a knight?" Estella asked.

"Mother hated violence, but she knew the wisdom of being able to protect yourself and your property." Germaine had a fleeting thought about his loss of Scot Hold. "She did not leave me completely untouched by her views concerning conflict. Many times have I wished that bloodshed was not necessary. It is a thought for which I cannot afford too much time or distraction." Germaine noticed a concerned look on Estella's face. Why had he let her know of his feelings against violence? *I have never revealed my dislike for violence to anyone, other than Adriana.*

Estella looked away from Germaine as they continued to walk along the wall bounding the courtyard. Germaine looked down at their footprints in the shallow snow. He wondered how many times they had walked around the courtyard without realizing the time. Germaine removed his skull-helm and brushed the snow from his shoulder with his free hand. He always wore his chain mail armor while guarding Estella.

Estella broke the momentary silence. "I did not know that a knight could be so sensitive. You must find your line of work very difficult at times."

Germaine swung his gaze back to her face and said, "Do not worry, my Lady. I do not carry these thoughts close to the surface while in battle." Germaine regretted that he had spoken openly to Estella about his feeling toward violence.

Estella reached over and touched his arm. "I do not worry about your resolve. I have seen you when you were required to kill. I am concerned for you. I can see that you struggle within yourself because of the violent life you live."

Germaine shrugged, "It is of no consequence, and I would as soon forget the subject." Estella dropped the subject, but he noticed the little pout of her lips that always occurred when she was deep in thought. He knew she would soon be talking with him on some other subject. As they walked, he enjoyed the time with her. Soon evening would come and, with it, the evening meal.

Germaine was happy with the ritual he and Estella had been keeping each evening. They would dine together, usually in the company of Bildad, Camron, and Mikial. On this evening, as most others, Germaine and Estella settled in the library to play board games after the evening meal was completed.

She had a very large collection of games, and she gladly taught him how to play those that were unfamiliar to him. Her nature was as competitive as his own, and he seldom beat her at many of the games. Germaine found his strongest game to be chess. He observed that Estella did not care for the long-range planning and tactics that were needed. He and Estella had just completed a game that had originated in Gaul.

Germaine retrieved the last game piece and placed it within the ornate box that held its comrades. He saw that Estella still had her triumphant smile in place. "You do not have to be so smug about defeating me. I have not fully mastered the moves that the Gauls designed in their invention of this game."

Estella shook her head and wagged a finger as she said, "Do I hear excuses from the Emerald Knight? Perhaps these games are too difficult for a warrior."

Germaine smiled at the teasing lilt of her voice. "Wouldst you consent to a game of chess, before I withdraw for the evening?" The knight knew what her reaction would be from past experience.

Estella tilted her head slightly and raised her right eyebrow in a high arch above her dark eyes. "You would want to play chess. You know very well that I do not care for the game."

Germaine laughed. "You mean, I know very well that you cannot beat me at chess." The hour had gotten late, and Germaine knew it was time to depart. He had not intended to stay longer, only mentioning chess to nettle her.

The knight watched as Estella waved her hand toward the shelves of games.

"Perhaps another game would suit as well?"

Germaine stood and stretched after the long hours of sitting. "No. It is late, and I must be about my rounds before retiring to my own chambers."

"Very well, Sir Knight. You have my permission to withdraw. Have a peaceful night."

Germaine stooped slightly to retrieve his helm that was sitting on the table. Estella's left hand was resting next to it. As he reached out, Estella's delicate hand reached out to grasp his. Germaine felt his heart skip a beat as he froze in that position and looked at Estella's face. Their eyes met with that tender contact of hands. Germaine looked into her eyes, and was almost lost within their depths. How long they remained unmoving Germaine could not tell.

Estella spoke, and broke the spell. "Thank you for spending the evening with me." She withdrew her hand from his. "I have enjoyed your company." Germaine saw a smile sparkle upon her lips and in her eyes.

Straightening up, he placed the emerald skull helm upon his head. "The pleasure is mine as well, my Lady." Germaine made his way to the door and hesitated. Turning to Estella, he said, "Good night." He almost said, "Fair damsel." Germaine was angry with himself over his boyish lack of control. His head and heart were awhirl with emotions. As Germaine made his rounds of the guards, he weighed the events of the evening and the stirring he had felt within his breast.

Because of his very nature, these feelings brought concern for Germaine. He was, after all, married and had been ever faithful to his wife, but he had feelings that he could not yet define concerning Estella. As Germaine tried to analyze his emotions, he did so knowing that he would be held accountable to his God if he harbored lust for her. *I have not been aware of any conscious desire to share her bed. I am feeling pangs of love for her. Can it be that love and lust are one and the same? I do not believe it to be so, but I must guard against developing too strong an emotional attachment to her. No,* Germaine thought, *these feelings do not seem to be wrong, in fact they seem to be harmless.*

As the winter bore on in its relentless march, Germaine came to the realization that he loved Estella. Not as he loved his wife or offspring. The knight found that his family's love for one another was a penetrating emotion, imbedded within the fiber of their being. It was as if they were bound by the same heart beat. His love for Estella did not feel the same as that for a friend. Germaine reasoned that friendship seemed to come more from the mind, than the heart. The love of friends springs from a well of common interests and trials. *Yes,* the knight reasoned, *the heart does play a role in friendship, but not as greatly as that of family love.*

Germaine concluded that his feeling for Estella was a love that he never knew existed. The capacity of the human heart apparently held more depth than he had ever imagined. When he was with Estella, it was as if the outer raiment of their physical bodies did not exist. He felt as if he dwelled within her mind and heart, and she within his. Germaine could not adequately define the feeling. It was unlike any he had ever felt. It was unlikely that Estella harbored any of these feelings in her heart. He would keep this newfound love hidden within himself. Germaine decided that he would not spend every evening with Estella as he had been doing. He did not fully understand his feelings, and he wanted to avoid any further strengthening of his love for her.

Germaine turned his thoughts more often toward his wife. Before the snows had been heavy enough to make travel difficult and dangerous, Germaine and Adriana had exchanged small gifts by way of couriers that sometimes carried the post between holds. The gifts were to be opened on Christmas Day. It had been a family tradition to celebrate the Savior's birthday by exchanging tokens of love. Germaine would celebrate the day alone, as it had no meaning for anyone else in Lyon Castle. When the day arrived and Germaine held the package in his hand, he tried to visualize Adriana opening her gift. He had sent a silver ring with a black pearl setting. The price of the gift was much higher than he normally spent, but Germaine knew how much his wife loved silver and pearls. With all the work he had lately, the knight could well afford this one extravagance. When Germaine opened his gift, he found a silver crucifix on a necklace. Germaine slipped the chain over his head as a tear came to his eye. This was the second Christmas he had been away from his family. Next year would be different, if the Lord willed.

As the winter blew its frosty breath against the walls of Lyon Hold, Estella found that the time was flying by too quickly. With the weather restricting outside activities, she had discovered great joy in the company of Germaine. He was so unlike any man she had known. Whenever she spoke to him, Germaine seemed intensely interested in every word. On many occasions, when they were playing board games, their hands would chance to touch. Actually, it wasn't so much chance as it was intent on her part to feel his touch. She felt at times as if her heart skipped a beat with the contact of their fingertips.

Estella found herself lying awake at night thinking about Germaine's smile, his lips. Even his walk was etched into her memory. She could almost see the twinkling of his eyes as he laughed at her humor.

Once, while brushing her hair, she asked her reflection, "Should you tell the knight of your feelings for him? What are your feelings, Estella? Do you at last feel love? Have you ever truly loved someone? No, you can't reveal your feelings for a man who is married. This relationship can be nothing more than friendship. If only I can convince my aching heart of this inescapable fact." As she lay her brush upon the table, tears streamed down her cheeks.

Estella wondered why the knight had all but ceased his nightly routine of visiting with her. *Perhaps he has recognized my feelings for him, and finds them distasteful.* She would not forget Germaine, no matter what the future may bring.

As spring pushed away the cold and snow of winter, Germaine observed the great meadow to the east become awash in a multitude of colors as wild flowers burst into bloom.

When not guarding Estella, Germaine spent time with the old sorcerer as he worked in his strange laboratory. Camron assured the knight his power was indeed increasing. Camron had told the knight on one occasion, "It seems that you are a man worthy of an old sorcerer's help."

Other than Germaine and Mikial, the old man kept to himself most of the time, studying from his many books of potions and spells.

Germaine discovered that the old sorcerer was eager to share the working of some of his spells with Mikial and the knight. In fact, in the dungeon one evening, Germaine witnessed a wondrous event. True enough, Germaine had heard of wizards and their arts in years past, but he had never been privy to actually seeing the real thing. On this evening, when Germaine had entered the sorcerer's laboratory, he found the old man standing near a table with a big bowl resting on the table in front of him.

Camron looked away from the bowl, toward Germaine. "Ah, Germaine.

You are just in time to witness the workings of Califern."

Germaine approached the table and asked. "Do you give names to your dinner-ware, Camron?" Germaine was smiling as he spoke. The knight found some humor in the scene. The old man had turned back to the bowl and was staring intently, as if looking for a bug that had fallen into his stew.

Camron answered as he continued to look at the contents of the bowl, "No, No. This is not a food dish. This is a cauldron that holds peculiar power. It is ancient. Come, take a closer look at the contents." Camron beckoned the knight closer, without removing his gaze from the cauldron.

Germaine gasped when his eyes beheld the roiling liquid that seethed within the cauldron. Parts of scenes were scattered upon the moving liquid. Germaine noticed that the liquid was beginning to calm and smooth out, so that its surface looked like a sheet of ice. Upon the face of that sheet was now a life-like, moving presentation. A great, white animal was running in a full stride across a grassy plain, a grassland of blue colored grass. The animal looked like, "A unicorn!" Germaine bent closer to look at the great detail before him. "Is it real, or a creation made with your sorcery?" The knight could not take his eyes off the beautiful animal. The beast's eyes were glowing red, like living fire. The animal's muscles rippled under its skin as it ran with a tireless rhythm.

"Oh, he is quite real. In fact, he has a name. He was named Snow, by a man who befriended him as a colt."

The scene began to fade as the roiling motion returned to the surface of the liquid. Germaine moved to a chair and took a seat.

"What is this wondrous Califern? Does it show you things that are happening in far away places on Terra?" Germaine had never experienced such a leap away from what he considered to be natural.

Camron moved a chair near to Germaine and took a seat as he spoke. "Far away scenes on Terra, yes, but the scene you just witnessed is not of Terra."

Germaine's head snapped around to look Camron full in the face. "Where is the unicorn?"

Camron laughed at the expression on the knight's face. "I hope that I have not revealed too much to you with one act of sorcery. The place you have seen is Midaron. It is called Middle Earth by many."

Germaine shook his head. "I thought the tales of Midaron were only fables.

And unicorns ..." Germaine's voice trailed off as he remembered the scene.

Camron stood and placed a hand on the knight's shoulder. "Yes, unicorns live in Midaron. There are many other wondrous animals and beings living there as well. Perhaps I will tell you more about the place sometime. Now, I have other things to do. I must also enure you to the sorcery that I perform. You must learn to accept my acts of sorcery as a normal thing. How would you like to see a small demonstration of levitation?"

Germaine was shown many wondrous acts of sorcery during the times he visited with Camron. The knight knew most of those events were witnessed by Mikial as well. The sorcerer may have thought that the knight would get used to the magic, but Germaine never failed to be deeply awed by the things he witnessed. While guarding Estella, he would sometimes think about something Camron had shown him. He would shake his head with the memory, still not quite believing.

During his rounds Germaine began to notice that men, suitors of various ages and rank, were coming to visit the Lady Estella. Germaine knew that they were seeking her favors. The knight found that, in at least one case, she was granting them, when he happened upon Estella and a suitor in the library. They were embraced in a kiss.

Germaine felt repulsion and anger at these dandies. They were, in some way, not of the sort she deserved. He realized that he was experiencing jealousy, and was in anguish at times.

He had thought her to be perfect and had allowed a part of his heart to house a love for her. Germaine tried to convince himself that Estella's personal life was none of his concern. In the convincing, Germaine was not too successful. The knight continued to feel pain because of his feelings.

"Why did I ever swear an oath to this hold?" Germaine asked himself one day. "If only my term was ended. I must be away from her before my sanity takes leave of me." He knew that his knight's code prevented him from deserting his post. His only alternative was to harden his heart. He would soon be leading scouting parties into the forest in search of clues to Craitor's plan. At least he would be away from the castle and in the open air of the forest.

One evening, Mikial asked Germaine if he felt ill. The knight reacted as if the boy had committed some crime in the asking. Germaine appeared ready to strike him before he apologized. "I am just tired. Everything will be all right, Mikial. Please forgive me for my edginess."

When he was alone, Germaine remembered a story that his mother had told to him about a man named David. The account was from scripture that the monk had related to her. David had been a man of God who sinned greatly for love of a woman. A part of David's prayer for forgiveness came to Germaine, and he went to his knees asking, "Lord, create in me a clean heart! Please do not turn your face from me if I have transgressed." Germaine found himself longing for those days when his mother would tell him of her scriptural knowledge.

Germaine sat afterwards and wrote a letter. It was not a letter to anyone, but a letter that held the words his heart could not speak.

It is believed by some that man has not the capacity to love, but only the baser need for survival, using sex as the defining act of love. I have found that, at least for me, love is much more than that! In fact, man has a great capacity for love. I have loved my wife, family, and friends for many years, and I believed this to be the limit of my heart's reach. Alas, I was wrong.

When I met one, whose eyes seemed to pierce to my very heart, and my eyes to hers, I found great joy in her smile and thrilled to the chance touch of her finger-tips with mine. It was a feeling I did not wish to lose, but lose I did. I found that love, no matter how strong, cannot survive on its own, unreturned.

It was my heart's undoing that she did not know love or even recognize its fragrance. Therein lies my agony, a two-edged sword. For if she loved me, I could neither accept it, nor give her my love. Unfortunately for me, there will always be a part of my heart that cannot be returned to me, but ever will it be hers.

When I fight my last battle, and lay breathing my final breath, my heart will remember her with its last beat. Be careful, lest you share my sorrow

Emptying the feelings within his heart upon paper had the effect of salving Germaine's pain.

One morning, around the time of the incident with Mikial, Crom came to the knight with a message. "Sir Knight, there is news of the Black Falcon."

Because of the earlier mystery about the insignia with the black falcon, Germaine and his men often used the name Black Falcon when referring to the enemy. They did so even though they now knew the true name to be Falchion Raptor.

Crom said, "About thirty of his men have been seen several miles to the west of the hold. Our observer reports that they have set up a temporary camp."

At last, thought Germaine, *some action*. "Muster a squad of twenty men. Weapons will be swords and long bows. We leave in fifteen minutes. Have the men mounted and assembled at the gate for my final instructions."

Crom thumped his chest in salute. "It will be done, sir." Then he hurried out of the room.

When they were assembled at the drawbridge gate, Germaine inspected the squad. He knew from his many hours with these men that they were the best among the garrison with the long bows that they all now carried. "Crom, you take ten men and ride out to the north for two miles, and then pursue a stealthy sweep to the west. When you get within striking distance, maintain conceal-ment and hold your position. Wait for my move. As far as we know, this may be but travelers passing through our lands. If I decide differently, you will know."

Germaine looked up at the sky then back to Crom. "I will lead my squad out ten minutes after you, but I will go directly west. If there are watchers, perhaps they will only be concerned with my movements and not yours. Good hunting, Crom!"

"May your sword be swift and sure, Sir Knight," returned Crom as he saluted.

As they entered the path into the western woods, Germaine fell into his warrior's mode. His eyes narrowed beneath the brow of his skull helm as he slowly swung his head from left to right, scanning the trees. Within a few hun-dred feet, he had marked the location of four spies watching their progress.

Germaine motioned to his lieutenant to pull his horse closer. "Byrone, I am leaving my mount shortly. When I dismount, continue with my mount and the men for about a quarter mile. Wait for me there." As they rounded a bend in the path, the Emerald Knight literally leapt from his mount to the conceal-ment of the trees. A startled Byrone kept his wits and continued with the men as instructed.

Germaine waited for the last of his troops to pass, and then began to scan the trees with his eyes. The watchers that he had spied would surely have signalers to pass information to the rest of the waiting enemy. Germaine removed the long bow from his shoulder. He knew that it would be best to carry the bow in his hand to keep it from rustling branches that it could touch while slung over his shoulder. While Germaine continued to probe the trees with his eyes and ears, he had quietly moved so that he could see the western-most watcher in the trees. Even as he watched, he saw a message arrow launched from the watcher. Germaine followed the arc of the message arrow as it fell to the ground within fifty feet of his position. A figure came out of concealment and grabbed the arrow. Germaine readied his bow as the man prepared to launch the message arrow toward the west.

Germaine loosed his arrow first. The would-be signaler fell dead, with the message still in his hand.

The knight looked back to the watcher who had sent the message. God had been with him. The watcher appeared unaware of his signaler's fate. *Now to retrieve that arrow*, thought Germaine as he moved stealthily to his victim.

After retrieving the arrow and concealing the body, Germaine continued his westward route. A quick glance at the contents of the message told him that haste was important. He knew there were other signalers and they could send word of his waiting troops. Before the knight reached his men, he disposed of two more signalers. After quick inspection of their bodies, he found the Falchion Raptor's insignia on each. There could be little doubt that Craitor was the author of this intrigue.

When Germaine reached a point that was even with his troops, he saw another signaler. This one, acting as spy, watched Germaine's men. Germaine crept through the trees. He wanted to take this man alive. The knight saw that the spy was wearing mail, but on his head he wore a cloth forester's cap that was similar to the one Germaine wore while hunting. He approached close enough to the man that Germaine could reach out and touch him. Instead, he cracked down on the spy's head with the hilt of his sword. He had his prisoner.

With the spy safely bound and seated against a tree surrounded by the Lyon Hold men, Germaine read the message he had removed from the arrow. It was a simple message. 'Emerald Knight and ten men-at-arms approaching, set ambush!'

Germaine knelt beside the bound prisoner. "What is the purpose of your comrades for camping in this forest?" Germaine glared into the man's eyes with a look that contained no pity. "Speak, and no harm will come to you."

The prisoner's eyes darted as he looked at the armed, angry men gathered around him.

Byrone spoke in a hushed, growling tone. "Sir Knight, allow me to loosen his tongue." Byrone slid his belt knife out of its sheath and brandished it in front of the prisoner's face. "He can speak as well with fewer fingers." The lieutenant's ominous presence served to spur the captive into speech.

"We were sent to set a trap for the Emerald Knight. Lord Craitor wants him removed from Lyon Hold." The captive's voice was tremulous with fear.

Germaine sharply asked, "What were your orders, after you successfully 'removed' me?"

The man trembled. He struggled to keep fear from his voice. "We were to send word to Craitor. That is all I know."

Germaine rose from the position where he had been kneeling by the prisoner. "Do you know what Craitor plans to do after my removal?"

The man shook his head. "I am only a soldier. I only know the orders I have told you about."

Germaine told Byrone to place a gag in the prisoner's mouth and said, "Let us find those awaiting us. I will continue on foot to the south of the path and neutralize the rest of the signalers. There should be two, maybe three, more, considering the distance the arrows travel. Give me a ten minute head start."

"What of the prisoner?" Byrone asked the knight.

"Leave him securely tied to the tree. We will collect him on the way back."

Earlier, as Germaine had left on his mission in the forest, Estella wondered about the reason for the knight's avoidance of her.

Estella was troubled. She knew that her chambermaid had noticed a change in the manner of her mistress in the weeks since winter. The maid had told Estella on several occasions that she noticed her lady was pale and had little appetite. Estella had lost weight from her already small frame.

What have I done, causing him to ignore me? Estella wondered to herself. *Can it be that he has realized that I enjoy his company too much? After all, he is married! But I have not sought physical love in return for my affections. If only he felt the same way as I feel when he's near me!*

Estella walked gracefully to the window and looked out over the brilliant colors of the meadow. True, he was much older than herself, but he conversed with her on a level that bespoke no difference in age. She remembered that she didn't have any particular feelings of attraction to him early on, but those developed as she spent time with him in those many long, winter hours. They just seemed to enjoy each other's company. Never had she spent so much time alone with a man without him making some advances to her. She had considered telling Germaine of her feelings but knew they would be misunderstood. Alas, she would have to keep her love for him locked deep within her heart!

"Excuse me, my Lady." The chambermaid broke her reverie. "The guard has relayed the message that Lord Cornado is in the study."

Estella almost frowned at the news as she thought, *I should be happy, but for now I can only use him as a diversion to forget my heart*. With this thought, Estella made her way to the study.

Meanwhile, in the western wood, Germaine and his soldiers come upon the enemy camp.

VIII

What Germaine saw made his skin prickle. Out beyond the tree line that now provided concealment for the knight's men, Germaine counted fifty of the Falchion Raptor's men assembled. He frowned. Either his observer provided a faulty report, or more men had joined the camp after the report was made.

The Raptor's men did not seem to be concerned with any unannounced company as they were busy having some evil sport. They had one of Lyon's men-at-arms stretched out and staked to the ground with leather thongs. The man was being tortured, with blood flowing from several knife wounds on his body. It was clear that they intended to use a metal rod that now lay with its end suspended above a fire to further the man's agony. Germaine could not see anyone questioning the prisoner. The scene the knight watched appeared to be an action that was not aimed at gaining information. To Germaine it seemed that they tortured the man solely for the purpose of providing evil enjoyment to the warriors clad in black.

Germaine looked to his men. "We are outnumbered lads, but surprise is on our side. Let us make these scourges pay for the torture they have inflicted on one of our own. Crom should have his troops in position by now." Germaine hoped the poor devil being tortured was not one of Crom's troops. That would mean Crom and his men were probably dead. If such were the case, they would have no help.

"Here is my plan. Each of us will fire as one, a volley of arrows. Use careful aim with that first shot, and we will have taken eleven men out of the fray. When your first arrow has been loosed, quickly mark a new target and fire a second time." Germaine placed his hand on the shoulder of a warrior whom he remembered stood out in archery. "You will remain here and continue marking targets. If any seek their mounts, make them your primary concern. We will leave our quivers behind during our assault, so you will have plenty of arrows."

Germaine then addressed the rest of the men. "When we have loosed the second volley, we begin our charge to meet them with swords. Perhaps we can level the odds more in our favor."

Germaine narrowed his gaze and scanned the faces of his men. "Spread out now and watch for me to draw back on my bow string. Count three and then loose your arrows."

Germaine observed that about six of the enemy fell dead or wounded with the first flight of arrows, and the second volley brought down another five of the black-clad warriors. As they broke from their cover, Germaine saw the enemy in a turmoil of confusion. Some were bending over fallen comrades, while others were drawing swords and hurrying toward their tethered horses. At least two were dropped by arrows from his lone archer.

Surprise provided their advantage as the knight's mounted warriors charged across the open area and were on top of the enemy almost before the arrow-pierced bodies of the second volley had hit the ground.

The Emerald Knight leapt from his horse with Stinger in his left hand and Lightning, cutting its emerald arcs, grasped firmly in his right. Germaine was vaguely aware that Crom and his troops had reached the battlefield as he was wrenching Stinger free of a foe's skull. Even as he had the small sword free to strike again, Lightning severed the hand holding a battleaxe from another warrior. A thrust of Stinger silenced the man's scream.

"You could have saved some of the action for us." Crom howled. "We have only the easy pickings left of this rabble." Crom's words were an exaggeration, but the battle was soon over.

The battle had been long over as Germaine evaluated what he had observed. While he considered the evidence before him, the men were tending to their wounds and the dead. All but two of the enemy had been killed while Germaine lost but three warriors. Crom had a minor head wound, and his red hair was swathed in a cloth applied by Byrone. The young lieutenant had his own battle scar evidenced by a bandage wrapped about his left forearm. Somehow Germaine had escaped this battle unscathed.

"Sir Knight, I would not be eager to face you in combat! Never have I witnessed a warrior who would jump in amongst so many foes and move the way you waded through their numbers. I thought you would surely be dead before we could reach the field." Crom's voice held awe as he spoke these words.

Germaine raised his hand in a motion to silence Crom. "God was with us today! Praise His support. Without it we would fail. The men we fought against today were poorly trained. Can it be that this Craitor is depending on sheer numbers of warriors to accomplish his goal?" *What kind of leader would so neglect the quality of his military?* Germaine wondered.

Germaine walked over to the pallet where the man who had been tortured was lying. Kneeling beside the stricken soldier, he spoke to the one who was binding the man's wounds. "Is he going to recover?" Germaine had never believed in using torture. The knight knew that he would have probably used more caution in this day's battle, was it not for the helpless situation of the captive.

The man tending the wounds answered. "Yes, Sir Knight, their purpose was to obtain information without dealing life threatening wounds."

Germaine thought, *More likely they wanted him to die slowly so as not to spoil their fun.*

The man on the pallet looked up at Germaine. "Thank you, sir, for taking my behalf! Some of the men told me that my plight caused you to attack even though you were greatly outnumbered."

"You would have done the same for me." Germaine rested his hand on the wounded man's shoulder as he said this. The knight allowed his memory to return to the long-ago scene that greeted him on his return to the destroyed Scot Hold. Several of his brave men had obviously died at the hands of a sadistic torturer.

IX

As the Emerald Knight stood up, a strange event occurred. A huge, gray hawk alighted on the ground next to where he stood, as if it were attacking prey. As he watched in wonder, a haze seemed to envelop the bird. No! A man now occupied the place when the haze began to disperse.

"Camron, how wondrous your sorcery! Are there any limits to your abilities?" Germaine had witnessed many things at Camron's lab, but never had he seen anything as strange as the transformation that had just occurred.

"There is no time to waste, Germaine. I am the bearer of bad news. I was in a farseeing trance and saw illness strike your wife. As her illness grew, she and the children returned to Fenn Hold seeking a healer." Camron paused, as if he struggled with the words he must speak. "She is beyond the help of men or sorcery. Adriana has little time left. Even now, Jahil has her at his hold, providing her with what little comfort his healers can give her."

Germaine broke in, "I must ride!" He called to Crom who was several yards away tending to a man's wounds. "Return with the men to the castle. Pick up our other prisoner on the way. There were four watchers that I left unaffected at the start of this trail. Take them if they are still manning their post. I shall return to Lyon Hold as soon as possible. Until then, maintain your vigilance, for the enemy may be ready to move." Germaine's mind now focused on remembering the illness of Ana's sister. He feared the same malady now held his wife.

"It shall be done, Sir Knight! God speed your return to my side!" Crom saluted the knight.

Camron caught Germaine's eye. "There is not enough time left to Adriana for you to ride. If you will but trust me, you will be at her side in a moment."

The knight nodded and turned again to Crom, "Take Silver Cloud with you. May your sword remain strong and true, warrior!"

Germaine did not know what happened next. One moment he stood watching his men mount up; the next, he had a sensation of falling. His eyes were bedazzled by a swirl of color. Suddenly, he was standing in the familiar surroundings of Fenn Castle facing a very startled Jahil.

"Germaine, you almost gave my heart reason to stop beating! I am not so sure that sorcery is a reliable ally if it allows one to scare the wits out of his friends."

"Forgive me, Jahil. I am afraid that the need for haste does cause problems at times. What of my wife? Where is she?" Germaine trembled with the realization that he could already be too late.

Without another word, Jahil led the knight to a bedchamber. Within, he found Adriana lying on a bed. Their two children, Daren and Durelle, were by her side. When they saw Germaine, they rushed to embrace him with tears of grief. Gently pulling from their embrace he said, "My little lights of love, please leave us alone for a moment." At this request the children stepped outside. As they walked out, Germaine noticed that Daren held his sister close in an effort to comfort her.

Adriana stirred at the sound of his voice. "Ah, my Emerald Knight. I finally get to see you again, Scotty!" She smiled faintly as she voiced her nickname for him.

Germaine looked at her pale face and thin arms that lay above the folds of her blanket. The knight dropped to one knee by her bedside with his face near hers. He suddenly removed the skull helm which he had forgotten was on his head. "Ana, what has befallen you?" A tear rolled down each side of his face as he grasped her tiny hand in his.

"'Tis nothing, Scotty, only life. God has chosen this as my time to meet him." Germaine could hardly hear her whispered voice as she struggled with the words. "I love you, Scotty! I know that times have not always been easy for us, but, through it all, I know God has been with us."

"He is with us, Ana, in our living and in our dying. I am just not ready to lose you. I love you so much!" Germaine felt his tears flowing freely now. All the time he had spent away from her now haunted the knight. *She has been the driving force behind my efforts to regain Scot Hold. Without Ana, life and Scot Hold will be without meaning.* Germaine now felt the pain that no enemy weapon had ever been able to inflict on him.

"Scotty, you never could hide your feelings. In battle, perhaps, but not in love. That is one of the things that drew me to you those years ago when we first met. For a man of such a gruff manner when dealing with conflict, you have so much sensitivity and love." Her voice was growing fainter now.

"My love is but a reflection of your own heart, fairest Ana." As the Emerald Knight spoke these words, the hushed breathing of Adriana came to an end. Germaine, still blood-spattered from battle, continued to kneel, bending his head to kiss for the last time those, now, stilled lips. He sobbed aloud at the reality of his lost love. Germaine felt, too, the pain of guilt. The feelings he had felt for Estella now seemed to be a violation of the trust that Ana had placed in him.

After some time, Germaine dried his tears and called to Daren and Durelle. When the children saw that their mother was dead, their eyes were filled with tears. Germaine embraced them in an attempt to ease their grief. Germaine then knelt and prayed for his wife's soul and the comfort of the children. The knight knew that God would hear. He could not understand God's reason for taking his wife. No, he could not understand, but he would accept that God's will had been done. It was not his place to question why.

Meanwhile, as Germaine consoled his grieving children, many miles away the lord of a skull-shaped fortress confronted one of his own men.

"The Emerald Knight! Can we not even rid ourselves of one thorn?" Scul Craitor bellowed at the man before him. "Let me make sure of your account. You say the knight, with ten men, rode into the western wood, and two hours later you noticed that your signaler was missing?"

"Yes, Sir Craitor." The man stuttered before Scul's wrath. "I sent a message arrow to him and watched as he retrieved it. That was the last I saw of him as I turned my attention to the trail. About two hours later I sent another arrow with a message asking for our orders. When the signaler did not come forth, I set out to find him, thinking that perhaps he had fallen asleep. He was asleep right enough, with an arrow through his heart! That is when the four of us watchers took to the woods in a wide arc away from the trail in search of our troops. When we reached camp, we found the men dead or missing."

"You expect me to believe that a knight and ten men overpowered at least fifty-six soldiers?" Scul glared at no one in particular. *This green knight is a formidable opponent.* He must make better plans in the future if he was to succeed in his quest to rule. Turning to his guard, he commanded, "Take this man and execute him for his failure and for bringing me bad news!" *What is it that causes this one knight to be so successful against my efforts? I would have had Fenn Hold in my grasp if not for his interference. Some of my best officers, and most of my best men, died in that conflict.*

As the man was taken hold of by the guard, Scul lashed out with a kick to the man's stomach. Scul smiled as the man doubled up in pain. Scul said. "Go on. Take him outside and make an example of him. I will not tolerate incompetence." Scul fell into thought as the prisoner was taken outside. *I had sought to bring Estella under my control. I would have married her to bring her realm under my benevolent rule. Now that my plan to kidnap her has fallen through, I want the skin of the Emerald Knight draped from a pole. As for Estella, imprisonment or death. I will follow my fancy when the time comes.*

The Raptor paced the floor. "Perhaps it is time to bring this contest into the open. I will not allow another season to pass without adding Lyon Hold to my domain." Scul paused and turned to his lieutenant and asked, "Have we succeeded in placing any more spies in Lyon Hold?"

"No, my Liege. They have put to use some very effective method for screening soldier applicants. We have not yet figured out their methods. It will take time."

"We have no time!" shouted Scul. "My support is beginning to dwindle. I wanted to make Estella my wife to bring her hold into my power, but, failing that, her death or capture will serve me just as well. In fact, I have an idea of how I may capture her." Scul paused, in thought. *I have avoided revealing my true nature and power. Perhaps one small use of it will not present a problem.* With this idea, he continued. "We will place the castle under siege, bottling up this troublesome Green Knight. Once the people get hungry enough, they will gladly give in to accepting me as rightful ruler of Lyon Hold."

"Please forgive me for making a suggestion, sir, but we have not the resources for an extended siege. This plan could backfire and cause our own—"

"Enough!" Scul cut off the lieutenant's words with this command. "I do not want to hear what we cannot do, but only what we can do. My plan will work!"

"Yes, my Liege. We will make the plans for the siege." The Raptor noticed the lieutenant was sweating as he made his answer. He knew the man found it better to grovel than to die by the hands of Scul.

As Scul watched the execution, far away in Fenn Hold, Germaine experienced a different pain. Germaine felt anguish as he tried to cope with the loss of his Adriana.

Germaine suffered during the two days that had passed since the funeral of Adriana. He tried to keep up a strong front for the children, but his mind would return to thoughts of his lost wife. Jahil informed the knight of Camron's arrival early on the second day after the funeral. The sorcerer did not arrive on a mystic spell, but on a horse, with Silver Cloud in tow. When Camron arrived with Germaine's horse, the knight asked why he had not used his transportation spell.

Camron shrugged his shoulders. "I cast two major spells within a short period of time. I maintained the guise of a hawk for an extended length and then transported you some distance. Both of these acts require a great drainage of power. It is difficult to explain, but picture a gallon of water. That gallon of water may put out two small fires. If you should happen upon a third fire, you do not have water to extinguish it. The container must be refilled. In a similar way, my power has to be refilled."

It seemed to Germaine that the old man's arrival helped lift some of the sorrow from his shoulders. To maintain his sanity, Germaine turned his thoughts to Lyon Hold. He feared the danger to his liege to now be at its greatest.

Germaine met with Jahil. "Thank you for the aid you gave to my wife. It is a debt I can never repay. I have another request that will only add to the debt. I must return to Lyon Hold to complete my oath and have no family near enough to leave my children with."

Jahil said. "My lodge is your lodge. Your children are welcome to stay as long as need be."

The First Prince refused payment when Germaine offered, citing his own great debt to the knight. "I will, however, save any gold that you send for the children. Their future will be secure."

"Jahil, I do not know how to ask this of you. Should anything happen to me, would you …" Germaine struggled to finish the question. With Ana gone, there would be no one for the children if something were to befall him.

"You do not need to ask it of me. I would gladly raise them as if they were my own children. I would not let them forget their true parents, not that they would. Just do not let anything happen to you for we would all miss you greatly."

"I will try my best, God willing." Germaine smiled as he spoke, and grasped Jahil's hand in friendship.

Germaine walked over to his children and embraced them. "I am leaving you in Jahil's safekeeping. Obey him, as you would me. I would not leave you now if it were not for the danger to my liege. Daren, you must take extra care for Durelle's safety in my absence." The young man nodded in understanding.

Germaine swung up into the saddle on Silver Cloud. "Farewell! If it is God's will, we will meet again under happier circumstances."

Again Germaine found himself departing Fenn Hold, this time with the gray cloaked figure of Camron riding at his side.

As they journeyed to the north, they encountered none of the enemy, though Germaine kept a sharp vigil. The constant expectation of trouble served to ease the pain in Germaine's heart.

Days earlier, after the foray into the woods and the departure of Germaine, the Lyon Hold men made their way back to the castle, and a curious Estella.

When Crom and the others returned from their battle in the western woods, he made an immediate report to Estella. When he got to the part about the wizard, she asked, "What did Camron tell Germaine that proved so important to take him away from his duty?"

"I do not know!" Crom shrugged his shoulders. "It was as if the old wizard cloaked his words so that only Germaine could hear his voice. All I can say for certain is that a great cloud of concern seemed to fall upon the countenance of the knight, causing him some anguish. Then, after telling me to bring his horse to the castle, he vanished in the grip of one of Camron's spells. It made my skin crawl. I have heard of such magic, but never have I seen it."

Out of habit, Estella walked to her window and dropped into deep thought. As she looked out over the meadow, her thoughts were on the knight. *Is he now gone forever?* She wondered. *No. His code would not allow him to abandon his oath.* "The old sorcerer would know! Bring him to me, Crom. Perhaps he can shed some light on this mystery."

"That is not possible, my Lady. On our return trip he disappeared along with Silver Cloud. I believe he was going to meet the knight at some agreed location. I have no idea why they did these things, but I know from my experience with Germaine that he will return as he said he would."

"Very well, Captain. Is Mikial still with us or did he go up in a puff of smoke also?"

"He is still here, my Lady. I questioned him upon our return, and he claims to be as much in the dark concerning this event as we are. I believe the boy is telling the truth for he showed great concern when we arrived without Germaine or Silver Cloud in our company."

As Estella absorbed these words, she again turned to look out beyond the meadow to the far hill. *Where are you, Emerald Knight? Does your departure mean that you believe us to be out of danger, or is it that you now go to face that danger?* Estella felt a small tremor of fear go through her heart. She wondered if that fear was for her hold or for the knight she missed so mightily.

A few days after Estella had wondered about him, Germaine began his journey to return to Lyon Hold and his duty.

After four days of travel, on the night before their arrival at Lyon Hold, Camron informed Germaine that he would perform a farseeing spell.

"My power has created a feeling of danger within me. By use of farseeing, I may be able to fathom the meaning of these feelings. You must protect my person, Sir Knight, for I am completely vulnerable while in this trance. Do not try to awaken me for any reason."

"It will be as you have said, Wizard."

Germaine wryly noted Camron's disdain for the name of *wizard*, but the old man tolerated Germaine's use of it. Germaine watched as the old man seated himself on a blanket and placed his hands limply on the ground beside him. The knight thought the sorcerer appeared to sleep in his seated position.

Germaine paced quietly at times, and seated himself at others, while patiently awaiting for the old sorcerer's spell to run its course. During the lonely hours, Germaine's thoughts were turbulent. With Camron sitting silently in his trance, Germaine was effectively alone for the first time since Ana's death. His mind wandered with the memories of their life together, and at times he would think about his own loss of Scot Hold. He tried to focus his thought on Lyon Hold and his duty to Estella.

At about one o'clock in the morning, the old man stirred. "It seems that I once again have the misfortune of being the bearer of bad news."

Germaine felt a knot well in his stomach. "What news?"

Camron stood up to stretch his legs as he spoke. "Lyon Hold is under siege by the Falchion Raptor's army."

Germaine at once felt guilt. "I should have been there, my oath—"

"Do not fret, Sir Germaine. As providence would have it, Scul believes you to be trapped in the castle with the others. That false assumption may be of value in defeating this siege, and the black army as well." Camron paused. "You must sleep now. It is my turn to stand guard while you get the rest that you will need to carry you through tomorrow."

Germaine did not think he would be able to sleep, but he began to doze off as soon as he lay upon his pallet. He vaguely wondered if Camron had woven some spell to bring him sleep as his eyes closed in much needed rest.

Germaine slept only a few hours, rising early enough to reach Lyon Hold before dawn.

 **X**

In the predawn light, the two shadowy figures watched from their place of concealment behind a fallen tree. The two, Germaine and Camron, could see the cleared expanse between the southern woods and Lyon Hold. Germaine could see that the castle and village were surrounded by soldiers of the Falchion Raptor. The enemy had drawn back to the tree line where most of their numbers could use the trees for a barrier to any arrows from the castle's defenders.

While the knight watched, a careless soldier was dropped by a lone arrow from the castle's ramparts. A smile came to Germaine's lips as he felt pride in that accurate shot. He knew that somewhere on that castle wall good men were giving the enemy something to think about. *They will not give up without a fight.*

The shadow wearing the skull helm motioned to his companion to fall back. "Let us withdraw and form some plan with which we can break this siege," the Emerald Knight whispered as he made his way farther into the woods.

"The numbers of the enemies appear to be about two to one in their favor. The fact that our soldiers would have to make an exit from the castle through the draw-bridge gate would cause the odds to swing further to the side of the enemy." Germaine was weighing his options.

"Perhaps," offered Camron, "you need an ally. Scul will not stop with this hold. It is quite possible that Prince Jahil stands to be the next victim of this scourge if Lyon Hold falls. He would have just cause to join you. Of course, the fact that he is your friend would probably have been enough reason to come to your aid."

Germaine narrowed his eyes and said. "I have considered that course. Jahil has done so much for me, and now—You are right, Camron. Tell me. Is your sorcery now strong enough for you to fly again as a hawk?"

Camron waved his hand for emphasis. "I have recovered power enough for that bit of sorcery. It is not like transporting someone else, as I did for you. I can make the trip. With a short rest at Fenn Hold, I can return to Lyon Hold in two days."

"Good!" Germaine cleared away a place in the dirt where he could trace the lay of the land for his idea. "I have a plan. It will take time to execute, and it will require you to carry the message to both Crom, in Lyon Hold, and Jahil. Here is the strategy. Jahil will divide his company into four equal groups. Three of these groups will take up positions to the north, south and west of the hold, behind the enemy hidden in the trees. These groups will move as close to the enemy as they can without being detected and wait for the sign that will come. The fourth group will form beyond the far eastern hill. If you make your flight to Jahil this morning, his troops can be in place by sundown about five days hence. At sunrise six days from now, the group beyond the hill will begin the battle by charging down the meadow with the morning sun at their backs. The blinding glare of the sun at our back should serve to confuse the enemy. The charge will draw the attention of the black army, and they will probably pull out of the trees and rush to meet the charge in force. When this happens, our men behind them will come out, catching them in a pincer. At this time, Crom will lead his troops into the battle. We will still be somewhat outnumbered, but surprise has always proven to be a faithful equalizer." *Surprise and the help of God. I pray He still smiles upon me.*

Camron grinned, "Excellent plan! I will fly to Jahil at once with the battle plan. If he agrees to it, I will then go to Crom and let him know that hope is still alive and in the capable hands of the Emerald Knight."

When Camron had finished speaking, Germaine watched as the sorcerer momentarily stood engulfed in a gray haze and, once again, lived in the form of a hawk. The hawk leaped into the air and flew southward with greater speed than any true hawk could hope to attain. Germaine knew his next days would be busy, as he would seek out the spies he knew would be watching for any would-be help that may come to the aid of Lyon Hold.

During the next few days, Germaine marked the location of several spies. He had not yet neutralized any, wishing to keep his presence secret until the last possible moment. He happened upon something that caused him to reconsider his time table for avoiding interference.

Germaine surveyed the scene from his hidden vantage point. He had spent the two days since Camron had departed scouting the woods for enemy watchers that might put a snag in his battle plans. The group he now watched had eight men, all armed with swords or axes. The leader seemed to be Scar, a name given to him by the knight for lack of a true name. Germaine observed that they had a captive, a woman about twenty-five years of age. She was tied spread-eagle on the ground, and most of her clothes had been ripped from her body by the Falcon's men. It was evident to the knight that she was about to be used by the men for their perverted pleasure.

"Release me, you buffoons! My father will have your hide stretched over an ant hill." The woman struggled against the tight, leather bonds that held her arms and legs immobilized.

The mean-looking thug with a scar across the left side of his head howled with a booming guffaw. "My little morsel, no one can stand against the black falcons of Lord Craitor. After we finish using you, we will cut your throat and leave your body for the vultures. Scream all you want. Your efforts will bring no one to your aid."

I cannot abide this! The knight's thoughts came as he pulled four arrows from his quiver. As he always seemed to do, he had formed a plan without conscious effort. As Germaine set his first arrow to the string, Scar had loosed the belt that held his breeches and let them fall to his ankles. Germaine made that to be Scar's last act as an arrow pierced his scarred eye and dropped him like a rock. The knight did not watch him hit the ground as he was busy sending three more arrows in rapid succession to find their marks. Even as the last arrow left the bow, Germaine was making his advance.

Throwing down his bow, Germaine slid his swords from their sheaths. Wielding Stinger and Lightning, Germaine ran toward the four remaining thugs. Germaine knew the men had found their swords too late. As he swung Lightning in its emerald arc, one man fell dead—almost severed in two—even as the knight thrust Stinger into the eye socket of a second man. Before that man hit the ground, Germaine sent Lightning through a path that took out the throat of the third man. The fourth foe actually got his sword clear of his scabbard, only to have Germaine slice downward, severing the arm. As the arm and sword fell to the ground in a gush of blood, Germaine did not let him suffer.

"Thank the stars. Thank heaven!" The woman sobbed as she spoke. "Please release me, sir."

Germaine started to go to the woman but stopped suddenly as he realized her nakedness. Turning his head aside, he saw a blanket laying on a sleeping pallet. Scooping up the blanket, he edged toward the woman with his eyes averted from her body as he tossed the blanket over her. Then, kneeling by her side, he cut her bonds. *This scene reminds me of my return to Scot Hold.* Germaine was remembering the evidence he had found upon his belated return to his destroyed hold. He had found several female bodies that had obviously endured ill-use before death had mercifully released them.

The woman had stopped sobbing and now stared wide-eyed at the knight. "Thank you, sir, for your kindness."

Germaine was blushing as he tried to act gruff. "No time for that now. We must hide these men and be away from here. Look through their kits and find some clothing to cover yourself." Germaine was still blushing as he began to drag the first man from the clearing. He turned his thoughts toward trying to figure out what to do with the woman. He could ill afford to be forced into seeing to her safety when he had the larger problem of the siege to take care of.

When Germaine had finished his grisly task, he found the woman dressed in baggy clothes. Her hair was mussed in a blonde halo about her head, and her face was quite dirty.

"My name is Ayana, sir. May I ask yours?" The girl's blue eyes were wide as she spoke. Germaine had been leading her to Silver Cloud's hiding place as she talked.

"My name is Germaine of Scot Hold and this," he pointed to the charger, "is Silver Cloud." Germaine swung up into the saddle and reached down to the girl. "I am afraid we will have to ride double." Germaine said this lightly, trying to set the girl at ease. He found no horses in the camp of the slain men, and figured that they had been reconnoitering on foot. As Germaine looked into the upturned face of Ayana, he could see the strain of her recent ordeal. She reminded the knight of a child that had been orphaned by war. Her tangled hair and dirty face put him in mind of Mikial, when the knight had first found the boy. Germaine felt compassion for her.

"You will hear no complaint from my lips. After what I have been through, walking barefoot on hot coals would be easy." Her voice was defiant as he swung her up and behind him. She wrapped her arms around his waist in a firm grip as they rode away.

"Where are you from, Ayana?" Germaine was trying to decide what to do with this girl. Surely she would not be able to keep up with him in the coming days, and she would be in great danger when the battle began.

"My family and I are from a far land that was invaded several times by barbarian raiders. Rather than continue being attacked by these people, we fled to look for a new land where we might be welcomed. We were refugees traveling in unknown territory when we camped last night about four miles to the west of here. I had gone with my friend, Emil ..." The girl choked back a sob. "We had gone to find water. We strayed too far away from the camp and those evil men fell upon us from ambush." She began to cry openly. "The one with a scar took a knife and cut Emil's throat while laughing at his evil deed." She wiped her eyes and then looked up at the sky. "I was so glad when your arrow took that one's life! I never in my life believed I could be so happy to see the death of someone."

Germaine turned Silver Cloud to the west. He would try to return the woman to her clan and then continue his task of spying. Finding her family proved easy. In fact, her people found him. They had traveled more than two miles when four riders confronted them. The four had swords drawn and blood shown in their eyes.

"Put away your swords. I am not your enemy." Germaine knew from the physical appearance of these men that they were probably of the girl's clan. Germaine noted that their beards and hair were of the same light color, and their eyes were light blue or green. These warriors did not wear the black clothing of the Raptor's forces.

"Father! I am safe! This man saved my life." The girl swung to the ground and raced to the leader of the band of warriors. The man was big, much like Crom, except for the blonde hair and beard. On the man's head rested a fearsome looking helm with two horns sweeping out from each side. In fact, Germaine noted that each of the four men wore a similar helm. Their upper bodies were clothed in animal furs, with leather sleeves covering their arms. The breeches they wore appeared to be leather as were their coarse boots. "He killed eight men single-handed. One of them was the man who murdered Emil."

The burly man looked at Germaine and smiled. "If any one other than my daughter had told me this tale, I would not believe that such a scrawny warrior could be so fierce."

"You are correct, sir. I am not fierce. The planets were smiling on me and luck came my way." Germaine smiled back at the warrior; the knight felt a kinship to him. *He reminds me of my old captain at Scot Hold. Not so much in physical appearance, but in his confident manner.* Germaine had always depended on his instincts concerning men, and this man was one that could be taken at his word.

"I am called Val Krul, sir, how are you called?"

"I am Germaine, Sir Krul." Germaine bowed his head slightly.

"Val will do. All my friends call me Val, and I now count you among them! My thanks, for the saving of Ayana's life." Val paused as he swung Ayana up behind him on his horse. "Please join us for a meal, and tell us about the trouble that holds this land in its grip."

"I would be honored, sir." Germaine was only too happy to agree to a good meal. He had been living on dried jerky and whatever he could find growing in the forest.

When they arrived at the camp, Germaine was surprised at how many kin Ayana had in her clan. He counted at least a hundred tents made of animal hides.

As they approached a tent with a standard flying above it, Ayana leapt to the ground as a blonde haired woman rushed out to greet them. "Mother, do not cry. I am safe by your side once again." Ayana hugged the woman and the two walked into the tent with their arms intertwined.

"Argund, show Germaine to a place where he can clean the grime of the trail from his person." Val indicated the rider to his left as he swung to the ground in a dismount.

Germaine alighted from Silver Cloud and removed his bundled kit from the horse. *It would feel good to be clean again,* the knight thought as he entered the tent that Argund indicated. Germaine had moved relentlessly the past two days, and he had figured out the pattern that had been set by the enemy in the placing of spies.

Germaine knew that he had time for this brief respite. Meanwhile, Estella and her people felt apprehension as the siege continued.

XI

Estella kept low as she moved along the rampart walkway. It had been more than two days since the forces of Scul Craitor had penned them up in the castle. Estella had discussed possible strategies with Crom, but none held promise of success. Estella calculated they had enough supplies and water to hold out for eight or nine more days if they kept to a strict ration.

Due to the possibility of attack, Estella had ordered all grains and preserved food items to be stored within the castle, instead of the usual storage sites in the village. She knew it was more than luck that the invaders had been discovered in enough time to get most of the remaining supplies from the village into the safer confines of the castle walls. Crom had set out distant sentries to warn of any assault in advance, and his precautions had paid off.

The enemy army had not attacked the castle, but surrounded it in a move that suggested to Estella they were planning on a siege. *We are now locked into a waiting game. It is a game that can have but one outcome with the odds the way they now stand.* She continued moving as she thought about their plight.

Estella was making an inspection of the ramparts, more in an effort to bolster the confidence of her soldiers than anything. She kept her head low in case someone in the enemy's ranks should try to send an arrow her way.

"My Lady," Byrone saluted Estella as she approached his position on the rampart walkway. "We have experienced some excellent target practice today. My men have given the burial details of the enemy some work to do. You would think that those fools would figure out the lethal range of our marksmen!"

"Perhaps their officers are intentionally sending them forth to make us waste our arrows." Estella would not put anything past Scul, even the intentional sacrifice of his men.

"That is probably their plan, but so far it is working in our favor. We have loosed twenty arrows, and we have struck eighteen warriors. My men are being very selective in the choice of targets. Besides, arrows are one thing we have plenty of. Germaine had our craftsmen make a large quantity of them. It would appear that he anticipated the possibility of a siege taking place."

The mention of his name brought Estella's mind back to the questions she had asked herself so many times over the past two weeks. *Where is Germaine? Does he know of our plight now?* While she was pondering this and other things, she was continuing her rounds of the rampart. As she moved along the north wall and came to the corner of the east wall, Crom came into her field of vision. He was standing on the terrace at the midpoint of the east wall where a catapult mount rested.

As she moved to join him, she was amazed to see a great hawk dive from the sky and alight next to Crom. For a moment it looked as if the warrior had been struck by lightning.

"This is the hawk! The same one we saw in the forest that day with the Emerald Knight." Crom stood without movement as he spoke.

Estella stared in awe as she watched a haze envelop the feathered intruder. Within a moment, the hawk disappeared, replaced by the sorcerer, Camron.

"Have heart, for I bring good news!" Camron said, "Crom, I must speak with you and Lady Estella."

"Let us go to my library, Camron." Estella spoke sharply. *Perhaps I will finally get an answer to my question.* Estella still felt displeased with the knight and his wizard because of their unexplained disappearance after the skirmish with Scul's men.

Once in the library, Estella held her peace as Camron began laying out the battle plans of the Emerald Knight to Crom and herself. She did not interrupt but listened intently as he detailed the entire plan. When he had finished, before Estella could say anything, Crom spoke up.

"By the planets! It is a good plan, Camron. I hate to admit it, but I had given up hope on you and Sir Germaine. I will never question your actions again." Crom saluted Estella. "I must go to my officers and give them news of this plan. Our morale is beginning to sag because of the great number of troops that surround us, but this is the best medicine to remedy that problem." He turned and hurriedly left the room.

As Camron turned to follow the warrior, Estella made a gesture with her hand for him to stop. "Would you please stay for a moment, Camron? I need to ask you about something that has troubled me."

Camron returned to face her. "How may I be of service, Estella?"

"What important matter arose that caused you and Germaine to desert our ranks these two weeks past?" Estella had one brow raised in an expression of genuine curiosity.

Camron answered, "He did not desert you, Estella. He had pressing business to attend, and I believe it best to let Germaine handle such questions."

"It will be as you wish, Camron. We are thankful that you chose to return for us. I know you are weary and in need of rest, so depart now to your quarters, with my thanks." Estella's voice was icy as she spoke. *I hope this wizard cannot read thoughts. Mine would probably make him leave the castle. Perhaps I will have a chance to question my errant knight.* Estella softened a little as she realized he could be killed, without her seeing him again.

"Thank you, Estella." Camron spoke in a tired voice.

Estella would have to wait for an answer to this mystery that piqued her curiosity, and her ire. Meanwhile, Germaine prepared for his meal with the Vordund.

When Germaine took his place in the dining tent, he noticed the chairs around his table were filled by men. Looking across the tent he saw the women were seated at tables separated from the men.

Germaine spoke to Val, who was seated to his left. "I have never witnessed this custom by which the men eat at one table and the women at another. Is it the usual way you dine, or is this a special occasion?"

Val was not wearing the coarse clothing and battle helm that he had on when Germaine met him in the forest. He was now wearing a brightly colored red and blue tunic. He smiled as he answered the knight's question. "It is a custom that has been handed down for many years. We were once a seagoing warrior race, and the men spent many months at sea. They lived, fought, and died together. When back in their home port, our ancestors would dine together and sleep in a common barracks. Thankfully we have not continued that last custom. In those days, the man only slept with his wife when the signs in the sky were right for conceiving a child who would grow to be courageous." Val laughed, as did the other men at the table. "Yes, I am glad that we do not hold to all the old traditions. Now tell us about the trouble that seems to seep through this land like the mist of a sea-dragon's breath."

Germaine told Val and his kin the important parts of his experiences at Lyon Hold. When he got to the part with the Vordund girl, they applauded his killing of the thugs.

During the tale, he noticed a beautiful, young woman at the other table. She kept staring at him and even seemed to be trying to catch his attention. The woman even fluttered her hand in a dainty wave as she smiled at him. He noticed that all the men and women were dressed in lighter, more colorful clothing than they had been wearing earlier. Germaine realized this could be the normal dress for the women, while the men had worn their warrior clothing earlier. The girl was wearing a light-blue dress that seemed to emphasize the blue of her eyes. Her hair was piled on top of her head in some manner he had never seen before. It had a stunning effect on her overall appearance. Germaine found her to be quite beautiful. Once, when Germaine had looked in her direction, she whispered something to the woman next to her. Germaine felt a little self conscious as the second woman smiled at him as well.

After the meal, Val stood up. "I must meet with my war council. My daughter, Ayana, will see that you are entertained while you wait. Ayana," Val called out while beckoning to the women's table. The woman in blue arose and made her way around the table to where they stood.

Germaine could now recognize this to be the same disheveled woman he had found in the forest.

"I am dressed differently than when you first saw me, am I not?" Germaine could see that Ayana smiled mischievously as she spoke.

Germaine felt his face flush. "Yes, my Lady. You are truly most elegant." The knight still viewed her as somewhat of a child, though a beautiful one. He could see Durelle, in but a few more years, in the mannerisms of Ayana.

Her dainty hand grasped his arm as she asked, "Shall we go for a walk?"

Germaine asked Val, "Is it permitted?"

Val smiled, "I feel that you will treat my daughter honorably. Your actions in the saving of her life tell me as much. Go now. We will summon you shortly."

Germaine allowed Ayana to lead him out of the tent. He walked with her around the camp for some time, as they talked. After a time, they settled down on a rough bench near where they had begun their walk. It seemed to Germaine that they had talked for hours.

Ayana said, "My people had been a seafaring race called by the name Vordund, which was the name of a country they once inhabited. Long years ago, they settled on a remote seacoast of Valeria and lived there in peace until recently. Our possessions and women became the target for raiding parties of barbarian pirates. They made life miserable for us. We are now seeking a place to settle peacefully." She paused for a moment, then Germaine detected coyness as she asked, "What about you, Germaine. What kind of life do you follow?"

"I really do not have much to tell. I am a warrior, much like your father. I have been a knight for most of my life."

Ayana interrupted before Germaine could continue. "A knight. A real knight?"

It was one of the things Germaine had not found to be important enough to tell the Vordund men while he was relating his brief history of the area. He was somewhat baffled by her apparent delight with this knowledge.

"I have heard sagas about knights but have never met one. I thought knights were merely a part of legends, like mythical dragons." With a coy look in her eyes, she asked. "Are you married, or promised to someone, Sir Germaine?"

As the question fell across his heart, great sadness weighed upon his shoulders. He had not allowed his thoughts to settle on Adriana's death in the days since he had last kissed her lips. His attempts had been aided by the dangers that kept him in his warrior's persona. A tear wet his cheek as he looked away from Ayana's gaze. "My wife's name is Adriana." He almost whispered. "She is not with me now." That was all he could manage to say as he choked back his emotions. *If only a warrior could kill emotions in the same way he can a flesh and blood opponent. Perhaps it was a mistake for me to leave the threat of death that dwells in the forest, for I now feel my will to forget is weakened.*

"Oh!" Germaine heard Ayana react to his answer. "It is sad that war is keeping you away from your lady. Maybe soon ..."

Her words were cut off by Val's booming voice. "Germaine! Come with me, sir. My council has words for your ears." This time Germaine felt Val's big hand on his shoulder as the warrior chief led him to the council tent. When they were seated, Germaine looked at one of the men whom Val now indicated at the table.

"This is Gorm, my lieutenant, and these others are the officers of my army. You have already met Argund, and this is Gavrik, and the last is Rolfe. They are good men, and true."

Germaine watched as Gorm raised a hand above his head, and all those present became silent. "Germaine of Scot, because of your valor and bravery on behalf of the blood of one of our own, we have named you as equal to blood kin with our folk. Your troubles are our concern. We will help you in this struggle. We further feel that this Falchion Raptor will be a danger to our people if he goes unchecked. It is common sense that we join with an army that has a chance to pull the claws from this Raptor's talon."

With this offer made, Germaine outlined his strategy for the coming battle. "I will be riding with the force that will strike from the east. That is where the greatest danger will lie, in that first attack on the enemy. I would be honored if you would join me."

Germaine watched as Val looked to his officers one by one. As his gaze rested on each man's face, a nod of agreement was returned. "We will ride with you, Germaine."

"If you will send for paper and quill, I will detail a map for you to follow. I have found the enemy spies that watch the trails. We will be massing for the attack three days from now." As Germaine paused, a Vordund man entered the tent with paper and quill. Germaine took the items and drew a map of the attack plan. After detailing the time and place, Germaine stood up. "I must return to my task in the forest. I will see you on the field of battle, my friends."

Val stood with the officers. Germaine grasped his hand, and the Vordund chief said, "May victory ride with your strong sword-arm, warrior."

Silver Cloud was led to the tent as he answered, "Let our enemies taste death by the steel of your sword and axe, warrior chief."

Germaine walked out of the tent and swung up into the saddle. He wheeled the horse and rode, without looking back.

Germaine spent the next two days pinpointing the spies who would be taken out first. With his task complete, he went to a place where he could watch for Jahil and his men.

✧ XII ✧

Germaine sighted the vanguard of Jahil's forces approaching from the south. On this, the fifth day since Camron's departure, he had been quite busy. He had eliminated all the spies on the southern approach and several that were potential problems to the west and north. He was soon reunited with First Prince, Jahil.

"Jahil, there are not enough words to thank you for coming to my aid." He slapped the prince on the shoulder as he rode alongside.

"My friend, I come also to my own aid. It is obvious that this power hungry Falchion Raptor would consume all of Valeria for his own domain. We must stand together, or we fall." Germaine saw that Jahil wore a fierce scowl as he spoke.

They had a short, fast council. Germaine detailed the plan to Jahil and the three lieutenants who would be in charge of the three battle lines to the west, south, and north. Germaine informed them of the remaining watchers and their approximate locations. He also told them of their new allies, the strangely dressed warriors of the Vordund clan. The knight did not want anyone to mistakenly take the life of one of Val's people in the heat of battle. With these last preparations made, Germaine called an end to the meeting and watched as the four groups divided. The knight watched with pride as the men he had trained at Fenn Hold regrouped, with a minimum of noise, and began moving to their respective positions.

"The unit that is traveling to the northern positions will have the longest journey. They will have a long night and be tired when the battle is met, but these men will stand tall even with fatigue." Germaine's plan called for the northern unit to follow the western group. Once the western group settled in place, the northern-bound men would pass behind their position to continue their way to the north. Before Germaine mounted his horse, he knelt in prayer.

God, grant us your strength and favor. Please allow these men to pass without notice of the enemy. Give the enemy into our hands.

As Germaine swung into the saddle, Jahil asked. "When will we meet your Vordund friends?"

"They will meet us beyond the hill of the east meadow an hour before first light. Let us make our way to our position. We should have enough time for the men to gain a short rest before dawn." Germaine wondered how many brave warriors would breathe their last breath on this eve of battle. *Perhaps my last breath will come on the morrow.* Germaine sat straighter in the saddle as the thought of death crossed his mind. He had never consciously thought about the possibility of being killed. At least not on the eve of conflict. He rode in silence as he wondered if this could be an omen of his own death. Other than his troubling thoughts, Germaine watched the night pass without incident.

Germaine had his men assembled and on their mounts as the sun broke above the horizon. An occasional rattle of harness and the clink of chain mail armor were but faint intrusions to the silence that surrounded the knight. In the distant hold, the cock's crows could be heard, breaking the news of a new day. The Vordund warriors had arrived and taken their position alongside the soldiers of Fenn Hold. They wore swords, these fearsome warriors of the Vordund, but they carried double edge battle-axes.

Germaine surveyed the line of cavalry with his eyes narrowed to bare slits. "It is a good day for battle! Today I ride in honor with brave warriors at my flanks. May your swords be strong and strike true for the side of right this day. If I should fall in this battle, and lie dying in the dirt, I will pass to the other realm with the great joy of knowing that I died a warrior's death with brave warriors fighting by my side. May God smile on us today and carry us to victory!" With these words, Germaine swung up to the saddle of his charger. The sun sent emerald sparks of light glittering from his polished skull helm. *If this is the day that I die, I thank God that He has allowed me the honor of having these good men at my side.*

"Ready swords!" The soldiers answered his command with the clanging in unison of two hundred swords as they slid from the metal necks of their sheaths. "To battle!" he bellowed as he leaned forward and spurred Silver Cloud into a gallop.

As Germaine led the charge down the hill with the rising sun at his back, the enemy began to roil in confusion. The knight knew the sun was blinding them enough that the oncoming cavalry would be hard to number. Black clad troops that had been spread out around the castle began to move from their positions to meet the cavalry charge. This was just what the knight had depended upon when he had laid out his plans. Even as they began engaging the enemy, the Fenn Hold soldiers that had been positioned in the forest behind the evil forces began to pour forth in a rush to catch Scul's men in a pincer. In their panic, the Raptor's troops did not maintain their positions commanding the drawbridge of Lyon Castle. Germaine caught a glimpse of the bridge dropping to allow Crom and his warriors to flood out into the fray.

The fighting proved to be the most fierce that Germaine could remember. He knew from his days of spying on the enemy that this would be the greatest number of antagonists he had ever seen in one battle. Even with the horn helmed Vordund added to their ranks, Germaine's forces were still outnumbered.

Germaine moved forward, still mounted on Cloud, as he hacked the enemy with both swords. He would rather be on the ground, but the enemy was so thick that he would be too exposed in a dismount. The Emerald Knight felt his arms tire from the awkward fight against men on foot. *It seems that the battle has raged for an hour, and there is still no end in sight*. Germaine felt a shudder race through Silver Cloud.

The knight tensed as Silver Cloud wavered, and then the great stallion went down, wounded. Germaine's quick reflexes allowed him to land on his feet, though an enemy sword pierced his side. He thrust Lightning through the armpit of the dark warrior that had wounded him. The enemy sword was still in his side, pushed up beneath the mail corselet. Germaine parried another enemy sword with Stinger, and, as he wrapped his hand that held Lightning around the sword that was in his side, he pulled the sword from the wound. A surprised enemy swordsman watched as Lightning burst his chest while the point of the second sword, held by the same hand, slid from Germaine's side. The moment he had it free of his body, the knight dropped the enemy sword and continued his desperate fight. Germaine felt pain in his side as blood flowed from his wound. *Must not lose control of my senses*, Germaine thought as he swung his swords in their lethal, emerald arcs through the enemy ranks.

Germaine continued his advance, taking the fight to the enemy, now swinging round to take out a black falcon warrior behind him, then another to his left. Stinger would thrust between a warrior's ribs, as Lightning would be ending the efforts of another warrior. He was surrounded by a sea of black clad warriors. It was as if they had orders to single him out from the rest of the hold's fighters.

Germaine felt like a ship caught in a storm, fighting against the wave of too many determined enemies. He cut desperate swaths through the enemy with his swords. An enemy sword pierced his left shoulder, and his now lifeless left hand dropped Stinger. Sharp pain wracked his shoulder as he continued wielding Lightning. He battled on against the protest of his own battered body. *I feel my end is near. God grant me strength to strike another of the enemy.*

The enemy was packed around him so closely that he took out three or four with each arc etched by Lightning. Then a blow to his skull helm brought blood in a blinding torrent over his eyes. He could not clear his eyes, so he simply continued swinging his blade. His purpose now was to take out as many of the enemy as he could before he died. Keeping his panic under control, he continued swinging his sword. The peace of darkness completely blanketed him as he helplessly felt himself falling to the ground.

Earlier in the battle, Scul Craitor had made his way, undetected, to a point outside the castle wall. Scul was near the castle drawbridge when it dropped. Seeing his army breaking their ranks to attack the on-rushing cavalry almost made him scream. *Those fools. Can they not see this was but a feint? I am surrounded by idiots.* Scul did not utter a sound. He did not want to give away his position to the warriors that were now crossing the bridge to join the fray. Scul was invisible to the eye. He had shared the secret of his true nature with only his most trusted officers. *I have no choice left but to chance revealing that I am a sorcerer. If I am discovered, so be it. I will not be denied my destiny.* Scul crossed the bridge before it could be raised. He made his way to the private chambers of Estella.

Scul saw the guard and knocked him out, gently lowering him to the ground to prevent any sound from alerting Estella. He then spun another spell that allowed him to become like a shadow. The shadow drifted under the door to Estella's chamber. As Scul reformed into a man, he saw that Estella stood at the window, watching the battle unfold.

Moving closer, Scul saw that she was watching the Emerald Knight. Scul watched with fascination as he saw Germaine lose his mount and fall to the ground. The knight was surrounded by attackers. Scul could only see him for a few minutes as he seemed to advance several yards and then was overwhelmed by the enemy from the force of sheer numbers.

"No! Germaine!" Estella screamed his name. It seemed to Scul that she was trying to overcome the din of the battle below. It was as though she sought to pull him free of that dark death with her very will.

What is this? Does the lady have feelings for the knight? No matter, now, he is obviously doomed. Scul carefully pulled the hood from his belt where he had carried it. He stepped closer to Estella.

With her attention riveted to the place where Germaine fell, Scul was smug with the awareness that she never expected his dark visit to her castle. Scul made that her last glimpse of the battle as he dropped the hood over her head. As she tried to scream, Scul struck a blow to her head, silencing her struggles.

Scul tossed the now limp body of Estella over his shoulder as one might do with a sack of potatoes. As he walked toward the door with his burden, the two began to shimmer, and a shadow again poured beneath the door, this time in escape.

While Scul made off with Estella, the Vordund leader, Val, witnessed the dire plight of Germaine.

Val saw Germaine lose his horse and fall among the enemy. It looked as though the Raptor's warriors were converging on the Emerald Knight as he continued to fight on foot. Val fought his way toward Germaine. The big Vordund now witnessed the strength of which his daughter had told him. Swinging his axe in lethal swaths through the swarm of enemies, Val kept an eye on Germaine as he advanced on his position. Suddenly, the knight went down under the onslaught.

"To me!" Val bellowed to his nearby warriors. "Nooo!" The giant jumped from his horse among a throng of roiling warriors, swinging his battle axe, reaping death. Val's huge battle-axe was swinging in a steady rain of blood as he virtually crumpled any of the enemy that stood in the way of his advance. Val had several wounds to his arms and legs, but he relentlessly cut his path toward Germaine. To either side of Val, now, waded two more of the fearsome giants, swinging their axes in death dealing arcs. The enemy warriors now tried to avoid the axes, running into their own men in an effort to escape. Val yelled above the din of battle. "Defend Germaine!"

Within moments, Val and his two Vordund warriors had surrounded the fallen knight, forming a protective perimeter around his still body. Val and his warriors received more wounds but stood their ground, as their great battle-axes continued to tirelessly heap bodies into a great circle around the Emerald Knight.

The soldiers of Crom and Jahil continued to fight on their respective fronts. Some of the Vordund continued to protect the fallen Germaine as the rest of their clan now engaged in the process of mopping up.

As the battle waned, it was obvious to Val that the day was won. Soon, the last of the enemy chose surrender over annihilation.

The gray cloaked Camron made his way to the fallen knight, with Crom following close by his side. The sorcerer heard Crom ask, "Why did you not use your sorcery to win this battle and keep Germaine from death?"

Camron cast a steely gaze upon the captain. "I will tell you something that is not widely known about sorcerers. Our power has limits, and certain circum-stances make them more limited."

Camron knelt beside the stricken, motionless body of the Emerald Knight. He ran his hands over Germaine's chest and bent his head to listen. "He is still alive!" With this exclamation he brought forth bandages and a vial of yellow powder from within the folds of his robe.

The sorcerer pulled the emerald corselet and tunic up to reveal the wounded side. He cleaned the wounds in Germaine's side and left shoulder and applied a generous amount of the powdery material to the wounds. As Crom watched, it appeared that the wizard used a kind of thin string, rather than the coarse, gut ties that were usually used to bind torn muscle together. He pushed the string through the flesh with a tiny sliver of metal. After pulling the wounds closed with the string, Camron then bound the shoulder in a bandage. For the wound that was just above the waist, the sorcerer placed a folded cloth upon it.

Camron then turned his attention to the wound on the knight's head.

"This is not as serious as it looks." The old sorcerer spoke more to himself than those around him. Once again he cleansed the area and used some more of the yellow powder on the wound. He then carefully stitched the wound closed with more of the tiny string. Camron wrapped Germaine's head with a bandage and then stood to survey the results of his efforts. "Get a litter and move him to my alchemy chambers!" The litter was already on the way, even as he had given the order to Crom.

"You did not finish telling me of your power limitations, Camron." Camron knew that Crom would not easily cease in his effort to understand the sorcerer's lack of aid during the battle.

Camron smiled and said. "I have told you more than I should, but, then, you do have a right to know." The sorcerer pulled Crom away from hearing of the others. "I can kill twenty or thirty men in a single blast of power. They must be within a close distance to me, and it takes a few minutes for me to recover my strength enough to strike again. While I recover, I am as vulnerable to death as you, and I do not have the skill to avoid a sword. Do not think me a coward. It is just that I know when to use my sorcery to its best advantage, as I now do to help Germaine recover."

The answer seemed to satisfy Crom, as he walked alongside Germaine's stretcher on its journey into the castle.

As Germaine was carried into the castle, Estella found herself an unwilling traveler on a long trek.

⇜ XIII ⇝

Estella spent the first part of her journey in a most undignified and uncomfortable manner. She awoke trussed up, gagged, blindfolded, and tied across the back of a horse. *This pain is unbearable. At least my wrists have grown numb to the pain of their lashings*. With the agony of her ill-treated body, Estella's mind would wander as she faded in and out of consciousness. Sometimes she would remember the scene of Germaine falling in battle. *Does he still live? How could anyone survive that onslaught? No. I must cling to the thought that if anyone could survive, Germaine will be that man. Thirsty. So Thirsty*.

When they finally stopped to camp that night, she was roughly taken from the horse, and the blindfold and gag were removed. Her captors then tied her to a rather uncomfortable tree, though it was much preferred to her previous perch. Estella ran her tongue inside her cheek. It felt as though her mouth was full of cloth. Her stomach felt bruised, and hunger was now gnawing at her middle.

When she could see her kidnappers, she found the leader to be a dark-haired man with a neatly groomed, black beard. He wore black chain mail armor and had the crest of the Falchion Raptor on his chest. The two men-at-arms with him wore similar, though poorer-made, uniforms. Estella realized that her captor must be Scul Craitor. *This is the man who ordered the death of my parents. Since he had my blindfold removed, perhaps my death is not far away.* Estella tried to marshal her energy. The pain in her wrists and ankles now grew worse. The bindings were biting deeper it seemed to the woman. *I must try to put up a bold front. I do not want to give them the satisfaction of knowing the amount of pain I am enduring.*

"So, Falchion Raptor, I wondered what the rotten stench was as I rode with my eyes hooded. I see it was only the aura of your evil personality."

"Careful how you speak to me! You are now my property. I will decide how you may best serve me, whether dead or alive." Scul bared his teeth in a wicked sneer.

"You will pay dearly for this evil deed." Estella was hoping in her heart that the gallant Germaine still breathed life. *What does it matter if he kills me? I do not believe anyone other than Germaine could deliver me from this cur.*

She winced as she saw Scul twist his lips in a sinister smile. "That is exactly what I want of you. The green lout has thwarted my plans for the last time. If he did not die in the battle, he will die by my hand when he tries to rescue you. Then, my loudmouthed lady, you will be placed out of your misery, unless I find another use for you." Scul threw back his head and laughed in a maniacal, shrill staccato.

Estella said nothing more to Scul. The evil seemed to boil from his skin. She recognized the man as a lunatic, and she knew that caution would be the better part of valor in dealing with him.

The next four days of the trip were at least a little more bearable, as Estella was allowed to sit on the horse's back. When they reached their destination, she found it to be a fortress with walls that formed a sinister appearance. Estella gasped as she realized the structure was shaped in the form of a giant skull. The gate through which they must pass to enter the fortress formed the mouth of the skull. Upon looking more closely, Estella realized the effect was more of an illusion than true construction. Once within its walls, the inside was as bleak as the outer walls had been. She saw cobwebs engulfing every corner and cranny. Estella's breath caught as she saw large rats roaming freely in the courtyard. She had a terrible fear of rats, forgetting her aches and pains as she watched their scurrying. She noticed that there seemed to be only a dozen or so soldiers in the hold, and they were keeping silent watch of the open plain which she knew stretched for some distance before the watching eyes of the skull. When her captors had reined their horses to a stop, they were at the foot of a stairway that stood in a state of disrepair. Some of the steps were partially missing, and pieces were crumbling. Estella grimaced as rats scurried about even on the steps of the stairway. The men dismounted and roughly pulled her from her horse.

"Show Her Ladyship her new quarters." Estella heard Scul growl to his fellow travelers before turning to Estella. "I hope you find the accommodations to be satisfactory." Scul finished with a roar of laughter that held no humor. Estella could feel only malice in his evil laugh.

When they had reached her accommodations, Estella found them to be a small cell in the dungeon. One of her captors kicked a rat out of the way as he opened the door on its squeaking hinges and shoved Estella inside. There was very little light. A foul, putrid stench assaulted her, causing her to gag. In the dim gloom of her cell, she could see the scurrying forms of rats. In a bunk along one wall she found the source of the wretched smell. A body lay there. It was more skeleton than flesh as she could see the rats working at it. She quickly turned away from that gruesome sight. *I cannot stand the sight of rats, but somehow I must survive among them.* She thought this as her eyes fell upon a chair sitting in a corner. She walked quickly to the chair and moved it to the middle of the cell. Sitting on the chair, she pulled her legs up under her, away from the rats milling about on the floor. She had her chair turned so that she was faced away from the body on the bunk. The rats did not seem to be paying her attention, but what would happen when they completed their filthy work with the body?

As she sat in misery, Estella realized that she had never experienced this much fear in her life, for herself or someone else. Even in her desperate state, she feared for the life of the Emerald Knight.

She shivered as a large rat placed a paw on a leg of the chair. The creature seemed to be testing the air with its snout pointed in her direction. Estella sighed as the rat pulled its paw away from the chair leg and continued its way toward the bunk. *I must control my fear. It is so thick that I cannot breathe. It may help if I turn my thoughts to memories of the times I spent with Germaine. The walks we took in the snow-covered courtyard. No rats. Only the clean white of the snow, and Germaine.* Estella knew that her only hope for sanity was to try to live in that world where she had no fears, only happiness. She would try.

Meanwhile, as Estella watched the rats in fear, Germaine was lying within Lyon's dungeon, unconscious with his many battle wounds.

Germaine opened his eyes, then blinked. He could see! *Am I alive or dead? If I am dead, could this be Hades? It seems too gray to be heaven.* He tried to move his head and felt pain. "No, I must be alive! The dead could not hurt this badly." Germaine spoke these words aloud, to no one in particular.

"Ah, but you are alive, brave knight." A sweet, lilting voice came from his right. Turning his head in the direction of the voice he saw a vision that gave him a start.

"I must be dead." *Can this be an angel?* His eyesight continued to be quite blurred, but he could see an apparition with a halo about its head.

"No, Sir Knight! I am not an angel, and my father would find it quite amusing for anyone to think such of me."

Germaine now recognized the voice and realized the halo was Ayana's blonde hair. He now noticed that she was holding his right hand cupped in her smaller hands. "How went the battle?" Germaine was hesitant to voice this question.

"You are still undefeated in battle, Sir Knight. Your strategy worked perfectly." Ayana then spoke to someone else in the room. " Go to Crom and Camron. Tell them our slumbering patient has awakened."

As soon as she finished speaking, Germaine heard footsteps running up the old stairway.

"How long have I been unconscious?" Germaine felt that it must have been at least several hours. Germaine began to lift his head, but the resulting dizziness brought an end to that effort. *I am thirsty. How long since I last drank water? This morning, just before the battle. I could do with some food.*

"Three days and nights. You have been resting most peacefully. I believe your sorcerer wove some kind of spell to speed your healing. While he was tending to the wounds of other men, I have been changing the dressings on your wounds, and they are knitting remarkably well."

"Three days? You said three days. Surely that cannot be true." Germaine could not believe his ears.

"So, my hard skulled patient has roused!" Camron sounded pleased as he came down the stair. "You shall live to fight another day, Germaine." Camron moved to Germaine's side and touched his head. "Do you feel much pain here?"

"No, just a dull ache." Germaine grimaced as he spoke. He felt as if a horse had stepped on his head. The ache surged in rhythm with his heartbeat.

"Good! The ache you feel is more of a side effect from the cure rather than the wound." Camron then began to poke and prod the left shoulder.

Germaine winced in pain, then regretted the sudden reflexive movement when his side felt as if it was stabbed by a fire brand.

"Very good, very good! Yes, I am a genius with medicine." Camron laughed. "I missed my calling. I should have been a great healer instead of a poor sorcerer. I have most of your wounded comrades back on their feet."

The knight smiled through his pain. Germaine found the old wizard's humor to be good medicine in itself. "How many wounds did I take? I feel as if every sword of the enemy must have struck me." Germaine's head started to spin with dizziness as he spoke.

"Ayana, would you be so kind as to get our patient some broth. Do not feed him too much at first, but we need to get his strength built back up."

Germaine turned his head slightly, toward Ayana as she arose from her seat. Suddenly the woman bent her face to his and kissed his cheek.

"I will prepare you some broth with my own hands. I've always wanted to fix a meal for a man who could not avoid eating my cooking." Germaine watched as she turned and left the room in a hurry. The young woman still put him in mind of his daughter.

Camron leaned close to Germaine's ear and spoke softly. "That girl has not left your side since she arrived here three days ago. What little sleep she has gotten has been with her head lying on your shoulder. I believe she was trying to will you back to health."

The knight said, "I believe she is repaying me for saving her life. In a sense, she has helped save mine."

"Sir Knight!" Crom's booming voice interrupted further words from Camron. "Welcome back to the land of the living."

Germaine turned his head to Crom and saw that Val was with him. "It is good to be once more with the living and to be able to see your ugly faces again." Germaine did laugh now, even though it caused an increased throb in his skull. "Camron, may I sit up?" *Perhaps I can better clear my head if I sit. Lying in this bunk for three days certainly has not helped.* Val had many bandaged wounds upon his body, as well. Crom had a bandage on his left forearm.

Camron nodded as he moved to help the knight in his effort. As Germaine pushed himself up into a seated position, his head began to swim for a moment, but it settled back quickly. Camron was still fussing with a cushion, propping it to support the knight as he leaned back.

"Tell me, my friends, what happened after I left the battle?" Germaine relaxed in an effort to ease his many pains. This was, indeed, the first battle he had not seen through to the finish.

XIV

Germaine listened intently to Crom as he recounted the events of the battle. When he told Germaine about how his life was saved by the Vordund warriors, he interrupted to say, "It would appear that I now owe you my life, Val."

"No, my friend." Val's face was somber. "How can we price a human life? When you gave my daughter back to me, her return was priceless. I can never save your life enough times to pay that debt! When my daughter told me of your attack upon the men who held her captive, I marveled that you would go against so many men for someone you did not know. Three days ago I witnessed you as you fought against overwhelming numbers, and I knew that you were placing your life on the line for others. Because of these things, I know you would lay down your life for me, or any of your friends. That is a great virtue to carry within your valiant heart."

"Thank you, my friend." Germaine felt himself flush as he nodded for Crom to continue the tale. In a strange way, Germaine felt vindicated of his perceived failure with the fall of Scot Hold. He had many times thought that his absence in some way contributed to the defeat of his hold. This battle for Lyon Hold had been won without him being there at the end. *Sometimes*, Germaine thought, *you cannot win. Then your best hope is to go out with honor.*

"That was basically the end of the battle. However, there is bad news of great evil that befell this hold during the fight. The Falchion Raptor somehow managed to gain entrance to the castle and . . . ," as Camron paused, Germaine could see that he struggled with the words, "He made off with Estella."

"What?" Germaine swung his feet over the side of the bunk and made an attempt to stand up. *I must go to her. I cannot fail her now. If he took her, he must have wanted to keep her alive. Surely she still lives.*

"No, Sir Knight!" Camron placed a hand on Germaine's arm. "Do not act rashly. You have not the strength yet. Please let the cure take its course."

Germaine stopped struggling to rise, more so because the room was now spinning than in response to Camron's pleading. He noticed that Ayana had reentered the room at some point in the recounting of events. He saw a strange look upon her face as she stared intently into his eyes. She stood at the end of the stairway, holding a bowl of broth on a tray.

"Have we any idea where she is being held?" Germaine gasped this question through clenched teeth.

Camron beckoned to the woman, "First you eat, and then I will tell you of my farseeing revelations."

"But," Germaine began, only to see that Val, Crom, and the sorcerer were already ascending the stairs, ignoring his attempt to ask questions. "Please, I must know—" The knight realized his words were falling on deaf ears.

The knight looked back at Ayana as she walked to the bedside. Placing the tray on a small table by the bed, she helped Germaine regain his previous seated position on the cot.

Germaine quietly watched as she scooped a ladle of broth. She puckered her lips and gently puffed across the contents to help cool them. She then put the ladle to his lips. The woman repeated the process many times, patiently waiting for the knight to finish each scoop of broth. Germaine had not realized how hungry he was, and soon had the broth eaten.

"You love Estella. Do you not?" Ayana's question was unexpected and caused Germaine to squirm a bit.

"Do not be ridiculous. I am sworn to protect her, and I have failed to this point. That is where my concern for her is rooted." Germaine spoke too loudly. "Have I said anything to lead you to this conclusion?" Germaine forgot his wounds as he thought about Estella.

He watched Ayana place the empty bowl back on the tray as she spoke. "When I looked into your eyes while you struggled to leave your bunk, I saw the spark of love in their depths. It was more than concern for a liege, or one in danger. Remember. I saw you in the forest when such a circumstance existed, when the life in danger was my own. Sir Knight, you may be unreadable in battle, but you are like an open book when it comes to your emotions."

Ayana's statement caused Germaine to stare blankly for several moments as he remembered his wife's last words to him. *What was it Ana said? You may be unreadable in battle, but not … Where is my memory? Have I so soon forgotten her last words?*

Seeing Germaine's hurt expression, Ayana asked, "Why that look in your eyes? Have I struck a chord that causes you pain?"

"You have, Ayana. The words you spoke just now mirror those that my wife had for me with her last breath." A tear in the corner of his eye betrayed the feelings of his heart.

"Your wife's last breath? I do not understand."

"My wife spoke of her love for me as she lay dying. Part of me has gone with her." Germaine wiped away the tear.

"Please forgive me, Germaine. I did not know of this great sorrow that you carry within your heart." Germaine felt Ayana's arms wrap about him in an embrace as she sat on the edge of the bed beside him. As she once again stood up, Germaine heard Camron descending the stairs.

"Ah! I see our patient has eaten well. Of course, it helps when one has such a beautiful server. Would you leave us for a short time, my dear? I have confidential tidings for Germaine."

Ayana bowed slightly to Camron as she gathered up the tray and then turned to go up the stairway. Germaine noticed the sad look on her face as she departed.

"I know where the evil knight has taken Estella. I will tell you this, and something else which is of great difficulty for me to reveal." Germaine gazed expectantly at the wizard as Camron moved to a chair and sat. "I should have told you this before now, but it is very distasteful for me to think about, much less talk about. I have been afraid to tell you before now. I feared that you might be disheartened by what I am about to reveal. I need not have worried, because you have proven to have a valiant heart. Scul Craitor, the Falchion Raptor, is also a sorcerer."

Germaine's eyes opened wide at this revelation. "Why is he hungry for the title of king if he is a wizard of power? Is he not like you?"

"There lies the problem. He is a sorcerer of the black arts. His powers have some semblance to my own, and yet they are different. My power can only be used on the side of a noble heart, one who is worthy. However, I cannot use my power to supplant the efforts of a worthy man. I can help in many small things, and the many small things become large when the final tally is taken. At one time, my sorcerer's powers were much greater. That was before."

Germaine watched as Camron stood up and walked to a table with some strange equipment upon its surface. He stared at the gadgets while he continued speaking. "Scul is of another sort. His powers are more limited, and can be used only for evil. Unfortunately, he is not under the same constraints that limit me. When he kidnapped Estella, he used an invisibility spell of some sort to enter and leave the castle. It drains much strength from a sorcerer to employ such a spell, much like the weakened condition I experienced after transporting you."

"Where did he take her?" Germaine could not allow her to remain in Scul's control.

Germaine noticed Camron frown. "He took her to Skull Fortress. The foundation of the Skull was set when Terra was young. Its builders are long for-gotten, but the evil that was woven into the stones is still there. That aura of evil emanates like tentacles to snare those who have power, like me. I could enter, but I would have to expend every ounce of my power to shield myself. I could be of no assistance to you, nor could I defend myself from physical harm."

"Has he harmed her in any way?" Germaine feared the answer.

"No. Not yet, for he needs her as bait for his trap." Camron now stared into Germaine's eyes. "A trap that he hopes will lead to your undoing."

"Why bait me into a trap?" Germaine could not remember ever meeting the man. *Why would he want me dead?*

"You have been a thorn in Scul's side for some time now. Even your recent action on behalf of Lord Jahil and Fenn Hold was an obstacle to Scul. His minions were leading that rebellion, and you were the one who put a stop to it. You have thwarted his plans at every turn, and he now wants to make you pay. He will probably challenge you to single combat to the death in exchange for Estella's freedom. Believe me when I tell you that, if he wins, Estella will die anyway. He will not abide by the codes of valor and he will use his powers, or whatever means lay at his disposal, to destroy you."

Camron now gazed at Germaine with twinkling eyes as he said, "I have told you that I do many of the little things. I have the ability to shield my presence from Scul's detection. I have also placed you under that same spell. I have sensed the black sorcerer's probing with his farseeing spell. He is beginning to doubt that you survived the battle. This fact will help you find him with his guard down. I have restrained myself from using my own power to keep track of him. It would be unwise to reveal myself too soon. Hopefully, Estella will not volunteer the information to him."

"Even if it appears hopeless, I must face this man! I cannot let him kill her. My only regrets in death would be leaving my children as orphans, and failing in my last Oath term." Germaine realized, as he finished speaking, the only faces he would miss were those of his children, and Estella. At least, in death, he would see Ana again.

"I did not say it is hopeless. After all, you do have a sorcerer of your own. You also have the advantage of knowing that he is a sorcerer while he does not yet know that you have me for an ally."

"Do you have a plan, Camron? I fear that, for once, I am at a complete loss." *How do I deal with a sorcerer? It has been difficult, at times, to deal with one as an ally.*

The knight watched Camron turn to the equipment on his table and pick up something wrapped in an oil cloth. Carrying the object almost reverently, he returned to Germaine's bedside. The old sorcerer pulled the oil cloth back so that Germaine could see the haft of a sword. "Have you heard of Titan's Blade, Sir Knight?"

"Is this Titan's Blade?" Germaine stared in awe at the sword before him. Germaine knew the sword as a legend. He had heard those who spoke of it as a real piece of history, but those believers were few. "It is said to be a weapon of great mystical power, power that is greater than that of mere sorcery. Legend says that the billet from which it was made was brought to a master swordmaker after it fell from among the stars." Germaine could not tear his gaze away from the sword.

"If you can wield this sword, you will have a powerful weapon that can destroy Scul. I must warn you that if you touch the hilt of this sword and are not accepted as worthy, you will die." Camron looked at the sword, and then to the face of the knight. "What do you say, Sir Knight?"

Germaine said nothing. *I feel as if the sword is tugging at me, urging me to take it up.* He reached out his hand and quickly grasped the haft of the sword. Titan's Blade suddenly burst into bright light. As Germaine raised it level with his chest, his hand began to glow. The aura of light continued traveling up his arm. Within seconds his entire body was glowing as brightly as the sword. Germaine felt a sensation of being filled with strength. The pain in his shoulder was completely gone. He shifted his legs over the side of the cot, then stood up. The glowing gradually began to fade, and soon Germaine was again returned to his normal appearance. He flexed his side, and found the pain to be gone. *I no longer have wounds. What power I felt from the sword! It was as if I were part of the air, yet filled with fire. I was among the stars, yet part of Terra.*

"Look at Titan's Blade!" Camron commanded.

As Germaine looked at the sword in his hand, it began to change color. The sword became emerald green. In fact, it now looked identical to his sword, Lightning.

"Why did the sword change form and color?" Germaine now cradled the sword in both hands as he examined it closely.

"It has adapted itself to be your protector. No one will ever suspect it is anything but your own sword unless you choose to reveal that it is Titan's Blade. This secret could prove to save your life. Remember, no one else must touch this sword's hilt or they will perish." Camron paused. "The powers of this sword will protect you from minor spells, and it will deflect major spells so that you can survive their impact. These facts will help you fight the Falchion Raptor on more equal footing. This sword does not make you immortal, so you must depend on your warrior's skills to defend yourself as you have always done. The difference between this sword and your own Lightning is that it puts you on a more level battlefield with a sorcerer."

Germaine looked at the sword as a question that had plagued him came to his lips. "Camron, do you believe in God?"

Camron smiled. "Most assuredly, why do you ask?"

Germaine held the sword higher in emphasis. "Is it right for men to use such powers as those held by you and this sword, I mean right in the eyes of God?" Germaine was trying to remember what he may have been taught concerning the subject.

Camron looked somber as he said, "I cannot say what is in the heart of God. I do know that God created all that we see, even this power. I have had the opportunity to read many of the scrolls of Scriptures that are kept in far lands, and I know from those writings that God frowns upon the misuse of what He has made. Unfortunately, most sorcerers are corrupted by the power they wield, and I fear the Creator will remove the ability of men to continue in that misuse. One day, sorcery will be but slight-of-hand in a magic show. This sword is used only on the side of what is good. I believe it was God who gave it into my keeping, and He, too, is good. There is one thing I do recall from a scroll. God used a man who was known to be a sorcerer to send a message to men. I believe his name was, Balaam."

Germaine had a far away look of remembrance in his eyes. "I do not remember mention of sorcerers during the days my mother taught me what she knew of God. She did teach me that the Lord would provide for the needs of His people. Perhaps your reason for being here with this sword is to provide the means for defeating this evil sorcerer." *Lord, I ask your guidance. Show me the path where I must set my feet. Because this sword will be used to fight evil, it cannot be of evil. I remember that Jesus said, "A house divided against itself cannot stand."* At least that was the way Germaine remembered the long-ago words of his mother.

Germaine walked to the table and found Lightning lying there in its scabbard. He removed his sword from its scabbard and replaced it with Titan's Blade, placing the true Lightning on the table. "The transformation of this sword is truly amazing. It seemed to be bigger than my own sword when I first held it. Now it fits my scabbard and has the same feel and weight as Lightning." He then strapped the belt holding the scabbard to his waist. He stretched out his left hand and picked up Stinger.

"Val found the short sword where you had dropped it during the battle and brought it to me for safekeeping," said Camron.

"I will need you, too, my little friend." The knight placed Stinger in its sheath on the right side of his belt.

"There is one more thing of importance, Germaine. Follow me to the stable." Camron turned and led the way up the stairs.

Germaine followed, flexing his left arm. The soreness was completely gone.

Once in the stable, he took the Emerald Knight to a stall and opened its door. Within was Silver Cloud. He was suspended above the floor by a sling.

The charger's right foreleg was bound with a bandage. "Some thought that we should put him down, but I would not allow it. He is healing slowly but will not be able to walk normally again unless the sword can be of help."

"You mean the sword can heal Cloud's wound just as it did for me?" Germaine hoped that this was so.

"I have been guardian of this sword for a long time, but I will never truly understand its power. I believe that the sword can heal your horse if it will be in your best interest."

"What must I do?" Germaine asked.

"Place the side of the sword against the injured area. One of three things will happen. Either nothing will occur, the wound will heal, or the horse will die of the sword's power." Camron removed the bandage from the charger's leg and moved out of the way.

Germaine hesitated, then gently laid the sword against the wound. Once again, he witnessed a bright glow from the sword that completely enveloped the animal. When the glow died out, Camron began releasing the ropes that held the sling. He slowly lowered the horse to the floor.

Germaine was elated as he watched Silver Cloud stand on his own. Silver Cloud began prancing his front legs back and forth as if to test them. Camron opened the gate to allow the horse to run free as he was released into the corral.

Camron pulled the sling to one side of the stall and secured it to a rail. "He seems well enough, but you should allow him a few days of rest before riding him again."

"It will be as you say, Wizard. I will select another mount for tomorrow's foray. I will ride at first light. Will you ride with me, Camron?"

"I will never be far from you, Germaine, but remember this. As I told you, my powers will be of no use against Craitor while within his lair. In fact, sorcerers seldom battle each other with their powers because there is a great possibility of a backlash. The wrong combination of opposing spells can cause the destruction of the wielder. As long as he is not aware of my presence, I can weave spells that will affect him when he is away from Skull Fortress." Camron motioned toward the sword as he continued. "The power held by the sword is not so restricted because it was not created by a sorcerer. Titan's power arises from a source beyond the ability of any human endeavors. As I have already said, the metal was forged among the lights in the heavens. That is why it can be unpredictable at times. You do not face an easy battle, but you have the means of victory in your scabbard. Remember all that I have told you. Do not feel that this sword will make you invincible. One of its previous owners died while wielding it in battle."

Camron paused. Germaine felt as if the old sorcerer was looking for any reaction on his part. The knight knew that death was a possibility, and he was not going to trust in the power of the sword to prevent such an end. He would trust in God, the sharp edges of his swords, and the sharp edge of his wits. All he expected was the level battlefield that Camron had already mentioned.

"Now, go, and get your rest. You will need it for your journey ahead." From a fold in his robe, Camron withdrew a map and handed it to Germaine. "These directions will lead you to the lair of Scul Craitor. May your sword be strong and true, Sir Knight."

"May your way be clear of troubles, my friend." Germaine answered. *Let my sword find Craitor's throat if he has harmed Estella,* Germaine thought, with a grim set to his jaw.

After selecting a mount and placing it within a stall for the morning, the knight returned to his quarters. When Germaine stepped into his chamber, he found a happy Mikial.

"Sir Germaine, it is good to see you away from your sickbed and back with me." Germaine saw a cloud of sadness cross Mikial's face. "Did you hear about Silver Cloud's wound? Some say that he will have to be destroyed."

Germaine smiled and said, "You need to go to the stable and check on him. I hear that Silver Cloud has made a miraculous recovery."

Mikial's eyes widened as he began to move toward the door.

Germaine placed a hand on the boy's shoulder and said, "When you return, prepare a travel kit. I will be riding at first light in the morning. I will need a nine-day supply of dry rations." He figured three extra days to provide for an extra person on the return trip.

"It will be done, Sir Germaine." Mikial rushed out without saying more.

While Mikial was at the stable, Germaine sat at the table with quill and paper and wrote two letters, one to each of his children. He wrote about how much he loved them and how he wanted to be with them. When he had finished, he folded them and placed his waxed seal on the letters, along with the names of the children. *I will place these in Mikial's safekeeping. Should I not return, he will see that the children receive my last thoughts of them.* Germaine rose from his place at the table and said to himself, "Now I must sleep. Tomorrow brings a long journey." As Germaine lay down on his bunk, his mind wandered to Ana. Somehow, the knight realized, he was no longer deeply saddened by the memories of his wife. In fact, he found comfort and happiness. He remembered how she was prepared to meet her fate. *She was brave in those final moments of life.* Germaine smiled as he remembered that Ana was as brave in facing death as any knight could be. As he fell asleep, she still filled his thoughts.

The sunrise found Germaine riding out of Castle Lyon Hold. As he crossed the drawbridge, he found two men on horseback waiting. "Crom and Val, what are you doing here?"

Crom thumped his chest in salute. "I ride with you, Sir Knight!"

"As do I," the big Vordund warrior added.

Germaine asked Crom, "Will the hold be safe without you here to command?"

Crom said. "Yes, the hold will be under the protection of Byrone. He is as able a leader as I. Besides, Craitor cannot have a very large military after his defeat here. I will better serve my lady by accompanying you, Sir Knight."

"I welcome your company, but this is a journey that will hold more than the danger you now expect. Camron has informed me that Scul is a sorcerer."

"I hear that a sorcerer can die by the sword. Is that the truth of the matter?" Val asked this question of the knight.

"It is true, warrior. Sorcerers are but humans with powers. They are difficult to kill." Germaine said this to let the two warriors know that the task would not be easy.

"Then we are wasting time talking. Let us ride." Crom's voice was bold and sure.

Germaine led the small group as they rode. Their goal was the sorcerer's lair.

As Germaine made his way to her, Estella continued to bravely face her ordeal in Skull Fortress.

XV

Estella sat perched upon her chair watching the movements of the rats as they scurried about the cell floor. On occasion she would use a short piece of wood, which she had found, as a tool to dissuade a wayward rat from climbing up the legs of the chair. She was thankful that the beady-eyed creatures had not shown true interest in her yet.

She found the only respite in her captivity the fact her jailers removed her from her cage twice a day to accommodate her toiletries and to allow her to eat at a table in the kitchen. The food was poor, but she hardly noticed due to her great hunger. A week had passed since she had arrived at her prison, and she now began to fear there was no hope of rescue.

Estella often thought about Germaine and wondered if he had survived the battle for Lyon Hold. The Falchion Raptor seemed certain Germaine still lived, but it was doubtful to her. There were times, in her cell, that she remembered her days with the gentle knight. She had never met anyone quite like him. They could never be more than good friends. After all, he was married. *I will be content with a relationship as friends. That would depend, of course, upon* **if** *I ever get out of this prison and* **if** *the Emerald Knight is, indeed, still alive.*

On her eighth day in the cell, she overheard two of her captors talking about Craitor.

"Scul has gone to get more soldiers from his holdings to the north," a guard, whom she thought of as 'Rat Face', spoke loudly to another. "I tell you, I think he will be lucky if he finds a dozen men to back him."

"Quiet, fool!" This from 'Mouse.' "Do you not realize that he could be listening to us with his sorcerer's powers, even now?"

Sorcerer! Estella shuddered with this revelation. *That would explain how he managed to enter my castle and then leave without being caught.* That thought had been bothering Estella. She had wondered if, indeed, another spy had been in the castle.

Rat Face cursed. "He has bigger troubles to worry over than us. Besides, he left early this morning and will not be back for four days. Let us relax and enjoy his absence. Perhaps we can even have some sport with our captive." Estella shuddered again when she heard this. She would rather stay with the rats. *If they enter this cell, I will fight. Perhaps they will kill me. That would be preferable to the alternative.*

"Tron, you know that Scul has some specific use in mind for the woman. If you touch her, you will die just as Eldon did, and Eldon's only crime was the bearing of bad news to Scul."

The conversation of the two guards faded away, as they were walking during their chat and were now out of ear shot for Estella.

That night, as usual, Estella slipped in and out of sleep while sitting in the chair. She was jarred wide awake by a loud noise that she thought was made by the rats. She soon realized the noises to be the sounds of battle in the fortress. The unmistakable clanging of swords resounded in the corridor outside. Estella wondered if the battle heralded her escape from captivity. She knew that with Scul absent it was possible that his ragged group of warriors could be fighting among themselves. She was afraid to know the answer. It could be that she was the cause of a fight over what was to be done with her.

Only a few short hours before Estella heard the commotion, Germaine and his comrades reached Skull Fortress.

The three warriors watched the fortress from their hidden vantage point in a great rift that was torn in the earth. Germaine surveyed the sparse tree line that lay just beyond the four-foot-deep ditch where they now crouched. He could see several sentries on the ramparts, if *rampart* would be an accurate name for an empty eye socket of a giant skull.

"They have an excellent defensive perimeter." Germaine grudgingly admitted. "There is no way to cross that open expanse without being seen." *It must be a hundred yards to the wall of the fortress.* Germaine continued to scan the terrain of the open expanse. He could not find any features that would provide concealment.

"Our best hope would be to wait for it to get darker." Crom spoke without conviction in his voice. Though well after sundown, the knight saw the low, flat land between them and the fortress had an illumination of its own. Crom voiced what Germaine had been considering. "The ground seems to be lit by unnatural means. Perhaps it will be darker after midnight. Then again, this could be some of Scul's sorcery work."

"As you say, I do not believe this light to be natural. The sorcerer probably set some sort of spell to aid his sentries." Germaine had seen stranger things than this since his association with Camron.

"By the sea serpent, look at your sword!" Germaine knew that Val almost yelled this warning, restraining himself at the last instant.

Titan's Blade was glowing with a faint, green haze. The knight had not told his companions about the sword being a thing of power. "Do not fear this sword, my friends. Camron thought some power of our own would be needed on this quest."

Crom asked, "What can this power do for us?"

"I am not sure, Crom." Germaine drew the sword from its scabbard as he spoke. "It would be helpful if it could allow me to cross this expanse without being seen by the men who watch." As Germaine voiced this thought, his two friends gasped and began looking about as if they had lost something. "What is wrong with you two?"

"I hear him, but where is he?" Val was asking Crom.

"Where is who? What are you looking about so wildly for?" Germaine was puzzled by their actions.

"Sir Knight, you have disappeared from our sight! It must be the work of your sword."

Germaine spoke, as if to the sword, "It would be helpful if the power of this sword would allow both of you to travel with me, unseen." Germaine watched the two warriors suddenly vanish from sight. "Come my friends. Let us pay yon fortress a visit before this spell wears off." As they walked in silence, Germaine could see their footprints form in the dirt. "Let us hope that the watchers ahead are not looking for disembodied footprints," Germaine whispered to his invisible comrades.

Soon, Germaine gained the base of the walls of Skull Fortress. As he had noticed earlier, the drawbridge was down with two guards standing watch on it. *The lowered drawbridge shows confidence that no one would approach this fortress, or it could be that we walk into a trap.* Germaine felt his skin itch with the anticipation.

Germaine did not want to leave adversaries at their backs, should the spell erode. 'Val, you take the man on your left. Crom, take the one on our right. Try for silent kills. I will pass between and gain the interior of the fortress." They trod very slowly on the bridge to avoid making any sound. As Germaine passed between the two guards, they both went down with their throats cut. Within another second, Germaine was within the fortress.

He heard his two warriors nearby and whispered, "Val, go up the ramp-way and take out the sentries on the rampart. Crom, you take the two men lounging by the gate mechanism. I am going for that stairway and the two guards at the top." When Germaine was within twenty feet of the guards, the spell wore off. The two men quickly drew their swords in surprise. Germaine could tell by the shouts behind him that his two friends were discovered as well. The clanging of swords reached Germaine's ears as he became locked in his own battle with the guards.

Germaine was swinging Titan's Blade in sweeping, emerald arcs with Stinger firmly held in his left hand. The two foes before him had the disadvantage of close quarters. They were crowding each other until Titan found the heart of the man on the right. Germaine parried two thrusts by the other man with Stinger, then he thrust Titan through the man's chest. With these two down, he hurried to the top of the stairs. When he reached the top, he found a landing with a set of stairs continuing upward, and another set that descended to a lower level within the castle. Germaine could not remember seeing such an arrangement before. *Why have two stairways leading to the ground level? Then again,* Germaine thought, *perhaps this stair leads down to a dungeon. Usually this is done from the ground level. Of course, there is nothing of the usual about this fortress.*

As he turned, Titan blazed brighter. A feeling of warmth tugged at Germaine. The feeling seemed to be inside his skull. He knew, somehow, that the sword directed him. "She must be in this direction." He flew down the stairs. At the bottom he engaged a rat-faced looking fellow who put up a fierce defense. They fought in the corridor, and Germaine caught a glimpse of Estella's face as she peered out through the bars of a dungeon cell door.

Germaine's strength seemed to surge with his realization of how near he was to his goal. He was battering Rat Face with a barrage of blows. Then a ferocious blow from Germaine sent Rat Face to his death.

Germaine could see Estella watching as he took the keys from the dead man's belt and came to her cell door, releasing her. She grabbed Germaine in a close embrace of gratitude and, with tears of joy in her eyes, pulled his face close to hers and their lips met. Estella's action caught Germaine by surprise. Germaine could not tell how long they stood locked in that embrace. It seemed like an eternity, and yet the moment must have been very brief, too soon broken by a yell from above.

"Sir Knight!" It was Val. "Where are you?"

"Here, Val. I am below you in the dungeon. I have found Estella!" Turning his face to the woman. "You seem faint, my Lady, can you make it up the stairs?" Before she could answer, Germaine lifted her into his arms and carried her up to where Val was waiting. *How light she is in my arms. I could carry her all the way back to Lyon Hold. She could never be a burden for me*. He sighed as he realized he would soon have to relinquish his hold of her.

When Germaine reached the top of the stairs he did not set Estella down, but continued to carry her down the stairway that led to the courtyard. Germaine reluctantly set Estella on her feet when they reached the courtyard.

Val was unmarked from the battle, but Crom had a gash in his right leg. Germaine saw Val putting something on the wound. "It is some of the wizard's ointment. He gave it to me just in case one of us was wounded." When Val finished wrapping Crom's leg in a bandage, he turned to Germaine. "There are horses in the corral, and these men will no longer have a need for them. I suggest we ride to where we left our horses rather than have Crom try to walk."

As Val and Germaine saddled the horses, Estella said. "I overheard two of my guards say that Scul Craitor had left for reinforcements. They also called him a sorcerer."

"Camron has already told me about Scul's true nature. Perhaps the spell Camron wove to prevent Scul from detecting me has served us this day. We did not have to face Scul's sorcery, and his absence would suggest that he did not believe me capable of showing up at his lair." Germaine mounted one of the horses and Val handed Estella up to him. He held her close as they rode out of Skull Fortress.

After they had retrieved their own horses, and Estella now rode her own mount, Germaine thought back to that long embrace and kiss. How easily he had melted into her arms. He wished that the embrace and kiss were signs of her love for him, but he knew that her action only expressed her deep gratitude and relief at being freed from captivity. He would have been content to hold her forever, with her sweet lips pressed against his.

Alas, he remembered the fine men of high upbringing that she exchanged favors with. *I can never be a part of her world!* His heartache increased with that thought. She could never love a man so much older than herself, not to mention a man without property or great wealth. No, she could never feel the same love that he felt for her.

Germaine found the trip back to Lyon Hold uneventful, but it seemed to take forever for the knight with the troubled heart. He wondered what the Falchion Raptor would do when he returned to find that his lair had been violated. Who could guess at the workings of a black sorcerer's mind?

During Germaine's journey to Lyon Hold with Estella, Scul returned to his lair, Skull Fortress.

Scul was maddened by his discovery of Estella's escape. He had the walls of his fortress as witness to the deed. The sorcery that dwelled within those walls revealed to Scul that the Emerald Knight was responsible for the release of his prisoner. By laying his head against a stone in the wall, he could see the images of the battle. The images did not reveal how the three men had entered the fortress. This angered Scul even more as he guessed that his men had been asleep at their posts. *Their fate was too good for them.* Thought Scul. *I cannot find enough men to build another formidable army, but I have an idea where to find an ally. An ally that no human can stand up against.* Scul laughed as he turned to his lieutenant and ordered preparations to be made for a journey.

Two of Scul's lieutenants rode with him. During the three-day trip to the mountain that held a great cave, Scul outlined his intentions to the two men. He could see disgust and fear on their faces when he told them about Iron Hide.

When they arrived at the mountain, Scul noticed that his men were nervous with their proximity to the cave. The Raptor and his men had to leave their horses some distance from the cavern because the animals were becoming unmanageable. Their horses pawed nervously with the sense of danger that lay ahead.

The entrance to the great cave reeked of carrion. Scul Craitor paused for a moment to look, again, for signs of movement within its dark recess.

"Old Iron Hide!" Scul called. "I come in peace for a counsel with you, O' Great One." There was still no sound from the cave opening. Only an occasional foul-smelling cloud of greenish smoke wafted from its depths. Scul turned to the two men who accompanied him. "Looks like we will have to go in to gain his attention."

"No, Sir Craitor!" The warrior to his right spoke. "We do not go in. You are the one seeking an audience with a dragon. We will await your return, should you indeed survive."

"This is the thanks I get from my officers. All right, cringe here like cowards while I go forth." Scul resumed his advance on foot through the cave entrance.

The stench of death was oppressive, even for Scul. Clouds of vapor, caused by the creature's breathing, wafted through the air. The steamy tendrils of dragon's breath limited Scul's visibility to a few feet.

"Great One, I am here as a friend. Please reveal yourself to me."

Scul had already woven a spell about his person. It was an ancient spell that would cause a dragon to suffer a great deal of agony if it tried to harm one so protected. The sorcerer knew that a determined dragon could choose to endure the agony if it wanted to kill him badly enough.

"What do you want, wizard? The aura of your power is plainly visible to me." Scul heard a great rumbling voice give life to these words.

"I have come to you, Great One, with a proposition. I have something you would be interested in, and all I ask in return is that you do a simple task to win the information."

"What could you have that would be of importance to me?" Scul felt his body quiver as the voice grew nearer to him. The ground seemed to vibrate with the dragon's deep rumbling.

"Another such as yourself. In fact, a *female* dragon."

Scul could make out Iron Hide's form, now visible through the mist. The creature was huge, much larger than Scul had expected. As his taloned claws scraped across the cave floor, Scul saw they were large enough to cover a horse. The huge scales covering the beast glittered as they were caught in the sunlight from the cave entrance.

He gauged the creature's height so great that its long serpent-like neck bowed down to allow it to move beneath the high ceiling of the cave, causing the hideous horned head to be just a few feet above Scul's. When the creature moved its mouth to voice rumbling words, Scul saw giant, yellow fangs flash into view. These appeared to the sorcerer to be three feet in length. With each breath it exhaled, greenish fumes would issue forth to add to the dense vapors that already enveloped Scul. The sorcerer watched in fascination as the great, leathery wings heaved up and down with the movement of the dragon's breathing. Scul's attention was drawn to the eyes of the dragon, huge, yellow orbs with a vertical black slit of a pupil splitting the center of each. Scul looked in awe at what appeared to be red embers in the nostrils of the beast. Without the spell that restrained the dragon, Scul knew he would be a quick meal for the rumbling Iron Hide.

"That is a lie! I am the last of my kind. You play a cruel joke on me, wizard."

"It is the truth! I know where a dragon sleeps the long sleep." Scul felt smug now. He had the old dragon where he wanted him. Scul had known for hundreds of years that the long sleep was a state that a dragon could enter, much like a bear would hibernate. The difference being that the long sleep could last for centuries, and the dragon would be cloaked in a disguise that could resemble anything, even a large rock. *Yes*, thought Scul, *they are very difficult to find when in the long sleep. Impossible for men, only difficult for a sorcerer such as me.*

"Where is this she-dragon?" Iron Hide growled in demand.

"Not so fast! I will tell you when you have satisfied my price for the information."

Iron Hide growled, "What is your price?"

"I must kill a certain knight. That will be no problem for me to accomplish for he is a mere human while I am a sorcerer. The problem is that I do not have an army large enough to consolidate my control of Valeria. That is where you come into the plan. At the dawn of the day following the next full moon, you will come forth and terrorize the hold. I will then come forward to 'thwart' you, and win the love of my new subjects. It would fit my plan if you devour Estella Merelda, the lady of the hold. That would make my leadership even more welcomed by the people of Lyon Hold." *I will bring my wrath to bear upon the Emerald Knight. He has been a barrier against me for too long. Violating my fortress is the last straw. He and the lady will pay with their lives.*

The dragon rumbled, "Who is this knight you must slay?"

Scul answered. "An insignificant cur who calls himself the Emerald Knight." Scul saw the great pupils of the dragon widen and then contract as it snarled.

"This knight carries green weapons?" The dragon drew his head up toward the high ceiling of the cave as he asked this question of Scul.

"Yes." Scul said. "He carries such weapons. How did you know this?"

Scul witnessed small spurts of flame from the dragon's nostrils flare as it said. "I have battled a knight with green weapons. That was hundreds of years ago. I was gravely injured by the knight, due to pure luck on his part. He managed to kill my mate when she came to my defense. My mate's action allowed me to escape. I did not know she was slain until she failed to return to the lair. Can it be that this human has lived that long?" Scul saw the dragon's pinions stretch in anger as it spoke.

"No, Great One. This man is no sorcerer. He cannot be the same man." Scul was now wondering to himself if it were possible for a mere human to discover some means of long life.

"What if," the dragon began, "this knight should get lucky and kill you instead? How will I get my side of the bargain?"

"If that should happen, and it will not, I suggest that you take your wrath out on this green slug for robbing you of a new mate. Perhaps he is descended from the one who killed your mate so many years ago. That possibility should be added motivation for you. No man could ever defeat you in battle. Do we have a pact?"

"It will be as you have said. If you try to renege on our deal, keep in mind that such a ruse will cause me to ignore your spell over me. Then you shall be my meal." The dragon punctuated this with a hideous growl.

"I will keep my word, Great One. I must now take my leave. There are preparations I need to make."

Scul rejoined his waiting men, satisfied that he now held all the answers. Meanwhile, Germaine and Estella were still free and within sight of Lyon Hold.

XVI

With Estella and her fellow riders approach to castle Lyon Hold, a great cheer went up as the people realized she had returned to them. Estella noticed, with a smile, that Germaine pulled in on the reins as he and the two warriors allowed her to take the lead as they rode through the drawbridge gate. Estella waved to the cheering crowds. She noticed a beautiful, blonde woman run to the Emerald Knight as he was dismounting. *I do not recognize this woman. Who can she be?*

As Estella watched, Germaine's feet barely touched the ground before he was grabbed in an embrace. "Ayana!" Estella heard Germaine manage to blurt out the name before the blonde woman's lips found his. As she saw the blonde move her face away from his, Germaine grinned. "Never have I received such a sweet welcoming to Lyon Hold!"

Estella could hear the blushing Ayana's words to the knight. "Please forgive me, Germaine. It is just that I was worried about you. After all, you were my patient one day and out on a quest the next."

Estella watched this scene, wondering. *Can this be Germaine's wife?* A sinking feeling churned within her breast. *I do not have the right to feel this way. It is a cruel twist of fate that I should lose my heart to a man I cannot have.*

"Estella!" Bildad's voice broke through her thoughts. "Are you all right? Did that black heart do anything to harm you?"

"No, my old friend! Other than squalid living conditions, I have not been physically injured. I must say that I am ready for some good food and a bed without rats dancing around it."

Estella noticed Bildad raise an eyebrow as he asked, "Rats?"

"I will tell you all about it after I have rested. I am grateful to you for persuading me to hire yon knight." Estella nodded toward Germaine. "Without him, I would not be alive now." Moving closer to Bildad she whispered, "By the way, is that Germaine's wife standing by his side?" She could not take her eyes off Germaine and the beautiful woman who was standing so close to him.

After giving Bildad a moment to look, Estella listened as he said, "I see whom you speak of. Oh, no. That is Ayana, daughter of Val, the Vordund leader. The Vordund warriors joined us in the battle to save Lyon Hold."

Estella raised her eyebrows as she thought. *Could this be the personal business that had taken Germaine and Camron away for those several days of absence?* A look of sadness darkened her already tired countenance. *I have been worried about my feelings for a married man, and it appears he is involved with someone else. I would not have believed him to be such a rat.*

"Yes, Bildad, a warm bath, a fine meal, and a good night's sleep are all I need, right now."

"Sir Knight," Estella heard Mikial call to Germaine, "Camron said to tell you that he must see you in his alchemy chamber at once." Estella noticed Mikial was wearing his biggest smile as he called out to Germaine. "It is good to see you, sir." Estella saw Mikial take hold the reins of Germaine's mount.

"I am glad to see you again, too. I know that Silver Cloud has been well tended while in your care."

"He is doing fine, Sir Knight. I rode him for a little while, yesterday. He seems to be completely recovered." Mikial then spoke to Estella as she passed near, on her way to her chambers. "It is good to see that you are safe, my Lady."

Estella smiled at the boy. "My thanks, Mikial. It is good to see you as well. Forgive me as I must be on my way to clean away some of the filth of Scul Fortress."

She hurried away, with thoughts of Germaine still plaguing her mind. Meanwhile, Germaine made his way to tell Camron of the events that occurred at Skull Fortress.

"Hello, Great Wizard." Germaine laughed as he entered the sorcerer's domain and noticed Camron's slight scowl at being called a wizard.

"It is good to see you once again, Sir Germaine. I witnessed some of your adventures with my farseeing spell."

"Camron, did you know that Titan's Blade can make one invisible?"

"Yes, I knew. However, be aware that the sword may not afford you the use of that particular spell again. I earlier explained that the sword's power is not derived from the sorcery that is known to men on Terra, but from a source among the stars. Over the years I have found that the sword can be uncooperative when the one who wields it seeks the use of its power. It cooperates at times, but not at others. Though it usually reacts in the best interest of its holder. The powers of defense against spells, as I told you of, are the only constants that you can be sure of. I must congratulate you on mastering the sword to use that power. You are truly a warrior worthy of Titan's Blade."

"Thank you, Camron. I am grateful for the use of the sword. The power made it possible for us to rescue Estella from Skull Fortress." His thoughts returned to the embrace he and Estella had shared. That kiss would not soon be forgotten.

He noticed Camron look for a long moment at an object sitting upon the table at which he was seated. "Bad news, I'm afraid. The Falchion Raptor is coming this way once more. He has become obsessed with killing you. His hunger for power is not driving him now. His motivation is his anger toward you."

"When will he be here?"

"That is hard to say. It could be within two weeks. He has been trying to raise another army, but he has not been successful. His control of the holds he has taken, has been weakened by the loss of so many warriors in the battle for Lyon Hold. Scul cannot remove his small garrisons from those holds for he will lose control of them, as well." Camron shrugged as he spoke.

Germaine turned to walk up the stairway. "My immediate concern now is to bathe and change into clothing that is not reeking of Skull Fortress and trail dirt."

"Germaine!" Mikial had appeared at the top of the stairs. "You are requested to attend a dinner with Lady Merelda and her party tonight."

"I hope that there will be enough time for me to bathe first." Germaine glanced at his dust-covered clothes.

"Yes, Sir Knight." Mikial said, "You have an hour before the meal."

"Very well, I shall be ready. Thank you, Mikial." Germaine found himself talking to empty air as Mikial had already turned on his heel and departed.

As Germaine walked up the stairs, he thought about the letters he had left in Mikial's safe keeping. He would have to retrieve them and add more to their contents of his thoughts for his children. *I will post them with the next messenger to travel to Fenn Hold,* Germaine thought as he made his way to his chambers. *With Scul's military strength weakened, perhaps the end of this oath is near. I am ready to spend some time with my children.* As he prepared for the evening meal, he realized that his thoughts of a quick end to Scul were premature. *I must not underestimate the Raptor. He has proven to be most tenacious in his quest for power.* As Germaine dressed, he placed Titan's Blade on his hip. *I will not be caught unprepared,* he thought as he left the chamber.

Germaine arrived on time and took his seat at the table. His dress tunic glinted with sparkles of emerald light. As he was seated, he noticed a man, whom he had seen in Estella's presence before, was seated next to her. The man was dark complected and was neatly groomed. Germaine noticed that he wore clothes that were very gaudy, with gold and silver trimmings on the sleeves and breast. He had dark brown eyes and an aristocratic nose that seemed to be lifted slightly upward in disdain for those around him. Germaine sensed a vanity about this man that sent the message that he knew himself to be comely. Germaine caught the man staring at him. The knight could detect some animosity in the man's bearing. *I believe this dandy to be resentful of my plain face at this table.* Germaine had always thought of himself as unremarkable in appearance. *Plain* was probably the better description of how he viewed himself.

At Estella's other elbow sat Bildad. There were several other people around the great table that Germaine had yet to meet this evening.

Seated in the chairs adjoining his was Crom on his left, and to the knight's right was a broadly smiling Ayana. The blue-eyed beauty was wearing an emerald green gown that glittered with light reflected from the oil lamps that were suspended from the high ceiling.

"It is good to see you again, Sir Germaine." Ayana held out her hand and briefly clasped his as he returned her greeting.

"It is my privilege to see you, my Lady. You are radiant in emerald." Germaine thought about how well that dress would look on Durelle, his daughter. Then he felt a brief sadness as he realized the emerald legacy may end with his generation. *Without a hold, what future is there for my children. Emerald may no longer be a part of their lives. It would be best if Durelle never owns another piece of clothing that is of that color.*

As Ayana withdrew her hand from his, she said. "I hoped you would like it. I bought it from a shop in the village."

Germaine's attention went to Estella as she greeted him, "Ah! My guest of honor is here. Welcome to my table, Emerald Knight."

Germaine stood and presented a bow. "Thank you, my Lady. It is my pleasure to be here."

Before Germaine could retake his seat, the man at Estella's right stood up. "Sir Knight, I am Arlis Cornado, Lord of Berne Hold. It is my great pleasure to meet you." Arlis bowed at the waist and then eased back into his chair.

"Thank you, Lord Cornado. I am honored." Germaine gave a half bow and then sat. *This man has shown me no ill-will, and yet I find a distaste for his presence.* Germaine silently asked the Lord's blessing for the meal.

"If the introductions are completed, let us enjoy this meal. I have been looking forward to good food for some weeks now." Estella laughed as she spoke.

"First!" Arlis again stood with his goblet of wine held before him, "I wish to offer a toast to the man that saved the life of the woman I love."

As everyone stood and presented their goblets in salute, Germaine's heart ached. He nodded absently and mumbled his thanks to the toast. His eyes went involuntarily to Estella who was smiling back at him with a look of—what? He could not tell.

"And now!" It seemed to Germaine that Cornado was not yet ready to sit down. "I am pleased to publicly announce my formal betrothal to Lady Estella Merelda!"

Now Germaine's heart experienced physical pain. Offering his glass to the salute without conscious thought, he turned his eyes to Ayana and saw that she was staring at him. He knew that the Vordund Princess was accessing the pain that he knew was written on his face. It seemed to the knight that Ayana looked hurt as well.

As the toast ended, everyone sat down to enjoy their meal, with the knight stealing another glance at Estella. She seemed to be looking at Arlis with shock on her face. Germaine saw that Estella said something curt to Arlis and then looked at Germaine. The knight quickly tore his gaze away from Estella and began to eat. Germaine felt as if each bite would stick in his throat as he ate in silence.

When he finished his meal, Germaine stood up and turned to leave. He saw Ayana looking at him with a tear gently tracing its way from one eye. The girl even lifted her hand to his wrist, briefly grasping it, then releasing her hold. Germaine thought her about to rise in an effort to go with him. *This gentle girl cares about my feelings. She should not waste her pity on me. I suppose that saving her life has caused her to feel concern for me*. Germaine's thoughts swirled away in confusion as he numbly made his way out of the castle.

Just a few short hours earlier, Germaine had been happy. Estella had been just as happy as she awaited the hour she would again see the knight.

The dinner hour approached, and Estella was eager to see Germaine again. She knew she would learn to accept the fact that he could only be a good friend, and not her lover. The only hitch Estella found in her preparations for the evening was the pesky Arlis Cornado. He had insisted on sitting beside her at the dinner. Estella had wanted to seat Germaine by her side, but realized that it would be better if she did not pull him too near. She would tolerate the presence of Arlis for this evening. Estella thought about how Arlis had known her for years, and during those years he had insisted that they would one day be married. *There was a time when I was quite attracted to his handsomeness, but that was before I realized how pompous he was. It seems that I can barely tolerate the man, of late.*

When the dinner hour finally approached, Estella felt as if she had been waiting for an entire day, instead of two short hours. Estella watched eagerly for Germaine to make his appearance. When he did enter the room, their eyes met for an instant and she felt happy. She wished for but a moment of his attention.

When the knight was seated, she saw that he was speaking with a woman who was sitting next to him. As Estella watched the exchange between the two, she felt a pang in her heart. *Does this woman not know of Germaine's wife?* She wondered. *She is the same one that met him with a kiss after our journey.*

As Arlis made his first toast to Germaine, Estella happily raised her goblet in salute. When Arlis had surprised her with that second toast, she nearly allowed the goblet to fall from her hand.

Arlis had spoken many times of his deep feelings for her. Though she was almost sympathetic toward him, she had never agreed to marriage. Not wishing to make a scene, she turned to Arlis and whispered. "I cannot believe you did this. I have not consented to betrothal. You must stand up and retract the statement." She glanced at Germaine and noticed that he quickly looked away from her.

Arlis smirked and said to her in a whisper. "I will not retract it now. It would not look right to the guests. Besides, you may grow used to the idea of marrying me."

Estella angrily looked away from Arlis, not wanting to cause a stir at the dinner. She would bite her tongue for the present. She tried to catch Germaine's eye once again, but he appeared to be intent upon finishing his meal. Estella ate without the relish she had looked forward to. Instead, she found the bites of food to be difficult to swallow past the lump in her throat. She, once again, found her feelings to be in a confused swirl. Arlis was a fine man, and she liked his company. The problem lay in the fact that she finally knew what love looked like and how it felt to the heart. Her feelings for Arlis were not those of love.

When the meal was over and Estella was alone with Arlis, she asked. "What were you thinking, sir?" Estella was red with anger. "I never settled on a betrothal to you!"

"Not in so many words, Estella, but a man knows when a woman is just being coy."

"Coy! I would not marry you now, not after your childish disregard for my feelings." Estella was exasperated.

"It is the Emerald Knight, is it not?" Arlis said. "I believe you have feelings for this man. That is understandable, what with him saving your life, but he is not worthy of your thoughts or time. Think about this. He has nothing but his code. He is a hired killer who cannot possibly commit his heart to a woman."

"You weasel! Leave my chambers at once! For all I know, you probably covet this hold as strongly as Craitor."

"But—"

"Out! Guard!" The man-at-arms on duty outside came into the room. "Escort this man out of my presence!" Estella was livid. *I have never allowed myself to lose my temper like this. Is it because Arlis struck so close to my heart with his accusation?*

"I am going, I am going, but you will see things my way tomorrow when you have given them some thought. You will see!" Arlis called over his shoulder as the guard ushered him out.

As the door closed, Estella ran to the eastern window crying. As she looked through her tears, she saw Germaine walking across the drawbridge. *See how easily you walk away from me, Sir Knight. I know you do not have feelings for me, as I have for you. Somehow, that makes me sad. I know that I must endure this pain of mine alone.*

Later that night, as Estella tossed in her effort to sleep, a lone horseman left the castle.

⇜ XVII ⇝

It had been two days of hard travel for the lone horseman. He left Lyon Hold like a thief in the night, and had been riding to the northwest in search of the Falchion Raptor. The horseman overheard two warriors in Lyon Hold as they spoke about the old man, Camron, being a sorcerer who held great powers. The rider knew this information would put him in a good stead with Lord Craitor.

On the morning of the third day, he awoke to find himself surrounded by warriors. They wore the emblem of the Falchion Raptor on their corselets, with a black helm that had a shield covering the face of each warrior. The face shield of each helm had rectangular eye openings and another opening for the nose and mouth. Mounted on each side of the helms were what looked to be vulture wings. A menacing statement was made to the traveler by the dark nature of their dress.

"I have traveled far to sit in council with the Falchion Raptor." He tried to sound brave, and sure of himself.

"Who are you that you should believe Sir Craitor would grant you a second of his time?" These words came through the black helm of the nearest warrior. The voice sounded like the growl of a wild beast.

"I am Arlis Cornado, Lord of Berne Hold. I have come from Lyon Hold to offer my aid to Lord Craitor. I may be able to provide him a service that will smooth the way for his plans."

"Come! We will take you to Sir Craitor and let him decide your fate." The growl-voiced warrior pointed to Arlis' horse. The warrior was ready to ride now, regardless of whether Arlis was prepared.

They did not ride more than a mile when the camp of the Falchion Raptor came into sight. Arlis was surprised at how few were the numbers of Craitor's army. His defeat at Lyon Hold must have crippled him much more than Arlis had believed. He now hoped that he was backing the right lord.

Arlis noticed they rode to the largest tent, located in the center of the camp. He saw a banner flying from its main pole. As the banner waved in the breeze, the image of a black falcon grasping a curved sword in its talons could be clearly seen by Arlis. After they had dismounted, the warrior who had done all the talking approached the open tent flap and saluted.

"Sir Craitor, we have a man here who seeks an audience with you."

"Where are your manners, Captain Cedral?" Arlis heard this question come from within the tent. "Show our guest in, so that we may meet."

When Arlis walked through the tent opening, his eyes took a second to adjust to the darkness within. When he focused on the seated Scul Craitor, he was surprised to find him to be a normal looking person. He had expected to find a grizzled, loathsome warrior.

"Greetings to you, Lord Craitor. My name is Arlis Cornado." As he spoke, Scul nodded his head in recognition.

"Ah, yes. The Lord of Berne Hold. What is it that you wish to discuss?" Scul well knew of Berne Hold due to the spies he had there. If his plans had stayed on track, he would have soon been adding that hold to his empire.

"Lord Craitor, I am aware of your great distaste for the Emerald Knight. I, too, have little use for the cad. It would be beneficial for us to join forces to get rid of him."

"Arlis, my good man, what makes you think I cannot take care of him myself?"

"Are you aware that a sorcerer is working in his behalf?"

"What?" Scul stood so abruptly that he knocked over his chair. *So that is how he defeated my men so easily? That would explain his entry into my fortress. This ally of his could have, indeed, created some difficult problems for me. Now that I know, the sorcerer is actually neutralized. He would not dare to use his power against another sorcerer. It could result in death for both of us.* "How can you help me? By pledging your army to my service?"

"No, I will not bring my hold into this conflict. I am sure that you can think of some way that I can help you from within the walls of Lyon Hold. In exchange for that service, I ask you to leave my hold unscathed and give to me the Lady Estella. I will be your loyal servant when you are High King."

"You ask for so little. I do have an idea about your part in this plan, an important role that will seal our bargain." Scul reached into a pocket within his tunic and produced a small vial that contained a green, liquid substance. He reached out and placed it in Arlis' hand.

"I will be coming to Lyon Hold within a few days to challenge the Emerald Knight to single combat. I will send forth a messenger with the challenge on the eve of combat. You must place this liquid into something he will eat or drink on that evening before he meets me in battle. You must not give this potion to him before that time. The spell is limited to a twenty-four-hour time frame."

"It will be done, Lord Craitor." Arlis bowed. "May I take leave, sir, to make my return to Lyon Hold?"

"By all means, comrade." Scul righted his chair and again sat down. "Until we meet again, my friend."

Scul watched as Arlis rode away. "What a delightfully devious person, Cedral. He is much too devious to be a trusted ally. Once we have finished our business with the Emerald Knight, you will kill him, and Estella, if she survives that long. Perhaps Iron Hide will have to make only a token appearance at Lyon Hold."

"As you have commanded, Sir Craitor!" Cedral saluted and left the tent.

Yes, I will soon have my plans moving in the right direction. It will not be long, now. Scul wondered what the Emerald Knight was doing.

Meanwhile, at Lyon Castle, Germaine was preparing for Scul, and trying not to think about Estella.

In the days since his return from Skull Fortress, Germaine avoided Estella. He had been practicing fiercely with the weapons of single combat. He wanted to leave no empty hours unfilled with work. To do so would open his mind and heart to more pain with his thoughts concerning Estella. When he had time to think, he directed his thoughts to his children. He had sent letters to them and received answers in return. He had almost worn the letters out as he read them so many times. Germaine was happy that they were doing so well. A letter from Jahil told him how well the youngsters were doing at Fenn Hold.

He practiced in full battle armor. As he rode with lance and shield against the dummy mounted on the jousting field runway wall, the emerald plume on his helm would bend in the wind with Silver Cloud's great speed. Val had asked Germaine a lot of questions about jousting.

"Germaine, I do not understand this custom you call joust." Val said to the knight. The Vordund warrior was visiting Germaine on the day the knight was setting the joust dummy in place. "Why do you call this spindly, two-foot tall fence, a wall?"

The knight smiled as he finished securing the dummy to its pole. The dummy did not actually sit on the wall, but a couple of feet away, on the opposite side of the runway that Germaine would occupy. Germaine checked to make sure that the dummy would tip over easily. "It has been called a wall because the knight cannot extend more than his weapons, or the arm holding his weapon, beyond it. The runway is the path the horse holds as the charge is made toward the opponent on the opposite end of the field." He had explained every aspect of the joust to Val.

The big warrior had told Germaine that there were too many rules involved. "It seems like a lot of trouble to endure. It would be easier to call the man out to battle in a field. All that would be needed are your swords."

Germaine was glad that Camron had spared the charger's life after he was wounded, not just because he loved the horse, but, the fact was, that it would be difficult to joust with an unfamiliar mount. It had been some time since he and Cloud had met an opponent in a joust, but he found no fault in the performance of the great, white charger.

He practiced with a sword several times a day. He also devoted time to battle mace and axe. Germaine had never chosen mace or axe in single combat, for he found them to be more brutal in nature, unlike the civilized swath cut by a good sword.

His only distractions came from Ayana. She made it her habit to ask him to supper as often as possible. He had ceased to wear his emerald clothing, other than his battle armor that he wore while honing his skills. He now wore a plain brown tunic and pants when not conducting guard or military operations.

At dinner one evening, Ayana asked him about the change. "Why do you no longer wear your emerald tunic, Germaine? Is it because your feelings for Estella have been dashed?"

Germaine snapped his gaze toward her eyes. "I have told you before that you are mistaken about my feelings. Will you ever let your suspicions rest?" The knight was uncomfortable. Ayana seemed to be able to read his heart as easily as one could read a letter.

"Germaine, you are driving your body too hard. If you keep this up, you will not be able to face Craitor due to fatigue."

"It will be all right, Ayana. A warrior knows his limits, and respects them." He took another bite of the meal Ayana had prepared.

"How is my cooking? Does it please you?"

"It is very tasty fare. I am surprised that you cook." Germaine gave her a grin, which had been rare for him of late. His time with Ayana was becoming his one enjoyment of life at Lyon Hold. She was pleasant, refreshing, and had become a good friend. Her only fault was her continual interest in his relationship with Estella.

"Why? Do not the ladies prepare meals for their lords?" Ayana had her brows raised in a quizzical expression.

"No, I am afraid it is a lost art. It seems that people in higher stations always have cooks, chambermaids, and many other servants."

"Well, it would not be a lost art with me. I would gladly prepare the meals for my husband. That is the way of the Vordund people."

Germaine laughed, "You will make someone a fine wife, a beautiful one at that." *At times, I wonder what is it that makes a man fall in love. I have felt so strongly about Estella, who has really given me little reason to do so. Yet, here is a woman who is physically more beautiful than Estella, and I do not have strong feelings for her. Life is full of mysteries, and I fear this one will remain unsolved.*

Ayana broke into his thoughts. "You say I will make someone a fine wife. Could you be that someone, Germaine?"

The question startled Germaine. The look on her face told him the full story. *How could I have been so blind? This woman has feelings for me that are greater than those of friendship. Let me say the right words. Words that will not hurt.* "Ayana, you would do yourself a great injustice to marry a man such as myself. You are so young. There are many fine lords who would be eager to make you their lady. I value your friendship too much to allow myself to fall in love with you. You deserve someone better than me."

Germaine finished speaking, then hugged Ayana and kissed her forehead. "I must be going now. The evening is growing late." *It is best I go before she can say more. She would grow to regret words that I would allow her to speak now.*

While Germaine was walking back to the castle, Val called to him. "A moment, Sir Germaine." The big warrior was hurrying to catch up to him. "May I walk with you, sir? I have to speak of a matter of importance."

Germaine clapped a hand on the big man's shoulder. "You have my ear, sir. What is the matter you speak of?"

Resuming their walk, Val began, "My people grow restless with our stay here. They want to continue our search for a new home. We are very grateful for the welcome we have had here, but we need to settle on land that we can call our own. The season is nearing summer and we will be hard pressed to weather the coming winter if we do not put roots down soon."

As Val was speaking, they walked across the drawbridge over the moat. Germaine found the road to be alive with people coming and going, each with his own business to tend.

Entering the courtyard, which fronted Germaine's quarters, the knight smiled at the sight of several young children at play. They made him think about his own children, at a time when they were younger. He could not help to think of the Vordund people and their children. They were in a difficult plight, and yet they had stayed their trek in order to help him. If not for Val and his warriors, he would be dead right now. He reached a decision. *With Ana gone, and my dreams of ever seeing Scot Hold rebuilt now a distant speck on the horizon. Why not do something worthwhile with what little I have left?*

"Val, I have an offer for you. I owe you and your people much more than I can ever repay. I do, however, own a considerable amount of land. It is good, rich land, but it lacks people. The buildings that were there are destroyed and much work will be required to make it a comfortable home place as far as shelter is concerned. As for your animals, there is plenty of grazing land and enough forage that you can store hay for winter. If you want it, the land is yours. All I shall keep is a small piece for a lodge, for my children and myself. I, too, am without a home. Together, we can help each other."

"That is too much for one to expect from a friend." Germaine could feel Val's penetrating gaze upon his face as the Vordund warrior spoke. "I have a counter-proposal for you to consider, Sir Knight. Allow us to live on your land with you, as friends. You will share in any success we may have. I will have to present this idea to my people for approval, but I feel they will accept such an offer. Is that agreeable with you?"

"What you offer is very fair, but I will still consider the land yours where you build your lodgings and other structures. It will be yours as long as you want it."

"Good enough. What is this place, and how do we find our way to it?"

"The place is what remains of Scot Hold, my castle. It was destroyed years ago by an army of barbarians. My castle and the village adjoining it were razed. With the people gone, there are no workers to rebuild. I have been selling my warrior abilities to those in need, trying to raise funds to finance the project. With my wife gone, I find the task hopeless, especially since I will be spending more time with my children after this oath is ended."

"To reach my lands, travel south for three days. The trail is well marked as it is the road to Fenn Hold. You will find a well-marked trail that crosses east to west. Take the westward trail. When you have traveled a little more than four days, you will find the ruins of Scot Castle."

"We are, once again, in your debt, Germaine. If they are in agreement, my clan will begin the journey in the morning."

"Wait but a moment." Germaine went into his quarters. After a few minutes, he returned with a scroll in his hand. "This paper has my pledge to you for the use of the land, and my seal is upon it. Should anyone question your presence, show them this document. I will visit you when this oath is completed."

"Sir Knight, I do not ride with my clan tomorrow. Two of my warriors and I have already decided to stay with you until this conflict with the Falchion Raptor is resolved. Though he comes to face you in single combat, the Raptor may have some of his minions in close company. My people will follow my second in command as they go before me and make preparations."

"As you wish, Val. The battle-axes and swords that your warriors wield with great strength are worth many times their number in battle. I welcome your decision to stand by my side." Germaine felt warmth within his chest. He found it a great comfort to have friends that were willing to stand by you when times were the most difficult.

With these plans made, Val departed to tell his clan of the knight's offer.

Germaine returned to his chambers, his spirit higher than it had been in days. He would sleep well that night.

The next morning would begin as another day of battle practice. For Estella, the morning would find her with a new strategy for bringing Germaine back to her close company.

In the days after the dinner fiasco, Estella hoped that Germaine would come to guard her as he had in the past. She ached for his company. The lady was glad that, at least, Arlis had stayed out of her sight. She hoped that he had left to return to his hold. She had considered ordering him away, but she did not wish to give him a reason to withhold future cooperation of his hold with hers.

On the few occasions she encountered Germaine, he said very little. He would answer her questions with short, curt statements. He seemed to be angry at her, but she did not know the reason. It seemed to her that the change occurred after the dinner following their return from Skull Fortress. *Could it be that this Ayana has said something to him? Possibly she sees me as competition to her affections toward Germaine. Or could it be possible that Arlis' announcement of betrothal—But that would mean—. No, it would be too much to hope for, and I would not want to be the rift between a man and his wife.* She did not know the answer, but she did have an idea that would force Germaine back into her presence. She would have a talk with Bildad.

"Why have you summoned me, Estella? Is there something amiss?" Estella read fatherly concern on Bildad's face as he spoke.

"Bildad, I am not doing very well. I do not feel as safe without Sir Germaine guarding me. Does he think the danger to me has passed by so he sends lesser warriors to protect me?"

"Estella, I do not know his reasoning in this matter. If it will set your mind at ease, I will ask him of this concern."

"It would, Bildad! Please do not tell him that the idea is mine. Let him think that you ask because of your concern for my safety. I would not want him to think of me as a frightened little girl."

"It will be just as you have asked, Estella." Bildad gave her a hug and left the chamber.

The time of day approached mid-morning when Germaine saw Bildad approaching him on the battle practice field.

"Sir Knight, I come to you with a troubled mind."

Germaine removed his battle helm. "What is the matter, Bildad?" Germaine could see genuine worry etched on his face.

"I am worried about Estella's safety! If the Falchion Raptor should again make an attempt upon her, well, I am not confident in her other guards. I know they would give valiant efforts in her defense, but they do not possess the great skill that is yours. Do you still deem her to be in danger?"

Germaine had considered this question many times. He felt that the Raptor would try to defeat him before making further attempts upon Lyon Hold. The men now guarding her had proven their worth in keeping her safe. They were, after all, now battle hardened. Yet he knew that he was not right in avoiding Estella. It was indeed his responsibility to keep her safe, regardless of his feelings for her. "Yes, I do believe the danger to her is not yet over."

"Why then do you not guard her as you did before? I felt much better about her well-being when you were protecting her."

Germaine looked down at the earth that had been torn and broken by the feet of many warriors. He could not escape the question, or the logic behind it. *Can I put aside my heart, and do what I must? I have no choice.*

"You are right in your concern, Bildad. I will honor my responsibility."

Germaine saw Bildad smile broadly in relief. "Thank you, Germaine. I am grateful for your understanding in this matter."

As Bildad left the practice field, Germaine made his way to his quarters. When he had reached the confines of his chamber, Mikial helped him remove the heavy, battle armor. "I am as ready as practice can make me, Mikial. Clean my armor for joust. I will not be using it for further practice."

After the knight had cleaned up, he donned his emerald, chain mail corselet with his tunic and breeches. Placing the skull helm on his head, he set out to find Estella. He found her in her living chambers.

He announced his presence at the door, and the chambermaid gave him entrance. Germaine scanned the room and found Estella seated by the eastern window. As he walked to a point a few feet from her chair, he could not turn his eyes away from her. She sat looking out over the meadow and did not show that she was aware of him. As he continued to look upon her, he wondered how he could have ever thought her not to be of great beauty. His knees felt weak, and his heart beat as if he were in battle.

"It is good to see you. Why have you come to me, Emerald Knight?" She broke the silence so abruptly that Germaine gave a slight start. She had not taken her attention from the meadow, but continued to stare out over its expanse.

"I am here to resume my duty as your guardian." Germaine forced his eyes away from her and looked out the window as well. The late spring heat had not dulled the beauty of the flowers that covered the meadow like a colorful blanket. Looking back at Estella, Germaine could not help but say, "I see great beauty. Beauty that is rarely appreciated by men." *I see that beauty in you. It is a beauty that I cannot hold in my arms. Only my heart and eyes can grasp it.*

"Yes, the colors of the meadow are beautiful." Germaine knew she did not realize she was the subject of his praise. "I gain much peace looking out over my meadow. When I was a small child, my mother would sit with me at this window and tell me stories to excite a child's fancy." He looked at Estella as she turned her attention from the meadow and looked upon his face. "Would you honor me by playing a board game, Sir Knight? It would lift my spirits."

Germaine did not answer at once. He felt that he should not allow himself to be so personally involved with her.

Estella's eyes seemed to hold Germaine transfixed, immobilized. It was as if their dark surfaces were not a part of reality, but pools of dark water without depth. "Will you not remove your helm, Germaine?"

Germaine lifted the skull helm from his head and placed it on the nearby table. *My will melts before her like snow on a hot day.*

"It would please me greatly if you would consent to endure a game with me, Sir Knight."

Germaine felt his resolve melt with the plea held in those fathomless eyes. A smile made its way to his lips as he spoke, "If it will please you, then it pleases me."

He was surprised to see Estella leap out of her chair and laugh. "To the library! I have the chessmen ready. I know that you favor that game, so I had it set up."

Germaine was infected by her happiness. For the moment, he would allow himself to enjoy her company. He found their time together that night to be like old times. When the hour was very late, Germaine took his leave, promising to check on the guards during the night. For the time being, the Emerald Knight did not suffer with the ache he had been carrying in his heart.

In the days to come, Germaine fell back into the routine of guarding Estella as he had done earlier in his oath term. Over the next few days, he once again found himself in close company with her. She was not accepting any visits from her suitors, so Germaine assumed it was due to her betrothal to Arlis. The knight found it to be extremely odd that Arlis was not making any appearances either. Cornado had sent requests for audiences while Germaine was in Estella's presence, but she had rejected them. Germaine had heard that Cornado had some sort of business that had required him to depart for a time without notice. The knight guessed that perhaps Estella was upset with Cornado for leaving without proper leave-taking. Even though he was curious at her behavior, Germaine did not broach the subject with her.

The knight had actually seen very little of Arlis in recent days, and that suited him just fine, as it allowed him time with Estella without her attention being centered on someone else. Germaine really could not like Arlis Cornado. There was something about the lord that he did not like. Though he had not figured out yet what that was, he did not want to face the fact that his feelings against Arlis were probably the result of jealousy.

Germaine's time with Estella was once again pure joy. They played board games, and some game using thin wooden, tokens that had numbers painted on their surface. Estella told him the tokens were called, *Cards.* Sometimes they would merely talk for hours. Actually, Estella would do most of the talking and Germaine displayed a good ear for listening.

It was around this time that Germaine had another old friend drop by his quarters to see him.

"Emerald Knight! It is well to see you up and in one piece, my warrior friend."

"Jahil! It has been long since we last spoke." Germaine realized that he had not seen the young prince since the beginning of the battle for Lyon Hold.

Germaine stood back as Jahil swung down from his horse. "You lead a charmed life, my friend. During our last battle, I saw you fighting against impossible odds. I tried to make my way to you, but the enemy did not see things as I did. It was fortunate that we had your Vordund warriors, or you would have been killed. Seeing those giants slogging through the ranks of the enemy, swinging those wicked axes, sent fear through me, and made me glad I was on their side."

"Enough talk about the battle. How are Daren and Durelle faring in Fenn Hold?"

Jahil laughed, "They are doing very well. I have found an excellent tutor. They are already smarter than you or me, but, then, they were that already." Germaine eagerly watched as Jahil pulled two letters from his tunic. "They asked me to personally deliver the post to you. They wanted to come with me, but I told them to wait until the danger to Lyon Hold is eliminated."

Germaine took the letters. "You were wise not to bring them to me yet. We are expecting Scul to arrive any day now. I am grateful that you have come to check on my welfare. You are a true friend."

The knight noticed Jahil fumble with the reins he still held. "I have been staying informed of your progress by way of messengers. I hesitate to tell you that there is another reason that brings me to you today."

"Do not fear talking to me, Jahil. I will be a sympathetic listener even if you have strong charges against me."

"The last time I saw you, Germaine, you were lying on a cot in Camron's laboratory. You were resting comfortably while a beautiful woman tended to your wounds. I had to return to Fenn Hold before you roused from your fitful sleep."

"Is that what is bothering you? Do not be troubled, my friend. There was no need for you to stay by my side."

"That is not exactly it either. What I mean to say is, the woman …"

Germaine roared with laughter. "Is that all? You had me worried that something serious was wrong. Her name is Ayana, daughter of Val, one of the warriors that saved my life."

Jahil cleared his throat. "Would you mind introducing me to this lady? If you have no objection that is."

Germaine had a broad smile. "Of course, I do not mind. I would be pleased to introduce you. Just remember that her father does wield a wicked axe." Germaine had to laugh again when he saw Jahil's expression after this last jest.

Germaine untied Silver Cloud from his hitching post. He had been preparing to take the horse on its morning ride when Jahil had arrived. "Val and several of his people remain at Lyon Hold, but the rest of his clan has left for Scot Hold land. Val has his tent set up near the northern edge of the village. He would not allow me to talk him into staying in the castle. He told me that he was beginning to feel closed in within its walls. Let us go there, and I will tell you about Scot Hold on the way." The two men mounted their horses and rode at a brisk trot toward the Vordund camp.

When they reached Ayana's tent and dismounted, Germaine called to Ayana as he walked toward the tent.

"Germaine, what a pleasant surprise it is to see you this time of day." Ayana's face glowed with a smile as she came out of the tent to greet him.

"Good morning to you, fair lady. I bring a visitor that wishes to be introduced to you." Germaine lifted his hand to indicate the waiting Jahil, who still stood by the horses.

Germaine watched Ayana as she leaned a little to look around him, in an effort to view her visitor.

"He wants to meet me? What are your thoughts about this?"

"Jahil is one of the finest young men I know. He is fearless in battle, which I know is a fact of little interest to you. He is a gentleman, and he is a good listener. It has been my observation that women like men to be good listeners." Germaine could not think of much else to say. He realized that he did not have any experience in introducing members of the opposite gender to each other. In fact, he could not remember ever introducing two people with the intention of hoping they would be attracted to each other. "I believe you would enjoy each other's company if given a fair chance." *I wonder if that sounds as lame to her, as I think it sounded to me.*

Ayana stared at Germaine for a moment. Germaine knew from his recent conversations and experiences with Ayana that she was interested in him. He detected a faint disappointment in her eyes.

As Germaine watched her reaction, she smiled and said, "You are not very eloquent when it comes to matchmaking. Yes. I would be honored to meet a friend whom you hold in such high regard."

Germaine motioned the prince to come forward. Jahil had a slight blush of shyness upon his cheeks as he walked up to Germaine.

"Lady Ayana, daughter of Chief of the Vordund, Val. This is Lord Jahil of Fenn Hold."

"I am pleased to meet you, Lord Jahil." Ayana held her tiny hand out to the prince.

Germaine watched Jahil take her hand gently, as if he considered it to be a piece of fine porcelain from a faraway land that he feared would break in his grasp. Jahil bowed slightly. "The pleasure is mine, Lady Ayana." He then kissed the back of her hand.

"Would you like to walk in the meadow as we talk?" Ayana asked the two.

After a short time of walking and listening to the two, Germaine interrupted their conversation. "If you will not object, I need to return to my duties. Do you mind, Ayana?"

"I believe myself to be safe in the company of Jahil. Please take your leave if you must, Sir Knight."

As he walked back to Silver Cloud, Germaine was happy to see how well the two were getting along. They really seemed to be enjoying each other's company. With that thought, his mind moved to memories of Estella and the many happy hours they had spent together. Soon, he would be back at Lyon Castle, enjoying her company. An ache came to his heart as he realized it could not last much longer. This business with Craitor would soon be settled, one way or another. *Scul's indirect methods of subversion, and his open attack on Lyon Hold, has caused him too much delay. He will soon cut at the heart of the matter, when he comes for me, himself.*

That evening, as Germaine was spending his time with Estella, he found her to be in very high spirits. As he entered her chambers, he found her to be dancing about. She laughed, and sat unceremoniously on the wide couch. She patted the cushion next to her. "Please, sit down. Today I have decided to allow my happiness to carry me. Life can be so enjoyable at times. There are days when it seems that the sunlight fills every corner of a room, and nights that seem as if the stars will light the darkest corner of a heart. Do you ever have feelings like that, Germaine?"

He saw that Estella looked intently at him as she asked the question. He was struggling with his thoughts. *How should I answer? These feelings that she speaks of are like my feelings toward her.*

Estella continued. "Even on a cloudy day or in late evening, one can some-times see bright light, if only in one's heart. In fact, warmth sometimes burns within the heart, searing away the cold of the evening. Remember our walks in the snow, this past winter?"

Germaine thought he saw sparks in the depths of her dark eyes as she talked. The knight felt a great burning within his soul. His feelings for Estella were rising too close to his lips. He knew that she would find it amusing that he felt more than friendship for her. "My Lady," Germaine began badly, "I …"

A loud knock at the door freed the knight from saying more.

"Sir Germaine, you have a visitor." The knight recognized Crom's voice to be raised in excitement.

"Come in, Crom. What is this news of a visitor?"

"There is an emissary from Scul Craitor downstairs."

The knight glanced at Estella, then returned his gaze to Crom. "I shall be right down. Go to Camron, and inform him of our visitor's presence."

"No need, Germaine. I already possess knowledge of this unpleasant visitor." Camron had appeared in the doorway without making a sound. "I shall listen to your meeting from a discreet distance." Germaine watched as Camron glided away to the stairs.

"Germaine." Estella placed her hand on Germaine's wrist. "Please, be careful. I do not trust Scul. While he held me as his prisoner, I came to realize that he is truly insane."

The Emerald Knight saw something in her eyes. Concern, yes, but some-thing else. Fear for him, perhaps. "I shall use caution, my Lady." Germaine turned to follow the path Camron had taken.

As Germaine descended the stair, the black clad warrior came into view. Crom was near the warrior, and a hold soldier stood on each side of the visitor. The man had removed his battle helm and held it under his left arm. His face had a scar that ran from the hairline above his left eye to a point on the right side of his chin. The scar almost divided his lips into two equal halves. His black beard covered the scar somewhat, but it had quite an unsettling effect for any who looked upon him.

The warrior thumped his chest in salute. "I am Cedral, Sir Knight, lieutenant to Lord Craitor. I come to you with a message." As he spoke, he pulled a gauntlet from his belt with his right hand and tossed it on the floor between himself and Germaine.

"So, I am challenged to single combat. What are Scul Craitor's terms?"

"He has placed no terms. He does not seek your hold or wealth. His only need is to kill you." With that, the split mouth broke into a roar of laughter.

"I am glad that you are so amused. Tell your master that I accept his challenge and that I choose the sword as the second to the lance. I will meet him at mid-morning tomorrow." *This is it. Now is the time to bring this conflict to a close.*

"One other matter, Sir Knight. Scul requests that you fight honorably by leaving your sorcerer out of the contest."

Germaine raised a brow. "I shall do just that. It is good to hear that this will be a fair fight." *So, Falchion Raptor, do you think me fool enough to believe you have honor?*

As Cedral left the room, Camron came out of the shadows. "It would appear that Lyon Castle is home to at least one more two-legged rat. We must be doubly careful."

"Yes! I wonder who went to that black heart with news of your existence? Can you use your science to divine the one responsible?"

"I will try, Sir Knight, though it is not always possible to see such things. My power can readily identify the men of Scul's ownership. Because I have not detected such, it would appear that we have a turncoat in our midst. I will have to examine each person within the hold closely." Camron departed for his laboratory.

"Germaine!" He heard Estella call out from where she stood on the stairway. "I heard the challenge of the Falchion Raptor. Must you face this man? I am afraid his sorcery will prove too much for even your brave heart to overcome."

Germaine heard a new voice break in. "Nonsense, my dear." Germaine and Estella turned to face Arlis. "I am sure the Emerald Knight can defeat this black-hearted Raptor. We should have a special dinner tonight to honor his gallantry in accepting the challenge of the gauntlet."

"Excellent idea, Arlis!" Estella grinned as she spoke. "I will go arrange for a small dinner, if it will please you, Sir Knight."

"A dinner sounds fine, but let's not announce this to the castle. I will be content to dine with just our immediate friends, and Arlis, of course. Make it a light dinner. There is much preparation to make. Perhaps Camron will join us as well." *I would have been happier if you had not shown your face tonight, Lord Cornado.*

Estella turned and hurried to the kitchen to set things in motion. As she hurried away, Germaine watched Arlis procure a flagon of wine and two goblets from a nearby cabinet. After placing the goblets on top of the cabinet, he turned to pour the wine. When they were filled, he handed one to Germaine. "Let me honor you with a toast. Here is to the Emerald Knight and his victory over the Raptor."

"To victory!" Germaine returned in salute as he lifted the drink to his lips and drank deeply of the dark liquid.

"I must prepare for dinner, Sir Knight. I will look forward to dining with you tonight."

"Until dinner then, Lord Cornado." Germaine made his way to the dining area. Perhaps he would simply sit and relax while he waited for mealtime to arrive. He needed to think to get his mind into the right set for tomorrow's combat. He would also spend time in prayer, always asking for the strong hand of his Lord to turn to his behalf before a battle. A joust was different from spontaneous combat for the knight. He was never nervous when entering combat. With an approaching joust, he would feel turmoil within his stomach until he actually suited up in battle armor. Why the difference, he did not know. A knight could be just as dead in either endeavor.

It was not long before Germaine found himself and the guests seated around the table. All except Arlis, who seemed to have fallen ill and could not attend. Germaine felt a little guilty at his happiness that Estella's fiancé was not able to be there. In fact, Estella had him seated at her right. Germaine was happy to see that even Camron had made time to be there. As the knight dined, light-hearted humor was bantered about the table, but he could feel a shadow of dread that lay just beyond his reach, yet close enough to taste. He had been nervous before a joust before, but this sense of dread was new to the knight.

When they had finished the meal, the guests excused themselves until only

Estella and Germaine were left. As the knight arose from his chair, Estella stood and wrapped her arms around his waist in a protective embrace. "Please come back to once again guard me, my knight." There were tears in her eyes.

"Do not fear so much for me, my Lady. Should death overtake me tomorrow, Scul will still not have enough of an army at his command to cause you trouble." *A warrior's death is the most a knight can hope for. I hope my words will ease her distress. I do not know what else to say.*

"Is that your greatest hope in life, Germaine, to die? What of love? Is it not worth living for?"

Germaine pulled himself away from her embrace. He wanted to tell Estella of his love for her. *Should I tell her how I feel about her betrothal to Arlis? No, that is none of my concern, nor do I have a right to interfere.*

"Germaine!"

He saw Mikial standing in the door opening.

"You must rest for tomorrow's combat."

"I must take my leave now, my Lady." The interruption saved him from opening his heart to certain denial from Estella. As the knight made his way to the courtyard, his mind began to work out strategies for the struggle he would face on the morrow. As he walked to his quarters, Arlis was seeking out his new ally.

⇒ XVIII ⇐

"Lord Cornado. I see that you, once again, seek the tent of Lord Craitor. This time, you scurry under the cover of darkness. Welcome to our camp, comrade."

"Thank you, Cedral. I have come to Lord Craitor with good tidings concerning his plan."

Scul watched the approach of Arlis, and waited impatiently for him to enter the tent. "What news do you bring, my friend?" A beguiling smile curled his lips. A smile he knew would conceal his true mind.

"The deed is completed! I have given the drug to the Emerald Knight just as you instructed."

"Are you certain that no one witnessed your deceit?" Scul still had the smile painted on his dark countenance.

"No one was present but the knight and me. I make an able ally for your cause, do I not?"

"You are, indeed, a very useful ally, Arlis. You have earned your part of the bargain. Perhaps you should wait until after I defeat our foe before you begin your journey to Berne Hold." Scul placed his hand on Arlis' shoulder in a show of friendship. *Only a show*, he thought.

"It shall be as you have said, Lord Craitor. I will not return to the castle tonight, lest someone should detect my part in this conflict. It will be safer for me to remain in the village."

"You may take your leave now, Arlis. I will see you again, before you depart for your hold."

As Scul watched Arlis ride away, Cedral entered the tent. "Sir Craitor, do you wish for me to kill that pompous Arlis now?"

"No, Cedral. He may yet serve us again if something unforeseen should happen tomorrow. I want you to take care of another matter. I do not trust

Germaine's sorcerer, and I do not know how powerful he may be. Hire an assassin to carry out the disposal of a problem. If something should happen that I cannot defeat that jackal tomorrow, I may have to use my powers to retreat so that I may live to fight again. If this should occur, our assassin should wait until the day Iron Hide arrives. When those within the hold are greatly distracted by the dragon, Estella is to be killed. Her death will injure him, if my sword cannot."

"Sir Craitor, I do not understand. Why can you not use your powers to get rid of this other sorcerer in advance? Would this not assure your victory?"

"The problem is that sorcerers can do little against each other. The power released against an opponent will actually feed back on the one who unleashed it. This other wizard could use a spell to enhance Germaine's resistance in some way, to defend him from my spells. Much like the shield I fashioned to protect myself from the dragon. If this were the case, I could probably undo the spell if given enough time. Without that time to study, haste could result in a backlash that would cause me serious damage. It is, of course, true that the other wizard is in the same predicament. If I can strike the knight down with lance or sword, the power question will be unimportant. If my estimation of the opposing sorcerer is not accurate, and I should have to flee, then Iron Hide's appearance will be of even greater value to my plans. The dragon should be here within a few days to rain havoc on the hold. I told him to arrive on the full moon. Now go and find an assassin to do our bidding."

"It will be as you have commanded, Lord Craitor," Cedral said as he left the tent.

That night, Scul slept fitfully. Meanwhile, Germaine found only conflict in his dreams.

❧ XIX ❧

Germaine rose early the next morning. His sleep had been filled with nightmares, the like of which he had never before experienced. In one of the dreams, he had battled a dark, tentacled beast with the insignia of the Raptor emblazoned on each writhing limb. In another, he saw a living skeleton strike off Estella's head with an axe.

As he sat up in bed, his head began to spin. "My eyes. Everything is a blur." The knight eased onto his feet and stood up. He felt weak, and his knees felt as though they were made of water.

"What is the matter with me?" the knight spoke aloud.

Germaine heard Mikial jump out of bed and run to his side. "Germaine. What is wrong? Are you ill, sir?" The knight was swaying on his feet. He felt like a tree being blown by a strong wind.

"I have fallen ill, can barely stand." Germaine's voice was weak.

"Germaine. You cannot go into combat in this condition."

"I must answer the challenge! It is a matter of honor." Germaine reached for a chair.

"Let me sit for a moment. Go fetch a cup of strong tea, and tell Camron of my illness."

Mikial was gone from Germaine's presence for only a few minutes when he returned with the tea. "Camron is on his way." He helped Germaine with the cup, because the knight's hands were shaking too badly to hold the cup without spilling it.

Germaine heard Camron enter the chamber and the old sorcerer was quickly at his side. Germaine felt fingers pushing his eyelids wide open.

"Open your mouth, Germaine. I wish to look at your throat." The sorcerer cleared his throat. Germaine knew that he had reached a diagnosis.

"I have failed you, Germaine." Camron's voice conveyed great sadness to

Germaine. "Someone gave you a sorcerer's drug last evening."

"Arlis!" Even in his weakened state of body and mind, Germaine remembered the toast that Cornado had made when they were alone. "It was Arlis Cornado. He gave me wine."

Camron turned and spoke to someone behind him. Germaine realized it was Crom, though the knight could not distinguish him with his vision blurred. "Crom, I suggest that you find Lord Cornado and detain him." Germaine heard Crom leave the room.

He shook his head in an effort to clear his blurred vision of Camron. "Can you use your powers to take away the drug's effect on me?"

"If I had discovered this deceit last night, I might have had enough time to conjure a cure. I would probably kill you if I tried to do anything in haste. Each sorcerer employs different elements to cast the same spell as another. Without knowing Scul's formula, I could cause his spell to explode in my face, killing you in the process." Germaine felt Camron's hand upon his shoulder. "You must concede victory to the Falchion Raptor!"

"Just as I do not understand the workings of a sorcerer's spell, you do not understand a knight's code of honor. I will not concede to Craitor! If it is God's will, I will die today, and it will not be a death in disgrace." *Is this how I will meet my end? I will not give in to this evil scheme. Death is a friend to be embraced compared to the disgrace of surrender.*

"You do not understand, Sir Knight. There is more at stake than one battle. There are things that I need to tell you. Things of great importance." Germaine felt desperation in Camron's plea.

"Do not tell me of these things if the knowledge would sway my hand from this course. I must engage in this combat."

"Stubborn man! Do you not have thoughts for anything other than your honor?" He heard Camron stomp out of the room.

Germaine knew that the old sorcerer would not give up easily. *It is a strange matter. Camron wishes me to give up without a fight, and, yet, he will refuse to give up trying to prevent the battle. He is probably on his way to talk Estella into summoning me for a stand-down of arms. I must avoid her presence. A knight under oath can only be ordered to stand down by his liege, in person.* Germaine did not know how much time had passed before a knock came at his door. He ordered

Mikial to give entry.

"Sir Germaine, it is I, Byrone."

Germaine's memory flashed to the day he had ridden with the young lieu-tenant against the Falchion Raptor's men. "Yes, Byrone, what brings you to me this day?"

"The Lady Estella asks that you come to speak with her before the joust."

Germaine struggled to clear his vision. "Tell me, Byrone, was Camron with Estella when she ordered you to bring me this message?"

"Yes, Sir Knight. He was there."

"You were not ordered to escort me to the lady, were you?"

"No, Sir Knight!"

Germaine smiled. "Please take this message to Estella. 'Forgive me for my lack of manners, but I am preparing myself for combat. I will come to see you before the contest.'" Germaine allowed this lie to pass his lips. He did not want Estella to see him in this drunken condition, and she could not order him from battle if she could not meet with him.

Byrone saluted. "I will give her the message."

As the lieutenant left the room, Germaine called Mikial to his side. "How long before mid-morning?"

"About forty-five minutes, sir."

"I know you have my battle armor burnished to a high shine, but I will not be wearing it, Mikial."

"You are not going to fight." Mikial's voice carried the feeling of relief to Germaine's ears.

"I will fight, but not in the heavy armor. I would not be able to carry its weight in my condition."

Mikial asked, in a voice that relayed his shock, "Surely you are not going to wear chain mail!"

"Exactly so." Germaine smiled serenely. *I must show the boy, through my actions, that this is my will. He must not go to Estella, as Camron did.* "I will need your help to dress, so let us begin."

It took some time, but Germaine was finally clad in his emerald pants with a chain mail sheath that reached to his knees. Over his emerald green tunic he wore the chain mail corselet.

"Mikial. Prepare Silver Cloud for the joust. When you have finished, bring him to the door and call to me."

As Mikial left the chamber, Germaine stood shakily and made his way to the wall peg that held his sword. Using great care, he lifted Titan's Blade from its resting place, grasping its belt, and hitched it about his waist. He could carry only one weapon other than the lance, so he left Stinger behind.

Germaine had one more important preparation to make. He moved to the table and placed his hands on the edge for support. Easing down so that he knelt on one knee, he prayed. His mind was so befogged that he simply said, "Lord, I ask that you give me the strength to face this evil foe. Guide my sword arm and my wits. If it is your will, and my death is certain, allow me to take account of the enemy. I ask this in the name of your son, Jesus. Amen."

Germaine arose from his prayer. He groped for and found his skull helm, which he tucked in the crook of his arm.

No sooner had Germaine completed his preparations than Mikial called to him from the door. Germaine gathered his strength and willed his feet to the task of carrying him to the door. His charger waited for him beyond. The Emerald Knight handed his helm to Mikial and mounted his steed.

After gaining the saddle, Germaine held out his hand to Mikial. "My helm." The knight's few words were the result of his illness. He was conserving what strength he had. *God give me strength to make the field of battle.*

Mikial handed the helm to Germaine. "If the Falchion Raptor's lance gets past your shield, the mail will offer no protection."

"I must do what I can to prevent that, my page." Germaine settled the helm on his head, then reached to the boy and took his hand. "Mikial. No matter what the outcome of today's combat, I am proud that you are my page. You have served me well." Germaine withdrew his hand and sat erectly in the saddle. "Now lead Silver Cloud to the field of battle, and my shield rack." He knew Mikial already had the shields and spare lances arranged on the rack.

Mikial led the horse in silence. When they reached the rack, Mikial handed Germaine his lance and then his shield. "May God ride with you, Sir Knight."

Germaine nodded to Mikial and then leaned close to the ear of Silver Cloud. "You will be my eyes, old friend. I am giving you the reins. It will be up to you to keep the runway." Silver Cloud bobbed his head as if in answer. *If Cloud does not keep me at the proper distance from the runway wall, I will not have a chance of winning.*

"Mikial. When the starter drops his banner, yell *go* at the top of your lungs. My blurred vision prevents me from seeing him or the banner."

He heard Mikial almost choke on his words. "I will, Sir Knight."

How can any knight go up against a jouster with the reputation of Scul Craitor, without full control of his senses? Any knight who holds to the code, as I do. His thoughts were interrupted.

"Combatants to your points."

Germaine heard the starter and nudged Silver Cloud. "To your point, Cloud." The horse moved into his position beyond the end of the runway. It was something they had done in joust and practice hundreds of times. Was it habit, or did the horse really understand?

Germaine could make out the blur that was the Falchion Raptor and his horse, at the far end of the run. At least a blur was better than nothing.

"Go!" Mikial's voice boomed in Germaine's head.

"On, Cloud." Germaine leaned forward as he nudged the charger's flanks. Silver Cloud reached full gallop in good time. Germaine had already decided in advance on a strategy. Normally he would adjust his moves to those of his opponent. Because he could not see, that tactic was not available to him. He would hold his shield high and to the front, leaving his left side exposed. At the last instant he would shift the shield to his left and at the same time swing his lance tip slightly right of its original angle. The problem was that he would have to rely on guesswork to determine that elusive last instant. Germaine knew that tactic to be all he had, if you discounted his many years of jousting experience. He hoped that his past experience would serve him today.

As Cloud's hooves pounded, the knight could see the approaching blur getting larger. *Not yet. Not yet. Now!* The Emerald Knight shifted his shield and lance, and immediately was rocked in his saddle with the impact of lances glancing off opposing shields.

As Silver Cloud slowed his pace and stopped at the end of the run, Germaine still could not see. *Is my lance still in one piece?*, Germaine asked himself as he strained to see his lance through the blurring. He solved the dilemma by running his hand along the length of the lance as he rested its haft on the ground.

"Another lance!" Germaine heard the Falchion Raptor bellow at the far end of the runway. Apparently his lance had broken.

While Germaine struggled with his lance, Scul struggled with his thoughts.

Scul could not believe it. How could the Emerald Knight have parried his thrust so effectively with the drug that surged through his veins? Could it be that Arlis had lied? His shoulder was aching from the impact that had almost unhorsed him.

Scul watched the Emerald Knight intently. *Yes! He is affected by the drug. See how he struggles with the condition of his lance, as if he cannot see that it is not broken. That would explain why he is wearing the chain mail. He cannot bear the weight of full armor.* While waiting for the next run, Scul was thinking furiously as he continued to watch Germaine.

As Scul made his way to his start point, Germaine moved toward his.

"Combatants to your points."

Once again Silver Cloud found his mark.

"Go!" Mikial's voice sounded its command.

Silver Cloud hit full gallop, and Germaine could just make out the blur that was the Falchion Raptor, closing on him. This time Germaine was going to take a big gamble. He rode with his shield more to his left, leaving his right chest exposed. As the blur grew, Germaine did not shift the shield as he had the first time. He swung his lance so that the tip would be to the left of its position in the first run. Hopefully, Scul would be expecting the same tactics the Emerald Knight had used the first time, since he knew that Germaine was blind

The impact was horrendous. Germaine flew from his horse and hit the ground. His warrior's reflexes recovered their balance and had him on his feet in an instant. He could hear Scul cursing.

"Green slug. We will finish this with swords!"

Germaine could hear the clang of armor as Scul must have been struggling to his feet. The Emerald Knight could just make out the blurred form of the Raptor approaching. Germaine felt hopeless. In the joust, he could depend on Cloud to keep him oriented and close to the location of Scul. Now he was hard pressed to keep track of his opponent, much less defend himself. Germaine knew he was about to die. *I may not be able to see it coming, but I will try to scratch him before he finishes me.*

As Estella watched helplessly, Germaine began to defend himself.

Germaine grabbed Titan's Blade and swung it up in defense. As his fingers closed on the haft, he felt a stinging sensation, then warmth. He could see a glowing blaze engulfing his arm, then his body. He could see! Titan's Blade had come to his aid again.

The Emerald Knight had no time to think, only react. Scul now stood in front of him, swinging his sword. Germaine parried and then struck a blow against Scul's blade that drove the Falchion Raptor backward. Germaine's chain mail now gave him a temporary advantage. He had greater freedom of movement and was able to pummel the evil knight with a barrage of blows. Germaine could see Craitor struggling against his bulkier battle armor.

Now Scul tried to parry Germaine's blows. Germaine could see desperation in the Raptor's efforts at defense.

Suddenly Germaine struck a mighty blow that broke Scul's sword. Releasing the handle of the sword, Scul swung his right arm toward the Emerald Knight. Germaine saw the movement and remembered Camron's warning on the day he first met the wizard.

Germaine quickly swung Titan's Blade in an emerald arc that brought it between himself and the weapon of the Falchion Raptor. Scul fired at almost the same instant. The bolt struck Titan's Blade just above its haft. The jolt of the impact knocked the sword out of Germaine's hand and caused him to fall backward. His right arm was numb as he helplessly watched Scul.

"You will die by your own sword!" Craitor grabbed Titan's Blade.

A scream from Scul's lips shattered the air as the blade glowed blood red, enveloping Scul's body in its light. With surprise still etched on Scul's face, a sound like thunder resounded with an accompanying blinding flash.

Scul was no longer standing over the fallen Germaine. In fact, Germaine could see no sign of him. Titan's Blade lay on the ground where Scul had been locked in its grip.

Germaine felt hands under his arms, and realized Mikial had rushed to him and now tried to help him up.

"Well done, warrior!" This time Germaine could clearly see Camron as he approached. "Forgive me for doubting you, Sir Knight." Camron reached for Germaine's left hand and helped Mikial bring him to his feet.

"There is nothing to forgive, sir. What happened to Scul? Did the sword kill him?" Germaine was feeling relief after the long morning he had just endured. He had never felt so helpless as he had on this day.

Camron stooped to retrieve Titan's Blade. He slid it into the scabbard on Germaine's belt as he answered, "It is possible, but highly unlikely. The truth is, I do not know. It is true that the sword is death to those whom it does not find worthy. In the case of the Raptor, the power of the sword was opposite in nature to Craitor's dark powers. The explosion we witnessed may have merely sent him far away. He may not be in a position to return any time soon. I cannot detect the aura of his presence, so he is at least farther away than the distance to his fortress. I will conduct a farseeing later to see if I can find him."

Germaine worked his arm in an effort to restore feeling. "Your warning to me about Scul's bolt weapon, when we first met, saved my life. Thank you, Camron. Perhaps we will be allies again in the future."

"I need to talk to you about that very matter. Will you meet me at the laboratory after you have recovered?"

Germaine smiled at the old wizard. "I will visit you this afternoon."

"May I help you to the gallery, Sir Knight?" Mikial asked Germaine.

"I would appreciate a shoulder to lean on. Thank you, Mikial."

For the first time, Germaine looked to the gallery for Estella. He found her standing with Bildad, Jahil, and Ayana. As he walked toward them, mixed emotions within him began to roil. They were feelings that he would not have felt a few short months earlier. He felt relieved with the knowledge that his oath term was nearly over, but he also knew sadness because he would soon be leaving the dark-eyed woman he now approached. He recalled his feelings of just a few short months back, when he had wished his oath ended so that he could escape Estella and his feelings for her.

"We must celebrate your victory, Sir Knight." The knight saw Estella's face aglow with relief as she spoke. "You have once again saved Lyon Hold. Take this favor, given in gratitude." With that she untied a wispy scarf from about her waist and reached out to hand it to Germaine. As he grasped it, she did not withdraw her hand, but left it laying softly upon his.

Germaine removed his skull helm with his left hand, and bowed slightly, touching his lips gently to her hand. He could smell her flowery scent as he kissed her, then, reluctantly he released his hold. *I would gladly hold that hand for the rest of my life.*

"I will never cease to marvel at your abilities, Emerald Knight." Jahil reached out his hand to grasp Germaine's.

"I am afraid the victory was more in the hands of sorcery than in my abilities as a knight. Today I am happy that we had such power on our behalf. Without Camron's help, and the sorcery of the sword, I would have been defeated by Craitor's spell." Germaine felt the victory to be empty because of his dependence on the sword.

Still holding Estella's scarf, the Emerald Knight addressed her again.

"My Lady. Have I fulfilled my oath to you?" As he voiced this question, Estella felt emptiness inside.

"We will not discuss that now. We will consider all of the possibilities concerning Scul Craitor before termination of Liege Oath is allowed. Perhaps his disappearance was a ruse." Estella tried to sound as confident as she could, but within her breast beat an uneasy heart. She did not want Germaine to leave.

The explosion and disappearance of the Falchion Raptor had brought Estella's emotion full circle. She had wanted to leap out of her gallery box and run to the side of the fallen knight. No! She had stayed in her place and awaited his approach as was customary for the victor. When she had presented her scarf as a favor to honor Germaine for his gallantry, she allowed her hand to rest upon his hand. Her heart fluttered as he gently kissed her hand. The touch of his lip was so light, as a gentle breeze might brush against one's face.

When he released her hand and asked the question about ending his oath, her heart felt as though it would stop beating. Her heart would never love another as it now ached for him. Life was not always fair where love was concerned. *Just when I have finally found that elusive perfect love, I must also relinquish its hold upon my heart. I will never be truly free of its memory.* Estella had to force her mind from these thoughts as Germaine responded to her answer.

"As you wish, my Liege." Germaine bowed as his mind worked feverishly. *Why do I not tell her that the battle is over? Has my very will given way to her command*? Germaine found that he grudgingly felt relieved that the decision was temporarily out of his control. Germaine made his way to the bath house. "Mikial, you served me well today. Without your help, the outcome could have been much different."

"Thank you, Sir Germaine. I am pleased to have been of use to you."

"Fetch a clean change of clothes for me. Whilst you do so, I shall begin to scrub the grime of battle from me."

Germaine's clothing was black with the battlefield dirt. "In fact, if I do not change soon, someone may mistake me for Craitor in this black armor."

"I will bring your things, sir." Mikial turned to carry out Germaine's orders.

"When you have returned with my clothes, take Silver Cloud to the stable and give him a royal treatment. He deserves a good rubdown and a fine feast of oats. I believe that gallant horse understands the human tongue."

Mikial smiled as he said, "Sir Knight, I know he understands!" With that, Mikial left on his errand.

Later, Germaine made his way to Camron's laboratory.

"Thank you for coming, Sir Knight."

Germaine noticed that Camron had been working with the cauldron he called Califern. "A man would be a fool not to honor the request of a friend." Germaine was still basking in his relief. This oath term had been the toughest to endure of any in his memory. It did not help that he had lost his wife during the same period. He was glad it was over. It would be good to move on. His regret was that he knew how much he would miss Estella.

Camron interrupted his musings, "I have something to discuss with you. It is the matter that I tried to reveal to you before the joust. Seat yourself and allow me to tell you a tale, one that affects you." Camron waited while Germaine found a chair.

"Because you are not one who has lived his life with sorcery as a second nature, you may find some of my words difficult to believe. Know it is the truth! A great number of years ago, darkness and calamity held the land we call Valeria in a death grip. Anarchy reigned as dark forces assaulted those who walked in light. It was in these dark days that Valeria was founded with the naming of its first high king. His name was Garth. He became king when he was presented with a unique symbol of power. That symbol was Titan's Blade. At the time of the sword's first appearance, I believe the date about 37 B.C., the weapons known to man were made of wood, stone, bronze, and a smattering of crude iron. Titan's Blade was different, more refined in its manufacture."

"Master craftsmen in a faraway land had made the weapon from a great metal ingot that housed mystical powers. It was soon discovered that the only men who could touch the sword, without dying, were the men that had made it. This touch of death created fear among the people."

"It happened that a powerful sorcerer, Volstad, heard of the sword and journeyed to see it for himself. When he reached the resting place of the sword, he approached it, being careful not to touch lest he should die. A strange thing happened in full view of the workers who had escorted the sorcerer. An aura of power glowed through the metal of the sword. The aura extended from the sword and enveloped the sorcerer. Without further hesitation, Volstad reached out and picked up the sword by its haft. That sorcerer became the guardian of Titan's Blade."

"When Volstad returned to his home country, and his laboratory, he found that his power had diminished. He would eventually discover that his power had somehow been tied to the mystical sword. The only power of any strength in his laboratory, was contained in two crystalline, power stones that he had procured years earlier. One was a clear, white stone that represented good, and the other was a clear red, representing evil. When great evil assailed the land, the red stone would pulse with energy. If there was a warrior worthy of leading the people in the cause of good, the white stone would throb with power. The white stone would actually reveal the existence of the next high king. When a worthy man was detected by the sword, it, too, would glow with power. With the arrival of a man worthy of the sword, Volstad's power would return to him, binding him to the new king."

Germaine finally interrupted the words of Camron. "You have said many times that I am worthy of your power, and the sword. Are you saying ...?"

"Yes, Germaine. You have been selected as worthy to reign."

"I am a man of meager standing. I have no wealth, no hold, and no support from the people. The stone and sword must have made a mistake." Germaine had never wanted to be a king. He looked at himself as a servant to others, a follower.

"Germaine, the power we speak of has never made a wrong choice."

"How can you be so certain? Is it in your power to see into the past?" Germaine stood up as he said these words and began to pace. *I am not worthy to rule a kingdom. I was not worthy to rule Scot Hold. The sword must have developed a flaw to select me.*

"I am certain because I was there. I am Volstad. My name was Simeron at one time, and Mordrod at another."

Germaine gasped. "No man could live that long!"

"Unless he found himself tied to the power stones and Titan's Blade as I have been. You see, Germaine, I was chosen to be a guardian, just as you have been chosen to be high king. You asked me several weeks ago if I believed in God. It is my opinion that He is the one who delivered the sword to my keeping. As I said, this is my opinion and not, necessarily, fact. This sword could not be some aberration of nature."

Germaine stood behind the chair. He placed his hands on the back and leaned on it. "This is a heavy burden to lay on unsuspecting shoulders. Do I have a choice in this matter?"

It seemed to Germaine that the sorcerer paused for a moment of thought, perhaps concerning the sword's candidates of the past. "You are not the first to question the choice of the sword. However, no one has ever refused it after considering the matter."

Germaine took a moment to gather his thoughts, then he reached for the haft of the sword in his scabbard. He pulled the sword free and handed it to Camron. "I must decide this matter without the influence of power upon my person. Please, keep Titan's Blade while I consider your words."

Camron carried the sword to a nearby table. Germaine watched as he gently lay the sword on a pad. He picked up Germaine's familiar Lightning and returned it to the knight.

Seeing a shadow of sadness on the old sorcerer's face, Germaine tried to ease Camron's concern. "I have not said I would refuse the sword's choice. I plan to leave for the site of my hold when Estella releases me from this oath. It would please me greatly if you would meet me there for my decision. I will arrive with Val and the remaining members of his clan."

"It will be as you ask, Emerald Knight. I am somewhat curious as to the progress the Vordund people have made in rebuilding Scot Hold. One more matter, friend knight. I know of the struggle within your heart. I do not see the details clearly, but I know that you must resolve the conflict within you before departing Lyon Hold."

Germaine's face reddened a little at this revelation. "Is nothing hidden from you, Camron?"

"As I have said, I know not the details. Only the turmoil within your heart is apparent to me." Germaine reached out to Camron. As they grasped hands in friendship, Camron continued. "I will depart in the morning for Scot Hold. Perhaps the Vordund built a suitable place for my laboratory."

"I will see you off, in the morning." Germaine released his hold of Camron's hand. "You have proven to be a good ally. You told me once, you would do many little things that would appear great when viewed together. Your aid to me has been that and more. I would not be standing here now if not for you and the sword. I thank you for that, Sorcerer." Germaine turned and ascended the stairs, deep in thought. He had believed his feelings for Estella to be the greatest of his concerns. Now his world was spinning with the decision he must make.

The early predawn hour came quickly for the knight. He had the most fitful night of sleep that he could remember in some time. After making their farewells, Germaine and Mikial watched as Camron rode into the Black Forest trail on the southern side of Lyon Hold. One of Val's Vordund warriors was riding with him.

"Well, Mikial, all we have to do now is wait for Estella to end my oath term. Then we, too, shall make our way to Scot Hold." Germaine felt strong emotions well up inside his chest as the name of his hold passed his lips. It seemed impossible that the hold would, once again, have people living and working there.

Germaine recognized Mikial to be in a relaxed mood as the boy lazily asked, "Do you think we will stay at Scot Hold for a while?"

"I do not know, Mikial. There is a personal matter in which I must make a decision. Our stay will depend on that outcome."

Germaine let his mind focus on the throne he had been offered. What would be the right thing for him to do?

"Sir Germaine." Crom had just joined the two as they had finished speaking. "We have not been able to find Arlis Cornado. In all likelihood, he ran back to his hold with his tail tucked like a whipped dog."

"He is of little importance, Crom. I believe he was but a lackey in this evil affair. Had I been defeated, Scul would probably have cut Arlis' throat himself."

Over the next couple of days, Germaine avoided Estella. He was trying to convince himself that he was over his love for her, but seeing Estella would always melt his resolve.

Germaine went on long hunting trips into the surrounding forest to further isolate himself from the lady. While on these hunts, he still treated his duty of Liege Oath seriously, and remained ever alert for agents of Craitor. He kept his vigilance honed in case he should have been wrong about the battle being over with Craitor's abrupt disappearance.

At the end of the second day of his excursions into the forest, Germaine returned to Lyon Hold long after dark. As Germaine entered his quarters that faced the castle courtyard, he tried not to disturb Mikial.

Mikial roused from his cot with a message for the knight. "The Lady Estella asks that you come to her. She said it is very important."

"Very well. I will go to her in the morning."

"No, Sir Germaine." Mikial was still shaking the effects of his interrupted sleep. "She said that you were to come to her tonight, no matter the hour."

Germaine had not the chance to sit down before this exchange with the young page. "I suppose it would be best to go to her and see what is wrong." Germaine had hoped to continue avoiding Estella. He had tried to push her face from his mind for days. Now he would have to begin his efforts again.

When Germaine reached the chamber door, Estella's two guards greeted him with salutes. *Wonder if she is still up at this hour*, he thought as he knocked on the door.

"Who is it?" The voice of the chambermaid sounded the question almost immediately after the knock.

"It is I, Germaine." *At least they were doing as I have instructed them to do, after the earlier incident with the traitorous guard and black falcon intruder*, Germaine thought as the door opened.

As he stepped into the dimly lit room, he could just make out Estella where she was seated upon a small couch.

"Come in, Germaine. Please, be seated." Estella patted the cushion next to her as she invited him to sit.

The Emerald Knight ignored her invitation of the cushion and moved to stand next to a nearby chair. He hesitated to sit. "Why have you summoned me, Lady Estella?"

"Please call me Estella tonight. We are alone and there is no need for titles. Please sit down, for a time."

He sat down, but felt uncomfortable. His heart was aching with clashing emotion. True, Estella's betrothed was no longer a factor, but he was still bothered by her closeness to Arlis. He guessed that her heart must be dashed by the betrayal of Lyon Hold by her fiancé. He felt some shame at his feelings for he knew that her relationships were none of his concern.

"Estella, is there some word of Scul Craitor, or have you some trouble that requires my attention?" Germaine felt a tingle down his spine as Estella looked into his eyes, as if she were trying to see something that she had glimpsed within their depths. As he struggled to maintain his composure under her scrutiny, she appeared to sadden as her face clouded. *Can it be that she has seen the love I hold within my heart? I have heard that the eyes are the windows to the soul. Perhaps the eyes are also windows to the heart, and she has seen that love, and recognizes how unworthy I am to feel that way about her.* Germaine hoped that he had not caused her too much sadness if she had indeed discovered his feelings for her.

"We had a minor problem, but Byrone has resolved it in your absence. I should have sent a message to Mikial so that he would not have sent you to me tonight."

Germaine began to rise from his chair.

"As you are already here, would you care for some refreshment before you leave?" Germaine saw what he took to be a pleading look in her eyes as she asked this of him.

"No, my Lady. I will allow you to return to your rest. Thank you for the offer." Germaine was forcing himself to move now. He felt as he did when the sorcerer's drug coursed within his body. *She needs company tonight, possibly to soothe her hurt feelings concerning Arlis. I do not wish to fill that role. My heart feels as if a great fist has it in a tight grip. I have never felt such pain before. Can something be wrong with me?* Germaine walked to the door and left, deep in thought.

Germaine's heart was in very real pain as he made his way to his quarters. At times he wondered if his heart was finally giving up its grip on life. He knew much younger men who had fallen dead when once-strong hearts suddenly ended their life's work. *It is possible that what I believed to be a heartache caused by love, could be something quite different. It would be a cruel fate to die of heart failure, rather than on the field of battle.*

Perhaps, the knight reasoned, the stress of his warrior life, the loss of his beloved Ana and his unrequited love for Estella were all too much for his heart to take. That night Germaine had trouble sleeping as the pain in his chest continued to torment him.

XX

The next morning, the knight rose late, still tired from his restless night. "I will not be going out today, Mikial. I am feeling unwell."

"Should I get a healer to come to you, Sir Germaine?"

Germaine shook his head. "No. I will be all right. I just did not sleep well last night."

About mid-morning, a shout went up from the guards on the ramparts. There arose a great commotion outside, causing Germaine to go into the courtyard to investigate. He doubted what his eyes beheld in the sky. He stepped outside in time to catch a glimpse of a huge form passing out of view beyond a rampart.

Germaine ran up the nearest ramp-way and gained the rampart walkway in time to see a fearsome creature attacking the village with its fiery breath. "A dragon!" Germaine exclaimed aloud to no one in particular. The beast was gigantic. The knight estimated the head of the creature to be greater in size than a brace of horses. He could see very large horns, one above each large ear, on the dragon's head. The long, serpentine tail of the beast seemed to be what the dragon used to steer itself in flight, as the tail seemed to move the opposite direction of turns that the creature made. Four great claws, mounted with wicked talons, were held close-fisted as the creature flew. Germaine noticed a horse grasped in one of those leathery fists. Even at this distance, about four hundred yards, Germaine could clearly see the giant, yellow eyes. Each marked by the great vertical slit of its pupil.

"How can something that huge maintain flight?" That question came from Crom, who was standing near Germaine. "Can such a creature be killed by men?"

Germaine watched the massive, horned head of the creature swing back and forth as it belched fire upon the edge of the village. People caught in that fire flashed out of existence.

The dragon now pumped its great leathery pinions that resembled those of a bat, as it climbed out of its dive. The ugly creature was graceful as it flew higher. Then the dragon began to roar words in a thunderous voice. "Send forth your champion that I may defeat and devour him, or send out Estella to appease my anger. I will return for battle.".

Germaine could barely understand the voice as it issued from a mouth not designed for human words. When the dragon had completed this challenge, Germaine watched as it flew to the east, over the distant hill.

"I did not know such creatures still lived in the land." Crom was looking incredulously at the knight. "Why would a dragon come to us? I have not heard of such creatures in years, not even rumors."

"Why, indeed?" Germaine's mind was working feverishly. "I must go speak to Estella and Bildad."

The knight knocked on Estella's door and was greeted by Bildad.

"What do you make of this evil event, Sir Knight?" Bildad allowed Germaine entry to the chamber.

The room was crowded. Germaine saw that Estella was there as were Val, Jahil, and Ayana. They were all talking at once, but silence fell on the room as Germaine raised his hands for attention.

"I regret that I was wrong in my views concerning Scul Craitor, my Lady." *I have underestimated Scul. A sorcerer seems to be much more difficult to predict than I thought.*

Estella approached Germaine. "What do you mean? Have you evidence of more villainy by Scul? Have we not enough problems now, with a dragon flying about?"

"We have all seen the evidence, my Lady. How else would the dragon know your name?"

Estella's face darkened as Germaine saw within her eyes the realization that Scul was behind this latest evil deed. "Then Craitor is not dead?"

"I do not know the answer to that. I believe the dragon's arrival to be a prearranged plan by Scul. With his army destroyed, he probably sought out the dragon to give him strength for completing his grip on Lyon Hold. It is only a theory on my part, but it makes sense."

"What should we do now?" Estella asked the knight.

"I see but one course of action available to you. You must order me forth to face the dragon." Germaine looked as calm as if he had just ordered breakfast. *I remember the legends that were told around the hunt fires when I was a child. A dragon was said to be unlikely to give up its prey. If a dragon marked a village as its own food source, it would not abandon that village until it was destroyed. This dragon will not quit its attacks upon this hold, unless I can kill it, or it kills me.*

"I cannot order you to your death. How could any mortal persevere against such a giant? Have you ever fought one of these beasts?"

Germaine knew that Estella was out of breath with exasperation as she nearly gasped the question. "No, My Lady. I have never seen a dragon before today. However, I have been told stories as I was growing to manhood about these dragons. It seems that at one time they were plentiful on the earth and many knights, 'sword warrants' as we were once called, earned their living by slaying the beasts. From the descriptions I remember, this beast seems to be much larger than most."

Germaine paused. "Though I have never faced one in battle, I do know how to kill a dragon if given the chance." *I remember well, the tales of knights concerning the weaknesses of dragons. I never thought I would find a need for such lore.*

Crom asked. "What kind of strategy would you use, Sir Knight?"

"That I do not know, for I have never witnessed their speed on the ground. From the serpentine appearance, I would guess they possess great speed. I would need some edge or luck to make the kill. I do have something that will prove useful, a shield that has been handed down for generations. I have carried it with my gear over the years, though I have never used it in combat. My father told me it was a shield to protect one from a dragon's fiery breath. Perhaps it is time to put it to the test."

"No!" Estella's shout rang in Germaine's ear. "You have placed your life in great danger for us more than enough already. I order you not to fight this dragon!" Estella shivered as she spoke. "There must be some other way to deal with this beast. Your wizard, perhaps?"

"He is gone, my Lady. It may be that he will have a vision, and, if the dragon allows enough time, he might come back. I do not understand how a sorcerer's power works." Germaine shrugged as he finished. *Camron will probably not perform a farseeing spell to check on me. He was quite sure the danger was over. This time, I will not have a sorcerer or a magic sword to help sway the outcome.*

Crom lay his huge hand on Germaine's shoulder. "Sir Knight, I have witnessed your mighty deeds in combat. I have great respect for your abilities. The fact that you are willing to face such a beast impresses me all the more. I must tell you I do not believe any human could hope to defeat such a dragon."

"It may be that defeat of the beast would not be necessary. I believe the main goal of this dragon is to slay me. If the beast kills me in battle, he will probably depart."

The knight watched Estella's face flush red. "Do you have a wish to die, Germaine? This is the second time you have made such a statement in my presence."

"No, Estella. I am being practical. If you send me forth, I will do my best to slay the dragon and live to fight again. I have merely stated the possibility that my death would probably have the same result of ridding this land of the dragon's wrath."

Estella was adamant. "My decision stands! No one is to go forth in answer to the dragon's challenge."

Germaine turned and left the room. *She does not understand. This creature will not be swayed until it has destroyed the entire hold. In that case, I will still be dead, but the life of the hold will have been forfeited as well.*

The next day, at mid-morning, Germaine watched from the rampart as the great dragon's leathery wings carried it above the eastern hill. His huge body was silhouetted by the morning sun as he rose high in the sky to, once again, dive on the village. The knight knew that most of the people were already hiding in the forest. The dragon's breath destroyed even more buildings in the village. Again he climbed high above the castle to issue his challenge.

Germaine watched with eyes that were narrowed. That challenge was his, and he knew it would have to be answered. To respond, he would have to do something he had never before considered. He would break his oath. *This is how I am to meet destiny, disgraced. I cannot stand aside and let this creature destroy innocent lives. I will not win, no matter the outcome. If I manage to destroy the dragon, the fact that I broke Liege Oath will probably bring an end to the*

Emerald Knight. If the dragon kills me, I die with the disgrace of disobeying my liege. Germaine sighed as he considered what he must do. The rest of the day was long, as he spent it in memory of his two children. He spent time in prayer as well. With all that weighed on his mind, Germaine slept fitfully that night, knowing in his heart that he was doing what was right.

Germaine rose early the next morning. "Mikial, wake up. I have a task for you."

Mikial sat up in his sleeping pad. "What is the task, sir?"

Germaine waved his hand toward his battle armor that stood on its rack in a corner. "I need my armor dusted off and prepared."

Mikial's eyes popped wide open. "You are going to face the dragon?" His voice trembled with the realization.

"You are not to speak of this to anyone. I am breaking oath, so I will not return if I defeat the beast. I will forfeit any pay that is due. A knight is dishonored when he breaks his oath, so I will no longer be welcome in this hold. No matter the outcome, you must take my gear to Scot Hold. Val will accompany you." *It is sad that Mikial will also bear some of my shame for this act. That is one of the things that befalls a page.*

Germaine looked squarely into the boy's eyes and continued. "If I should lose to the dragon, please see that my son gets my equipment. I know that it may mean nothing to him because of my absence in his life. If Silver Cloud survives, he is yours for your faithful service. Now get my armor ready. I will also need that old shield we have been carrying with my battle shields. You know the one."

Mikial had tears in his eyes as he turned to do his work. "Yes, Sir Knight. It will be as you have commanded."

An hour before mid-morning, Mikial brought Silver Cloud to the door of Germaine's quarters. Mikial had placed the emerald tabard and skull helm upon the great charger. The Emerald Knight strode through the doorway in full battle armor. His head was still bare as he carried the helm in the crook of his left arm. The only weapon he would carry today was his sword, Lightning. When Germaine stood beside his horse, he drew forth his sword and placed it, point down, in the soil with a thrust forced by both hands. Still holding the upright sword by its haft, Germaine knelt on one knee in prayer. After a moment, the

Emerald Knight raised his eyes to the heavens and said these words as he concluded, "Lord God. Give me the strength to face what your will brings, in the name of your son, Jesus. Amen!" *It is the most I can ask of you. Please guide my children and this young page.*

Mikial held the knight's helm as he mounted. When Germaine had placed the helm on his head and lifted the visor, he reached for the shield that Mikial now held out to him. The shield had a leather loop on its back that slipped over a saddle hook above Germaine's left thigh.

There was nothing left undone in his preparations for battle. The only regret that he felt was for the things he had left unsaid to Estella. He now realized how insignificant his reasons were for not telling her of his love. With this thought, he prodded Silver Cloud into motion and, at a casual trot, the horse headed toward the castle gate, and Germaine to the fate that lay beyond its passage.

While Germaine rode to the east hill, Estella was in her chambers. A loud knock at the door brought her abruptly to her feet. She had been sitting on her couch thinking about Germaine. This morning she felt emptied of all emotion and strength because of her open disagreement with Germaine, and had spent her time alone with memories.

The chambermaid opened the door to an excited Crom. Crom was breathless. "My Lady. Look out your window to the meadow."

Estella turned from him without a word and walked to her window. When she saw the knight riding toward the far hill, she sank to her knees. "No, no! Crom, you must stop him." She turned to Crom with cheeks wet from new tears, tears she did not think she had left.

She saw Crom look at the floor, to avoid her eyes. "My Lady. He has broken oath. He is no longer under your liege."

Estella turned back to the window and looked to the sky. "It is almost midmorning." She turned from the window and raced to the door with Crom following close behind her. She did not stop running until she had reached the ramparts.

The distant knight was now at the foot of the far hill. Looking about her, Estella found that the rampart walkway was filled with people watching the knight's advance on the hill. She knew that the news had traveled fast to the people.

Estella was vaguely aware that Ayana and Val had come to stand by her side.

She heard Ayana ask, "Estella, did you order Germaine forth?" Estella could see fear shading Ayana's countenance as she momentarily turned her eyes from the Emerald Knight to look at the Vordund Princess.

"No. I wish that I could will him back within these walls." Estella's tears were flowing freely as she felt Ayana put an arm around her in an attempt to comfort.

"You love him greatly, Estella?" Ayana still held her arm about Estella as she asked the question.

Estella pushed away and started to deny her heart, but she found herself nodding, affirming her feelings for Germaine.

"Have you not told him so? Do you not know that he loves you as well?" Ayana asked.

Estella lifted her downcast eyes to Ayana's. "You are wrong. He loves his wife and longs to return to her side. I have no right to harbor the feelings that live within my heart."

Estella saw the light of understanding cross Ayana's face. "Has no one told you of his wife Adriana? She fell ill, early in his service to you. Adriana died with Germaine at her side."

Estella's thoughts leaped back to the mysterious disappearance of Germaine and Camron before the siege of Lyon Hold. Estella now realized how much she stood to lose to the dragon. *If I had taken him in my arms, told of my love ... If only I had told him. Perhaps he would not be riding to certain death. Three days ago, when I summoned him to by chambers because I ached to see him, I was going to tell him. But he seemed so aloof, so uncaring on that night. He would not even consent to stay for a short while. I thought he was uncaring, but now I see his heart ached for me as well.*

"We must hope that Germaine's God does not forget him today. It will take a miracle for him to survive." Estella could see no hope as she watched Germaine's progress.

 XXI

As Germaine made his approach to the hill over which he knew the dragon would appear, he went over what he could remember about the things he had been told as a boy. The most important fact, he remembered, concerned the location of the beast's heart. It lay beneath the flesh that formed the chest area directly in the middle, between the two forelegs. Germaine had heard the armor-like scales, which covered most of the dragon, did not cover his soft-skinned chest or underbelly.

Another vulnerable spot was the eye. Germaine remembered a knight who had claimed that he had pierced one of the eyes of a dragon, and the beast could no longer breathe fire because of the great pain. Germaine hoped that the stories told him as a boy were based on facts and not some minstrel's musings.

As the knight continued his advance, he went over in his mind, the lethal weapons of the dragon. The talons were its most versatile instruments of death. The tip of its tail contained a sharp-edged, bony plate that the beast could use as a battle-axe on attackers at its rear. Germaine realized the fangs of the beast would be instant death with their wicked, sharp points and the crushing power of the jaws that held them.

The Emerald Knight knew that, at best, he would get one chance to strike a blow. If providence smiled, he might have the opportunity to use his blade a second time. That was the most he could hope for. He did not know for certain that the shield he carried would deflect the terrible flames of the dragon's breath.

Germaine neared the top of the hill and heard a loud sound. The noise sounded like the snapping of a loose sail flapping in a gale. Suddenly, the great leathery wings of the beast appeared above the crest of the hill. The body of the huge beast came into view. The dragon's head was swinging side to side, as if hunting for prey. Its big eyes settled on Germaine.

He heard the dragon's voice roll like thunder. "Ah! A brave champion comes forth to die. You must be the green slug." The dragon pulled in his wings and plummeted from the sky.

Germaine lifted the shield from its hook and drew his sword as the dragon dove toward him. Silver Cloud reared in fear at the unexpected attack from above, throwing Germaine to the ground. The knight's reflexes had him on his feet, with the shield held above his head as the dragon unfurled his wings and slowed to attack.

The flame struck the shield with tremendous force, driving Germaine to one knee. The shield was deflecting the flames away from the knight, but the heat was warming his armor. As sweat rolled down his brow, Germaine saw the beast land forty feet from him. The beast was no longer spouting flames. The knight could see the dragon's muscles were visibly tensing for a leap.

The dragon sprang as the Emerald Knight made a quick move to his right in an attempt to avoid the giant claw that was sweeping toward him. Even with his warrior-honed reflexes, Germaine was not as fast as the dragon. The beast was agile, despite its great size. The giant's sweeping left claw swung through a wide arc as dust was rising in a cloud from the sudden moves made by the dragon. For some reason, the action of the dragon stirred within Germaine's mind the image of a cat batting at a mouse.

A single talon of that huge claw raked across the left side of Germaine's chest, staggering him. Had he not moved to the right, his entire rib cage would have been removed with that swipe. The knight knew he was badly hurt, but he could not waste a moment in concern for his wound as long as he was still standing. The dragon's head was swinging in a snake-like motion that was bringing it toward Germaine. *When he tries to grab me with its fanged jaws, his eyes will be within reach.* Germaine watched as the horned head continued to glide toward him. He knew this to be his last chance.

Germaine had never seen a dragon's face before, but this one had a surprised look on its ugly head as it swung in what seemed to be an effort to take a closer look at the knight's wounded chest.

The Emerald Knight did not have time to wonder about the dragon's action as Germaine's opportunity to attack was at hand. The knight timed his leap perfectly. He drove Lightning into the right eye socket of the dragon with all his might. Green, putrid liquid poured from the eye as the dragon, screaming in pain, reared upward on its hind legs. In its effort to move its wounded eye away from the knight's attack, the dragon picked Germaine from the ground as he continued to hold onto his sword. The sudden movement caused Germaine to nearly lose his grip on Lightning. Fortunately, the sword slid from the eye socket allowing the knight to fall to the ground with the sword hilt still held tightly with both hands.

A thought raced across Germaine's mind. *Why is my wound not causing me pain?* He knew, without looking, that his chest had been opened by the dragon's blow. There was no time to think further as he saw an opportunity for a second attack on the beast as it reared up on its hind quarters. Germaine ran to the exposed chest of the beast and quickly drove in his sword to the hilt with all of his weight behind that thrust. He hoped he had found the heart, because he could not pull the sword free to strike another blow.

The dragon roared this time as it pawed the sky with its forefeet. As the beast began to topple, the knight realized he was going to be crushed by the falling dragon. Germaine ran, but did not get far before he was smashed to the ground.

The crowd came to life as a mighty roar rose from the dust-covered battle field. An eerie silence followed that roar. Estella wondered if that roar was a trumpet of victory rising from the dragon. Could the beast now be preparing for further attack on the hold to destroy it and devour more helpless people? Estella and the others on the wall stood in silence as they strained to see the beast through the dust.

Estella swayed in a state of shock. She was staring at the scene as the dust was settling. She feared what that cloud might reveal as it lifted its veil. *I fear what I will see, but I cannot turn my eyes away.*

Estella gave a start as Crom's voice shattered the silence. "There! There is the beast. It is dead! See how lifelessly it lies."

A roar went up from the crowd as they recognized that the knight had killed the giant beast.

"What of Germaine? Does he yet live?" Estella was straining to see his form somewhere on that field of battle. *Before the dust obscured the battle, the dragon struck a grievous blow. Even from this distance I could see more than glittering shards of armor.*

"I see him!"

She heard Mikial as the boy pointed excitedly.

"Under the dragon's right wing. See. He struggles to free himself."

Estella saw that Mikial was right. Even as he spoke, another great roar went up from the walls as the people cheered their hero. Estella was yelling as loudly as a hoarse voice would allow.

As she watched, she could just make out the form of the knight struggling to free himself from the dragon's lifeless wing.

Germaine, having not lost consciousness, realized he was pinned beneath one of the huge wings. He struggled and finally gained his freedom from that giant, leathery pinion. Feeling some pain now, Germaine shrugged out of the remains of his armor corselet and placed his hand over his chest, as if to cover his wound. Only now, did he permit himself to look at the damage to his breast.

What he saw beneath his hand gave him more pain than the ragged wound itself. *How can such a thing be possible?* He now realized what the dragon was looking at so intently that it had allowed an opening for the attack on its eye. *My heart! My heart has become a thing of stone. How can this be?* Germaine noticed with fascination that the stony surface of his heart had been slightly scratched by the dragon's talon. The stony casement had allowed him to survive long enough to slay the creature. Germaine felt himself weakening. He knew that he did not have long to live.

Germaine turned away from the castle as he saw people beginning to pour through the drawbridge gate, rushing out to meet him. He did not want them to see him like this. "Here, Cloud." Germaine's charger ran up to him. "Steady, boy," as he mounted the horse with difficulty. The wound was now giving him pain, but the thought of what lay in that damaged breast brought ever greater agony. Germaine turned Silver Cloud away from the castle and yelled, "On, Cloud." He spurred the charger to its fastest gallop. "I must get far away so that none may follow." Germaine clung to the saddle with the strength he had left. When he died, he wanted to be alone, away from Estella's view. He now realized that it was for the best that he had never told her how he felt. His mind numbed and emptied of thought as he drew further away from Estella.

Estella could not understand what her eyes beheld. Germaine was riding away from the hold at full gallop. Looking down at the crowd filling the gate,

Estella could see that none were mounted on horseback. The knight would be out of sight before anyone could set out after him.

As Estella turned to Crom, she heard Ayana scream in warning.

"Estella, look out!"

As she turned to see what was happening, Estella caught a glimpse of Val, who was standing beside her, throwing his belt knife toward a section of the crowd. Her eyes darted ahead of the flight of that projectile. Val's target was a man who stood aiming an arrow at her!

The knife struck the assassin in the throat. In the same instant, he loosed the arrow. Estella had time to scream when the arrow struck. Then darkness engulfed her.

As she fell, Germaine rode beyond the view of the castle. The knight continued to spur the horse with what little strength he had left.

Germaine did not know how long he had been clinging to Silver Cloud. He knew the horse had long since slowed to a trot. Lather covered the horse's neck. The knight wanted to say something to the poor horse, but he could not force any sound from his lips.

As night began to fall, Germaine knew he had been riding for hours. No one would find him now. He released his grip and fell to the ground. Looking up at the heavens, he could see the stars in their glory. *At least I will die in peace, with God's blanket above me. Thank You, God, for your grace.* Germaine felt his thoughts dimming. *Like the embers of a dying fire. My thoughts flee from me like the small sparks that leap from a fire. Soon. My end comes soon.*

As he lay on the ground, Silver Cloud moved close and nuzzled him. He knew the horse was trying to rouse him.

With these last views of Silver Cloud and the stars above, Germaine's thoughts turned to Estella. His lips formed the words, but no sound came from them. "I love you, Estella. I love … you." He saw a gray hawk as it lighted near his face. The Emerald Knight closed his eyes and drifted.

Far away, in Lyon Castle, Estella lay with her own serious wound.

Estella opened her eyes slowly. A deep, dull pain was throbbing in her left arm. "What happened?" She asked this as she looked at the ceiling, not knowing if anyone heard.

Ayana's face came into her view. "You were wounded, Estella. My father tried to kill the assassin before he loosed his arrow, but he saw the man too late."

"As I recall, you were the one who screamed the warning." Estella forced a smile through her pain. "Thank you for saving my life." Suddenly Estella remembered the wounding of Germaine and started to struggle out of bed. *What about Germaine? Did he survive his wounds? I must go to him.*

"No Estella! You have lost much blood. Do not force open your wound again." Ayana held her hand against Estella's right shoulder to restrain her. "Relax, Estella, please."

Estella lay back in her bed, weak from the exertion. "What happened to Germaine?"

"Crom has been searching for hours, but we have no word yet. Do not worry. Crom will find him." Ayana did not sound confident to Estella.

Estella put her right hand to her forehead. "I should be out looking for him. Does anyone have an idea what caused him to ride away?"

"Mikial said that Germaine told him before riding out that he was breaking Liege Oath and would thus be unwelcomed as a dishonored knight." Ayana fixed her gaze upon the floor as she talked. "Mikial said that Germaine instructed him to take the knight's equipment to Scot Hold, whatever the outcome of the battle."

"The man slays a dragon for our sake, suffering a serious wound in the fight, and he would think himself unwanted! I do not believe I will ever understand men, much less this gallant knight and his inflexible code of honor." Estella was exasperated. "When I find this particular knight, he shall never leave me again, if I have my way." Estella's memory returned to the sight of the dragon wounding the chest of Germaine. *Could he possibly survive such a wound?*

A few hours before Estella awoke, a distant Camron had felt a tug of danger in his power. The old sorcerer ceased his work on Scot Hold and went to his lodge to investigate.

Camron had been sitting in a trance watching with his farseeing talent. He saw the fight with the dragon and Germaine's flight into the forest trail. As he roused from his trance, he went to the place where he had hidden Titan's Blade. After placing the sword within the folds of his robe, he once again transformed into the gray hawk. With the change complete, the hawk leaped into the air and flew with great speed. He knew that it may already be too late to save the stricken knight.

From his lofty vantage point, Camron found the knight in time to see him fall from his horse. Within minutes he was landing beside the fallen Germaine. As the hawk turned into a sorcerer, Camron recognized that Germaine had already slipped into the deep sleep that comes before death.

When Camron looked at the wound, he realized that Titan's Blade had played an unexpected role in the battle with the dragon. The sorcerer knew that only the power of the sword could have created the rocklike shell around the knight's heart. From within his robe, Camron withdrew the sword and laid it by Germaine. He then brought forth, from another fold, a vial containing a powdery, blue substance he sprinkled over the open chest cavity. The powder twinkled with blue sparkles of light as they fell. Placing his hand on the haft of the sword, he removed it from the sheath and gently lay it on the chest of the Emerald Knight.

A soft glow seemed to radiate from the sword and the body beneath it. The light became a blinding blaze. Camron had to avert his eyes because of the brilliance. After several minutes, the glow subsided and then disappeared. He bent to look at the wound, a wound that no longer existed. The sorcerer placed his hand above the knight's heart. By concentrating, Camron utilized the power of the blue powder to see what lie within Germaine's chest. The heart was still encased in stone, but was functioning as a normal heart, except that it beat very slowly. After counting the beats, Camron realized that Germaine's heart was beating slower than that of a normal sleeping person. "It seems Titan's Blade was trying to protect your heart from something. I do not believe it was the dragon. What could it be?" Camron's memory returned to the conversation he had with Germaine, the night before departing for Scot Hold. *So, you did not resolve your problem of the heart. I fear that I will need to figure out that problem before Titan's Blade will allow your heart to return to normal.*

The knight slept still. Camron reasoned that, though his body was healed, the Emerald Knight was still suffering the exhausting effects of the battle and the long ride to the place where he had fallen. Camron left the sword lying on the knight's chest as he set about making a litter. He would transport the knight to Scot Hold as was Germaine's plan. Camron set a couple of spells that would keep him awake, and Silver Cloud rested.

Through the rest of that night, Camron had to deal with wolves. When they had been traveling about four hours, the sounds of a hunting pack startled Silver Cloud, almost throwing Camron. "Easy, Cloud. We will be all right. I will protect you from those wolves." Camron pulled the silver wand from his robe. *I have used much power today, flying as a hawk to Germaine, and now maintaining spells to keep the horse and myself alert. I will place another spell on Cloud that will cause him to see the wolves as harmless. For the wolves, perhaps some sparks from the wand will suffice.*

Soon, Camron could see the eyes of some of the beasts as they caught light from the bright moon. "Let us see how you like a little light, and noise." Holding the wand above his head, Camron said. "Send forth!" The old man watched sparks leap from the wand. The sparks would arc out to where the wolves were lurking and then burst in a loud pop. It was a minor trick that the sorcerer had used on many occasions to entertain himself and, at times, children. It was a harmless trick, but he smiled at the reaction of the wolves. *Look at them dance. I do not think they appreciate my talent.* Camron watched as the wolves ran in terror. He would find the rest of the night to be without trouble, as he continued his slow journey.

The journey proved a long two days for the old sorcerer. He did not stop for sleep. He did allow a few brief halts, to allow Silver Cloud to graze. He kept the horse at as quick a pace as possible, without jostling Germaine too badly. He did not fear the knight being thrown from the litter because he had bound him securely. His greatest concern was the knight's continued sleep. *Why does he not awaken? He seems to be well in all respects, except for the condition of his heart. He should have awakened by now.* Camron kept turning in the saddle, expecting to see the knight struggling to free himself from the litter. He kept constant vigil for the remainder of the trek.

XXII

Camron was glad to see Scot Hold come into view, marking the end of his journey. He had hoped that Germaine would be awake to see the progress made by the Vordund people. Camron knew that over half of Prince Jahil's soldiers were there as well, helping with the project. When the old sorcerer had arrived at Scot Hold, after Germaine's joust with Craitor, he arrived to find what was to have been a surprise for the Emerald Knight. The Vordund, and Jahil's men, were actually beginning to rebuild Scot Castle. Val had told Camron that Jahil had ordered his men to take an old drawing of the castle, which had been in the library of Fenn Hold, to use as a rough plan. It would not be identical to the original, but Camron knew it would be close.

Camron had used powerful spells to set many of the walls in a single day. The old sorcerer had been resting from his use of the power when he had seen Germaine's plight. Camron knew this to be the greatest reason for his powers to be so weak when he went to Germaine's aid.

Between the efforts of his magic and those of the toiling people, Camron estimated the castle to be about three-quarters complete. Had he not needed to go to Germaine, the castle would now be whole. "Sir Knight, I do not know if you can hear me, but I must now conserve my powers to try and find an answer to your malady. Your castle is now the least of our worries."

Camron took the sleeping knight to the small lodge that had been built for the sorcerer. He washed the grime of the battle and journey from Germaine's still body. The old sorcerer talked to the knight, hoping that he could draw the sleeping man away from the spell that held him. "You would have been surprised, Germaine, if you had seen Scot Hold on our arrival. You must awaken to see it." The knight still slept, as if in death. Camron had removed the sword where he had bound it to Germaine's chest, thinking that perhaps the sword held him in a protective sleep. For one of the few times in his long memory, Camron was at a loss for an answer to this deathlike sleep. He sat in a chair by Germaine's bed, deep in thought. *I must look through my tomes and see if there is some spell that might bring him back. If I use a spell, I will have to be absolutely certain that it will not react unfavorably with the one that now holds him. This will mean a long time will be spent in research. It would help if I knew the source of his inner turmoil at Lyon Hold.*

As Camron pondered the questions that assailed his memory, he stood up with a sudden motion, knocking over the chair in the process. "Of course! I have been walking around with blinders upon my eyes." Camron bent close to Germaine, so that he could whisper in the knight's ear. "It is Estella. Is that not so, my emerald friend?" Camron saw a small movement of Germaine's mouth as it formed a smile. "I am right. Your troubled heart has ached for Estella and you suppressed those feelings for some reason. That would explain the stone casing about your heart. Titan's Blade tried to protect you, even to hardening your heart in an effort to eliminate your pain." *An old sorcerer has once again found something new under the sun,* thought Camron. *Never has the sword acted on the behalf of one of its owners such as it has now. Perhaps this is the first time that the circumstance of love has caused turmoil within a bearer of Titan's Blade. How can I cause the sword to relinquish its misplaced help?* Camron again spoke to the knight. "Estella may hold the key. I will use my farseeing trance to see what she is now doing. I will send for her. No. That will take too long. I will wait a few days for my power to fully recover, and go to her as the hawk." Camron righted the knocked-over chair.

"I must rest, but first, let me check the rhythm of your heart." Camron listened for a few minutes as a frown deepened the creases on his forehead. "Oh, no!" The old sorcerer said in despair. "His heart beat has slowed even further. Let me see. I counted the beats, what ... two days ago. Now they are reduced to ..." The old man stopped in mid-sentence as he realized the knight had only days left. *I would waste my time going for Estella. I am not sure she could do anything to help. I must conserve my strength and try to find a spell or potion that can reverse the efforts of Titan's Blade.*

Camron picked up the sword and said. "If you understand the needs of Germaine enough to have made him invisible, why do you not see that you are killing him? You misguided sword, release him!" The old sorcerer looked back to Germaine and saw that there was no change. "I have an idea. Perhaps if I send you to Midaron, you will be far enough away that your influence will be ended here."

Camron carried the sword to a table near the wall, and laid it in the center. On either side, he set the white crystal and the red one. He then brought out his silver rod and waved it above the sword as he chanted a spell. The sword grew hazy, and then winked out of sight. Turning from the table, he walked back to Germaine and saw that his face turned blue. A quick check told Camron the knight's heart was almost completely stopped. The sorcerer hurried back to the table and quickly reversed his spell, bringing Titan's blade back from middle earth. As the sword materialized, he hurried back to Germaine's side. Camron found the knight's heart beat now back to the count it was before the separation from the sword.

It appears that the sword is using its power to maintain the function of Germaine's heart. What will happen when the knight's heart beats its last time? Will the sword restore him when death is finally eminent? The old sorcerer shook his head. The journey, and Germaine's condition, had been much for an old man to endure. Camron walked into the adjoining room and fell across his bed. His thoughts were about the times he had seen Estella and Germaine together. Some things were now much clearer to the old man, as he slipped into a slumber.

Meanwhile, Estella was at Lyon Hold, worrying about Germaine.

Estella grew restless. Three days passed since she had been wounded. The wound was still tender, with her arm supported in a sling to immobilize it. Ayana had told her that the sling would help her arm heal more quickly. Estella could now work off some of her anxiety concerning Germaine by moving about freely within the castle with her arm supported in the sling. As she walked around her room glancing occasionally at the meadow, she heard Byrone at her door. She called to her maid. "Give Byrone entrance."

Byrone entered the room and approached her. "My Lady. Crom has returned from his search." The lieutenant's face was sad.

A knock at the chamber door, and a gruff voice announced to Estella that Crom had arrived close on the heels of his lieutenant.

As Crom entered, Estella saw a look of helplessness in his expression. "I could not find Germaine, my Lady. His charger appeared to leave no tracks at times. I would search and finally pick up another trail, only to lose it again. It is hopeless."

"Byrone. Have Mikial and the Vordund people left yet for Scot Hold?" Estella had an idea. *If he still lives, Germaine will try to reach his hold. He did tell Mikial before the battle with the dragon that he would meet him there. Perhaps his wounds were not as serious as they appeared at the distance we were from the battle.*

"No, my Lady. They were awaiting Crom's return, in the event he carried news. They will be leaving soon."

"Inform them that I will be riding with their party. Have a horse saddled and waiting for me. Have an escort of four men-at-arms provisioned and ready to ride."

"It will be done, my Lady." Byrone and Crom left the chamber as Estella turned to her maid.

"Pack a travel kit with riding clothes. I will not need any gowns or frills." The maid set to work as Estella changed clothes. It had been a while since she had last worn breeches and a tunic. As she pulled on her riding boots, her thoughts were on Germaine and her hope that he would be at Scot Hold.

When Estella joined the assembled group of travelers, Crom was with them.

"My Lady." Crom saluted. "Do you wish that I accompany you?" She saw a pleading look in his eyes.

"Yes, Crom." Estella nodded to Byrone who stood behind Crom. "Byrone is quite capable of commanding the soldiers during our absence. We may have need of your sword should we meet someone of Scul's followers."

"Thank you, my Lady." Crom half bowed and then mounted his horse.

Estella looked over the party she would be traveling with. Beside Crom and the four men-at-arms, she saw Mikial, Val, Ayana, Jahil, and Gillam. Gillam was the warrior who had remained with Val when the other had journeyed to Scot Hold with Camron. Estella wondered about Jahil's continued presence. *I had thought he remained here solely because of concern for Germaine, but I see he has another reason that holds him here.*

As the journey began, Estella noticed that Jahil and Ayana had grown very fond of each other. Estella watched them laugh as they talked together. She could see they were happy just to be in each other's company. A tug came to Estella's heart as she watched Jahil reach for, and hold Ayana's hand as they rode close beside each other. Estella could not help seeing herself and Germaine in that relationship. Looking back, she could now see clearly that Germaine did, indeed, love her as she had loved him. They had wasted too much time apart. *If he still lives and still loves me, we will make up for that lost time.*

Estella had known the journey would be a long seven days. Her body protested the long hours in the saddle by hurting in places she had never been aware of. She knew that she could endure the aches. It was the ache in her heart that bothered her more. She was often finding herself jealous of Jahil and Ayana. The two were so wrapped up in each other that Estella doubted that they were even aware of the passage of time and miles. She knew how they felt. She had experienced such feelings when she traveled from Skull Fortress with Germaine by her side. *If only we would have yielded to our hearts on that journey. How different things could be now.*

Estella was thinking about the fact that they were in the fourth day of their journey. She wondered if the wolves would continue to be a threat. They had killed several wolves on each night of the journey. Estella was glad that the remaining wolves had been satisfied with turning on their wounded pack members, at least until now.

The lady's thoughts were interrupted by a loud yell.

"To arms!" Crom bellowed.

Estella saw that one of the men-at-arms had been knocked from his saddle by an arrow. She realized they were under attack. *Are they Scul's men?*

Estella drew her own sword but did not have time to use it as an arrow buried itself in her left side. As she felt searing pain, she did not black out as she had with her earlier wound. She half fell and half dismounted as she landed with a painful jarring thud, on her feet. She was vaguely aware the men-at-arms had used their own bows to exact a quick answer to the attack from men in the trees, as Crom, Val, and Gillam were using swords and axes to cut down men that had charged out of the undergrowth. Estella sat down, and looked at the arrow protruding from a point just below her left breast. Quiet soon reigned once again as Estella allowed a moan to escape her lips. The arrow felt like fire burning within her chest.

She saw Crom, examining the body of his last victim. "Are they men of the Falchion Raptor?" her voice came out raspy.

"No, my Lady. They appear to be thieves. It was ill for them to chance upon us." Crom turned to face Estella as he answered. "Lady Estella! I did not realize you were wounded." Crom rushed to her as he spoke. Ayana was close at his heels.

"Move aside! Allow me to examine her." Ayana pushed her way past Crom.

Ayana knelt beside the wounded Estella and gingerly cut away some of the tunic from around the arrow with her belt knife. "Not much blood. You must remain still."

"Can we cut the arrow off and push it on through her body?" Crom asked Ayana.

"No. The arrow is too near her heart." Ayana answered. "We must stop our journey and keep her still while someone rides ahead for Camron. The old sorcerer has a great knowledge of healing."

"No. I will not stay here. I will continue to Scot Hold." *I must go to Germaine. I feel within my heart that he needs me.*

Ayana said, "Estella. You are seriously wounded. I do not know if you will survive long enough for the sorcerer to get back to us. If you die, you will be of no help for Germaine if he still lives. We do not know that he is still alive."

"I feel he is alive, and I must go to him. Perhaps his God has deemed that we should die together." Estella's voice carried the tone of deep resolve.

Estella watched Ayana stand and say to Crom, "Construct a litter. Her mind is set, and only further damage will be done to her if we cause her to struggle."

Crom responded. "It will be done, Lady Ayana. We must also bury the soldier that was felled by the first arrow."

"Lady Estella." Crom said. "We will be ready to continue shortly. Try to take a short rest while we finish with the wounded." Estella noticed that two of the men-at-arms had received minor wounds. Estella marveled that she still felt well enough to travel, though the wound continued to burn.

Jahil had received a slight wound as well. She noticed his smile for the nurse that now tended him. He was being well cared for by Ayana. The sight made her remember the joust, when she had wanted to go to the injured Emerald Knight. She had wanted to tend Germaine's wounds. *I remember the day I wounded the Emerald Knight with a wooden sword*. She smiled with the memory. *I remember the feelings that surged through me as I touched his wounded chest. Oh, that I can touch him again.* Estella winced as a sharp pain stabbed at her, breaking into her thoughts.

When the attack had occurred, Estella and her group had just turned from their southern track to a westward one. Within an hour after the robbery attempt, the rain began to fall. At first, Estella welcomed the cooling rain that fell as she was pulled along on a litter by the horse she had previously ridden. She would soon come to wish that the rain would stop.

The conditions were miserable. It rained steadily through the fifth and sixth day with the nights being spent in wet blankets. Neither Estella, nor the rest of the party, slept much, so their nightly stops were cut shorter than usual. It was less uncomfortable to ride while drenching wet than it was to try to sleep in puddles. After midnight of the sixth day, Estella awoke from a brief sleep to find that the rain ended its relentless assault on them, and the sky cleared. The main concern on her mind, now, proved to be the knowledge that she was growing weaker. *I can no longer feel my legs*. She struggled to raise her right arm. *I can barely move my fingers, much less my arms. If I can only stay alive long enough to see him one more time.* Estella smiled, a weak curve of her lips, as she realized she loved Germaine more than herself. She knew that she would give her life, if it would save him.

When Scot Hold came into view on that seventh day of the journey, the clothes they wore were stiff, but dry.

Mikial caught Estella's attention as he let out a whoop as they approached the nearest buildings that were completed. "Silver Cloud!" Mikial turned his horse toward the small pen where Estella now saw the charger as well.

Estella's heart leaped in her chest. *Could Germaine be alive and here, or did some instinct bring his horse without its rider?* As they approached the small lodge near the horse pen and stable, Camron came out of its doorway.

"Camron! Does Germaine yet survive?" Estella could not control her emotions as she tried to talk to Camron. Her voice came out almost the croak of a frog, as she could only manage a whisper. *Please let him be here.*

"Yes, Estella. He lives, but in a deep sleep that I cannot break. What about your injuries? You look like death, itself. Let me tend to your wounds."

"I am going to him." Estella began to struggle. With the effort, she could feel some control over her limbs.

"Hold, my Lady!" Camron's command came in a loud voice that stopped Estella in her struggle to rise from the now halted litter. Camron was looking at her wound. Estella could see deep concern on his face as he turned to Ayana. "There is rot about the wound. I may be able to save her life with a spell." Turning back to Estella, Camron said. "Do not struggle to move. We will carry you to Germaine. We must speak of something before you see him." Camron held up his hand in a motion for silence as she started to protest. The old sorcerer motioned to Estella's fellow travelers and said. "Allow us to be alone but a moment. I wish to talk to Estella." Estella tried to mouth another protest, but Camron said, "Germaine is not going anywhere."

Estella saw the others move away as Camron continued, "Germaine was gravely wounded in his battle with the dragon. He would have been killed if not for a very strange circumstance. His heart was sheathed in stone."

"What! How could such a thing be possible?" Estella felt her strength rise, as if her body was marshaling itself for one last effort.

"To answer that I have to go back to a conversation I had with Germaine on my last night at Lyon Hold. I told him that he had a struggle within his heart that must be resolved before he left that hold. I did not then know the source of that conflict in his heart, but I do now."

Estella closed her eyes. A pain stabbed quickly at her wound as she thought. *Could that conflict of Germaine's be the same that I felt within my breast?*

"I believe the conflict which he did not resolve to be a love that he was trying to deny. His love for you, Estella." Camron paused as Estella felt a tear spring to the corner of her eye. Reaching into a fold of his robe, Camron brought forth a cloth and dabbed at her tears. "I see that it is possible you love him as well."

Estella would no longer deny that love. "Yes! Yes! My love is greater than I ever thought possible, and now he is lost to me." Her tears flowed freely. "How could I have denied my love for him?"

"There now. Stop crying. I did not say Germaine's condition was hopeless.

Let me finish my appraisal of his illness. I believe he has loved you in some way, perhaps even before his wife died. It may be that he felt great pain in his heart because of guilt about his love, or he may have thought your love to be unattainable by a man such as himself. There could be many factors that caused his heart to ache in conflict at the sight or thought of you. Whatever the cause, he had wielded Titan's Blade during these times of heartache. I believe the sword sought to protect him by shielding the heart that beat in Germaine's chest. In a manner of speaking, Germaine is liege to the sword, and the sword is his protector. Unfortunately, in trying to protect him, the sword may actually kill him."

Estella looked up toward the tree branches above, with a look of great sadness. "I wish that the past could be changed so that I might remove the grief that turned his heart to stone."

"Not so, Estella. If not for that stone sheath about his heart, Germaine would be dead and the dragon yet alive. His heart aches for you and Titan's Blade formed an unexpected shield that helped him defeat the dragon."

"Will he recover from this death sleep?" Estella felt hopeful now.

"I do not know. I believe if you were to spend some time in his presence, talk to him as if he were awake, it may be that his heart will respond. If my theory is correct, the knowledge of returned love by you, combined with the sword in the same place, may be the medicine he needs. If the sword recognizes the love between you, then it will no longer be necessary for it to protect Germaine's heart. It is worth a try, though I admit to be grasping at a single straw."

"Take me to him, Camron. Germaine and I have kept our hearts from each other for too long."

When Estella was carried into the room, she found it to be dimly lit. There was the one she loved. She saw him lying on a cot in the middle of the room.

Estella heard Camron giving directions to some of the men who had followed them into the room. "Clear that table, and move it over near Germaine's bed. We will place Estella on it."

As Estella was moved closer to Germaine, she could see on the bed, by his right arm, lay the sword. He looked so peaceful, with a slight smile curving one side of his mouth. As she was settled on the top of the table, Camron moved to the knight.

Estella watched as the old man straightened and said sorrowfully. "It is too late. He has only moments of life left. Perhaps I should now tend to your wounds, Estella. I fear that you will not survive much longer than Germaine."

"No! Move me from this table to that chair by his bed."

"Estella. If we set you in the chair, I fear your death will be hastened."

"If you do not move me, I will move myself." Estella began to ease up on her right arm as she spoke. "Cut this arrow off, where it enters my skin. I no longer care about survival." *I know my fate is to die with him. I must go to his side.*

"Stop struggling. We will move you." Camron picked up a sharp knife and quickly cut through the arrow shaft. "I am afraid that your death is now sealed."

Estella grunted as Jahil and Crom moved to her and gently lifted her from the table. As they set her in the chair, she said. "Leave us alone. Let us spend our last moments together."

Camron spoke a warning. "Do not touch the sword for it has always meant instant death to anyone it has not chosen."

Estella smiled, between stabs of pain, at the sorcerers words. *I will soon be dead, and he is still concerned with me killing myself.*

When everyone had left the room, she leaned close to the bed as she heard Camron close the door behind him. For a time, she stared intently upon his face. Then she leaned close to Germaine's ear and spoke softly. "Do you smile because you are dreaming, dreaming of us?" A pain brought a gasp from her lips.

"We are alone, once again, Emerald Knight. I do not have gaming boards with me, but I long for you to return with me to the rooms where we enjoyed each other so. Did you enjoy our long talks as much as I?" Estella felt as if she needed to cough. She tried to suppress it as she continued. "I want to do these things and more, Germaine. I want you to return to my side so that you may once again protect me. My love! Yes, I say it aloud. My love for you is greater than I have ever felt for another. Please come back to me so that we can share that love. Please!" She did cough now, and an intense pain shot through to her toes. *I must feel the warmth of his skin against mine. His touch always gave me joy.*

Estella reached out her hand and gently cupped Germaine's cheek. "I love you, Emerald Knight." As Estella's elbow was resting on Germaine's chest, above his heart, she felt a warmth that was growing hotter. She looked away from Germaine's face to view her arm, and she saw a white glow on the knight's chest where her elbow was touching him. She started to withdraw her arm, but something inside told her differently. *So strange. I feel as if this glow belongs inside of me. It seems to urge me to some action.*

Without knowing why she was so compelled, Estella rose from her chair and moved to gently lie alongside Germaine on the edge of the bed. With great care, as if in fear of hurting him, she shifted her body partially over the knight's left side so that her breast, with her heart beating rapidly beneath it, was directly over his heart. As they lay there, heart to heart, Estella placed her cheek against his. She felt the warmth that radiated from his heart penetrating hers. Moving her left hand, she reached across Germaine and gently lay her hand on the sword. A blaze of light illuminated the room, and a clap like thunder sounded.

As a tingling sensation surged through her body, she vaguely noticed that Camron had rushed into the room and stood nearby as if mesmerized by the scene before him. Estella knew that she, Germaine, and Titan's Blade were all enveloped in a white blaze of power, just as she had witnessed at the joust when Germaine had grasped the sword. Suddenly the blaze died out, and Estella found the room, once again, dimly lit.

"What ...?" The voice was scratchy as a now awakening Germaine tried to speak. She could see his sudden awareness as he recognized her. Estella realized the pain from her wound had gone. Something lay under her breast, between Germaine and herself. She shifted her body, and reached under her to find the remainder of the arrow. Estella smiled. "It is a long story, Germaine. If you are willing, we have a lifetime to talk about it. I want you to tell me everything about your God. I want Him to be my savior, too. Through all that has befallen us these past months, there have been more than a sorcerer and a sword guiding your steps. The very way you live life, trying to do what is right in all that you do. I want to be that way, too."

Estella heard Camron loudly clear his throat. "Well, I see my attention is not needed here." He hastily made his way out of the room.

Germaine looked deeply into those dark eyes. He would never avoid them again. "Estella. I love you. I wish—"

Estella placed a tiny finger on his lips. "I love you, Germaine. Never leave my side again." She removed her hand from his lips and pressed her lips to his as their hearts finally met in a love that could be ignored no longer. She felt Germaine's arms move to encircle her.

How long they were joined in their love, Germaine could not say. He only knew that the time had raced by too quickly as they ventured out of the lodge to face what remained of the day.

Later that evening, Germaine and Estella arrived at a feast held in Germaine's honor. The great tables were set up so that the partly rebuilt Scot Castle served as a backdrop. Lanterns were set about, and Germaine remarked that the stars provided a magnificent canopy.

Jahil and Ayana sat beside each other as they waited for all the guests to be seated.

Mikial was seated next to Germaine's right, while Estella was to his left. *This is much better than the seating arrangement that met me on my return from Skull Fortress.* He looked at Estella, and her eyes were on his. He reached for her hand and held it gently, atop the table.

"Sir Germaine." Mikial sought his attention. "How are you feeling? Do you have any ills left from the battle?"

"No Mikial. I have found the best cure for my illness." Germaine gave Estella's hand a little squeeze. "In fact, I feel very well after the days that I have slept. I do not believe I will ever have to sleep again."

Germaine noticed that the men and women were all dining at the same table. He wondered, with a bit of humor, if the Vordund had changed their dining habits, or if this would be the new order of things in Scot Hold.

Crom stood up to offer a toast. "Here is a salute to the bravest man I know. He is also the only one I know who has slain a dragon. To the Emerald Knight!"

The entire party rose up and presented their goblets. "To Germaine!"

As they took their seats, the Emerald Knight remained standing. "I wrote a letter while at Lyon Hold, during a time when my heart felt deeply troubled. I will not bore you with the contents of that letter, but I would like to bring one thought from its lines to your ears. I had written that 'it is believed by some that man has not the capacity to love.' The love that I spoke of was a love so deep that it has no end. I have that kind of love for Estella." Germaine paused as he turned his smile to Estella, and his eyes met hers. "I want to ask for her hand and her heart in marriage, but first there is a matter I must resolve."

Germaine reached to his scabbard and drew his sword. He held it high for all to see. "This sword is Titan's Blade." As he held the sword aloft, the sword shimmered and resumed its original appearance. Germaine heard several people gasp at the transformation.

A buzz of people talking began when Germaine paused. Germaine realized that the Vordund probably knew very little of the legend, but Jahil's soldiers were now excited at his revelation.

"This sword was presented to me by its guardian." Germaine pointed to Camron. "Many of you may know the meaning of this sword being placed into my care. I must admit that I did not realize the full ramifications until after my joust with Scul, and Camron informed me. It seems that the sword has selected me to be high king. I did not ask to be chosen for this responsibility, but I am willing to shoulder it if that is the will of the people. Normally, a king is born into the position, and the people accept him because of that birthright. I do not have such a birthright to give me authority to rule. Some kings gain their authority by taking it forcefully. I will not force myself on the people. That is why I want the people behind me. That would be my authority, my birthright. I know that all Valeria cannot be asked, so I will accept the verdict from all of you here, and I will honor whatever it may be. Do you accept me as High King of Valeria?"

Germaine found the roar deafening as the crowd cheered for the Emerald Knight.

Another stood up. It was Jahil. The prince held up his hands for quiet. "The Emerald Knight has conquered great foes. I have witnessed him performing the great acts of valor that most never see in ten lifetimes. And yet, with his prowess as a fighter, he has also proven to be wise beyond measure. Without his guidance, my hold would not be healthy, if it were to exist at all. I watched helplessly as he defended Lyon Hold, with his life seemingly forfeit. It is with certainty that I now endorse Germaine as High King and pledge my hold to his service." The crowd roared its approval of Germaine.

This time Germaine silenced the crowd. He turned to Estella and reached out his hand to help her up. As he faced her, with his hands holding hers, he asked. "Would you consider marrying me, though I would be king?" *If you do not, life will be next to meaningless.*

Estella looked into his eyes with those dark-brown eyes he had grown to love so much. "I would marry you if you were a pauper. I love you now, and forever."

Germaine reached for their goblets and handed Estella hers. "I have one more toast to offer. This is to my betrothed, my beloved Estella."

With his toast made, the crowd erupted into a roar that went on for some time.

Camron stood up and waved his arms to get the crowd's attention. "With all that said, let us get down to the business of eating. This old sorcerer is famished."

Germaine ate heartily and happily as he realized all of his friends were with him. He wished that Daren and Durelle were there as well. He knew that he would soon have them by his side. They would be a family from now on.

*   *   *

"Well, old Gryph, it has been several months since I brought you to Lyon Hold. What do you think of my sorcery now?"

The old owl winked at Camron.

"Be obstinate. I thought you would prefer this dungeon to our damp cavern. At any rate, I must tell you of a strange dream I had. This dream had the feel of power to it. I was serving a new high king, about two hundred years from now. I did not get his name, but he was a descendant of Germaine, through his daughter, Durelle. We lived in a most splendid castle called Camelot."